PRAISE FOR Willful Machines

★ "From a first-person perspective, Lee fumbles from self-deprecation to self-confidence. As varied as his opinions are of himself, so too is the landscape, mixing technology with gothic settings à la Poe and Stoker. Gothic, gadget-y, gay: a socially conscious sci-fi thriller to shelve between *The Terminator* and *Romeo and Juliet*."

—*Kirkus Reviews*, starred review

"Smart, brave, and utterly original, *Willful Machines* asks questions that matter. Tim Floreen's unforgettable debut will stay with you long after you've finished reading."

—Amie Kaufman, *New York Times* bestselling author of *These Broken Stars* and *Illuminae*

"*Willful Machines* is as exciting as it is heartbreaking. A deft mixture of science fiction, gritty action, and sweet first love, Tim Floreen's debut is everything I want from a book."

—Shaun David Hutchinson, author of *The Five Stages of Andrew Brawley* and *We Are the Ants*

"*Willful Machines* is a thought-provoking thriller wrapped around a fascinating concept—skillfully mixed in with basic human dilemmas. Tim Floreen's tale convincingly depicts a world where machines can pass as human, but humans still struggle with age-old questions: 'How much control do I have over my own life? Who can I dare to trust? Who can I dare to love?'"

—Margaret Peterson Haddix, *New York Times* bestselling author

Also by Tim Floreen

Tattoo Atlas

willful machines

Tim Floreen

Simon Pulse

New York London Toronto Sydney New Delhi

SIMON PULSE

An imprint of Simon & Schuster Children's Publishing Division

1230 Avenue of the Americas, New York, New York 10020

This Simon Pulse paperback edition October 2016

Text copyright © 2015 by Tim Floreen

Cover photographs copyright © 2016 by Thinkstock

Cover design by Regina Flath

Interior design by Dan Potash

Also available in a Simon Pulse hardcover edition.

All rights reserved, including the right of reproduction in whole or in part in any form.

SIMON PULSE and colophon are registered trademarks of Simon & Schuster, Inc.

For information about special discounts for bulk purchases, please contact Simon & Schuster Special Sales at 1-866-506-1949 or business@simonandschuster.com.

The Simon & Schuster Speakers Bureau can bring authors to your live event. For more information or to book an event contact the Simon & Schuster Speakers Bureau at 1-866-248-3049 or visit our website at www.simonspeakers.com.

The text of this book was set in Minion Pro.

Manufactured in the United States of America

10 9 8 7 6 5 4 3 2 1

The Library of Congress has cataloged the hardcover edition as follows:

Floreen, Tim.

Willful machines / Tim Floreen. — First Simon Pulse hardcover edition.

p. cm.

Summary: In a near-future America, a sentient computer program named Charlotte has turned terrorist, but Lee Fisher, the closeted son of an ultraconservative president, is more concerned with keeping his Secret Service detail from finding out about his developing romance with Nico, the new guy at school, but when the spiderlike robots that roam the school halls begin acting even stranger than usual, Lee realizes he is Charlotte's next target.

[1. Computer programs—Fiction. 2. Terrorism—Fiction. 3. Presidents—Family—Fiction. 4. Gays—Fiction. 5. Science fiction.] I. Title.

PZ7.1.F59Wi 2015

[Fic]—dc23

2014030181

ISBN 978-1-4814-3277-1 (hc)

ISBN 978-1-4814-3278-8 (pbk)

ISBN 978-1-4814-3279-5 (eBook)

For Ada and Lucy

1

◇◇

The first time I set eyes on the new kid, he'd just pressed himself into a handstand on the stone wall above the cliff. Right away my heart started pounding and my shirt collar seemed to tighten around my neck—I had a complicated relationship with heights—but I couldn't tear my eyes away from him either. His feet seemed to float there, as steady as a hot-air balloon, under the black, low-hanging clouds. Only the flexing and relaxing of his fingers on the rough stone hinted at the effort it took to balance like that. His hair, longer than regulation, hung down from his head in bronze-colored curls, and the dark blue necktie of his school uniform dangled to one side of his grinning face. Below him, the river that ran underneath Inverness Prep roared. I couldn't see it from where I stood, but I could picture it on the far side of the wall, crashing down over the cliff face like shattering glass.

Beside me, Bex stood on the toes of her scuffed black

combat boots to see over the crowd. An upswell of rapturous giggles came from a trio of girls on her far side. "That's right, ladies," Bex muttered. "Good looking and he can do a handstand. Obviously, this guy's the whole package." She hadn't noticed me silently freaking out. Landing on her heels, she said, "What's your expert opinion, Lee? Gay or straight?"

I cut a look at her.

"Relax, Walk-In. Nobody heard me."

That was Bex's name for me: the Walking Walk-In—a semiaffectionate allusion to my closetedness.

My gaze slid back to the boy. I tugged at my collar and tried to pull myself together. "How can you tell he's good looking? He's upside down."

"I can tell."

"All *I* can tell is he tied his tie wrong." Trying not to sound too interested, I added, "Know anything about him?"

She shook her head. "He picked a hell of a day to start, though."

By then everybody on the terrace had turned to watch the show. A loose crowd of students had formed around him, the FUUWLs and a few others. Their pucks hovered in a cluster over their heads, the palm-size disks held aloft by softly whirring rotors. Bex wandered closer to get a better look at the kid, but I kept my distance. I noticed Dr. Singh, the robotics teacher, hunched in her wheelchair near the school entrance, having a smoke and observing the proceedings. "What a goddamn idiot," she muttered in her wheezy smoker's voice. But she didn't make a move to intervene, which didn't surprise me. She wasn't exactly a disciplinarian.

Meanwhile, my heart still felt like it might punch through my chest any second. In my mind, I could already see the boy losing his balance and vanishing over the edge. I imagined it happening fast, like a magician making himself disappear. I knew the FUUWLs must've put him up to this.

Bex and I called them FUUWLs (pronounced *fools*) because you could practically see the words "FUTURE UNSCRUPULOUS ULTRAPOWERFUL WORLD LEADER" tattooed on their foreheads. The pack of them had conquered Inverness Prep the way other kids might conquer a video game, ruthlessly mowing their way to the top in every category: academics, sports, popularity. Just seeing them around school, with their flawless hair and calculating eyes, never failed to turn my stomach.

A ragged wind gusted across the terrace, ruffling the boy's curls and whipping the cuffs of his khakis around his ankles. The crowd gasped. One of the trio of girls let out a thrilled scream. Several pucks shot higher, ready to capture the kid's final moments on video. My heart jackhammered against my rib cage. But his legs didn't budge.

I edged closer to Dr. Singh. "Do you think I should go find Headmaster Stroud?"

She exhaled a dribble of smoke but didn't answer. Her salt-and-pepper hair, in its usual messy ponytail, stirred in the breeze. Her eyes, still fastened on the boy, had taken on a strange intensity.

The FUUWLs had also appointed themselves enforcers of Inverness Prep's time-honored traditions, including the Freshman Stand. At the start of each year, while everybody waited on the terrace to be ushered inside for the Welcome Assembly, the upperclassmen would dare the boys from the incoming freshman class to stand on that wall—not on their hands, just on their feet. That was terrifying enough, especially when the wind kicked up, which it always did. The older kids would laugh and hurl insults at the petrified freshmen half crouching on the wall, and they'd torture the ones who hadn't had the courage to do it even more mercilessly.

Although in my case, things had played out differently. I suppose that year's upperclassmen couldn't resist the temptation after everything they must've read about me on the Supernet. When I refused to climb up, three of them grabbed me and deposited me there themselves. When I tried to scramble back down, they formed a barrier to block me. So there I stood, my body shaking, my glasses misting with spray, the wind shoving at me as if it wanted to join the game too. The whole time, the boys standing below me chanted the nickname the sleaziest gossip sites had coined for me a few weeks earlier: "Leap. Leap. Leap." Probably knowing they'd get in serious trouble if Headmaster Stroud caught them taunting me, they repeated the name—or was it a command?—in a whisper, their voices blending with the brutal smashing of the waterfall.

Before the Welcome Assembly my sophomore and junior years, I'd made sure to skulk in the main hall so I wouldn't have to watch the ritual. Today, though, it had taken me by surprise. The school year had started a month ago, and the new boy didn't look like a freshman, but the FUUWLs had clearly decided the tradition still had to be observed in his case. They were sticklers that way. And it appeared he'd taken them up on their dare and gone one step further.

My hands in fists at my sides, I glanced up at Stroud's office window, all the way at the top of the school, wishing he'd look down and see what was happening and put a stop to it. He always seemed to see everything. But today he must've already come downstairs for the special assembly.

A mechanical thundering filled the sky, drowning out even the noise of the waterfall. I looked up again. A black helicopter slid into view above the school. While everybody else gaped at the huge chopper hanging over our heads, my eyes jumped back to the boy.

"Oh, God," I murmured.

Another blast of wind, much bigger this time. The kid's legs wobbled, then scissored frantically back and forth.

"No!"

Before I could make a move, a hand grabbed my wrist, the fingers digging into my skin like an animal's claw. Dr. Singh peered up at me with eyes that had turned huge and wild. "Please, Lee," she rasped. "Just let him fall."

"What?" I sputtered. No time to make sense of it. I wrenched my arm out of her grip and barreled forward, shoving people out of the way. Others had noticed the boy flailing now, but they were hesitating, unsure what to do. The wind smashed into him. His hands staggered a few steps to the left. Ten feet from the wall, my shoe caught on a flagstone. The floor flew up and slammed into my cheek. All the air blew out of my lungs.

I rolled onto my back, my eyes squeezed shut. I knew what I'd see when I opened them: the boy, vanished.

My eyelids lifted. Above me, dark clouds. The boy's feet, as steady as a hot-air balloon. His grinning upside-down face. "Gotcha."

The wind had slackened. The helicopter had disappeared. It must've circled around to land on the school's front lawn. A few kids snickered, like they'd known all along he'd been faking the wobbling. A soft purring came from my inside blazer pocket: Gremlin, trying to calm me down.

A voice growled, "Mr. Medina, get down from there at once."

I lifted my head. Headmaster Stroud glared at the new kid from the entrance to the main hall, the grim expression on his craggy face matching the one on the stone raven carved into the wall above him. The boy's feet smacked the terrace next to me. He grabbed his blazer and shrugged it on, his flushed face still wearing a breathless grin. "Sorry, sir."

Stroud frowned a second longer but didn't say anything more to the boy, or to the FUUWLs, either. Officially, the school administration condemned the Freshman Stand, but I hadn't ever heard of anyone actually getting in trouble for instigating it. "You may come in," he told us, "and line up to enter the auditorium." Then, to me, "Get up, Lee."

"Yes, sir."

Technically, Stroud was also my grandfather, but that didn't mean I was entitled to special treatment—unless you considered an extra share of contempt special treatment. While the other kids crowded toward the doors, their pucks swarming along with them, a hand appeared above me: the new boy's. I flinched as I took it. His skin felt hotter than I'd expected.

"Thanks."

He gave me a wink and melted into the crowd. For a second I stood staring after him like an idiot, my face burning. Then I remembered Dr. Singh, and her hand clutching my wrist. *Just let him fall.* A cold breeze blew in from the lake, chilling the back of my neck. I looked for her, but she'd disappeared too.

2

✦✦✦

The Spiders had left the main hall even more immaculate than usual. The dark wood paneling gave off an oily shine, and the crystals dangling from the drapey, oversize chandelier glittered. Even so, a gloom hung in here, and not just because of the dark clouds outside. Inverness Prep was always gloomy.

A line had formed at the auditorium entrance. We didn't usually have to line up for assemblies, but today a body-scan machine had appeared in front of the door. Students had to step into a glass booth one by one and wait for a green light to flash before a guard waved them through.

"You okay?" Bex drew up next to me and brushed off the front of my blazer. "That was very gallant of you."

"Try mortifying."

I almost started to tell her about the weirdness with Dr. Singh, but her attention had shifted to the hall around us. "This place is a circus. Just think, Lee: all this for your dad."

I glanced at my father's staff cutting back and forth across the hall like they owned the place, all of them in sleek dark suits, their heads bent down, their pucks glued to their ears, their shoes ticking over the worn stone floors. And then there were the burly men in sunglasses standing here and there, failing to look inconspicuous. All this for Dad—it did feel strange to think of it.

"Hey." Bex elbowed me and lowered her voice. "I told you he was good looking."

Ahead of us in line, the new kid had just entered the body scanner. Bex was right: he was handsome. Not in a boring way, though. His good looks contained a hint of strangeness that made you think of words like "striking" instead of words like "cute." Maybe it had something to do with his fuzzy ethnicity. He had one of those faces that could've passed for black, white, Pakistani, or Eskimo. Or maybe it was the huge mop of twisty hair that sat on top of his head. With his friendly face and bronze curls and tan skin, he seemed too warm for a cold place like Inverness Prep. Even though he wasn't balanced above a cliff anymore, I still felt my heart pick up speed as I watched him. "He's going to get in trouble for the tie," I said.

The red light above the boy's head flashed, which meant the body-scan machine had found something. The guard glanced at the light, frowning. A split second later, the machine changed its mind: the red light flicked off and the green one came on instead. The guard gave the control panel a couple of sharp raps with his knuckle, shrugged, and waved the boy through.

"Damn," Bex said. "I was hoping we'd get to watch a strip search."

A few minutes later, when the time came for her to step into the booth herself, she fussed with her bobbed hair and smoothed her pleated skirt like she was about to have her picture taken. Inside the glass chamber, she looked even tinier than usual, like a doll in a display case—albeit one that wore combat boots and smudgy black eye makeup.

Green light. My turn. The booth's overhead light blazed down on me, and I could feel all the kids behind me in line watching. I imagined what they saw: a skinny guy with chunky black glasses and cropped black hair that made his already big ears appear even bigger. Bex always claimed she liked my look. In my school uniform, she said, with my dark hair and pale skin and serious face, I reminded her of a cute mortician. But when the other kids at Inverness Prep looked at me, I knew they thought only one thing, and today more than ever: That *boy is Henry Stroud's grandson and John Fisher's son?*

The green light flashed. I shuffled out through the booth's far door. Inside the auditorium, more suits sliced up and down the aisles, shouldering their way past students, and more hulking men with suspicious gun-shaped bulges under their jackets lined the walls. I noticed Trumbull among them. He gave me a grim nod, but I knew he loved days like this. It had to beat following me around from class to class, that was for sure.

High over our heads, news cameras wobbled through the air, watching everything. A mahogany podium stood on the stage, with a banner above it that read, JOSEPH P. INVERNESS PREPA-RATORY SCHOOL TERCENTENNIAL, and below that, FOR THREE HUNDRED YEARS, SHAPING THE LEADERS OF TOMORROW.

Bex and I found places and settled in, at least as much as we could. The hard wooden seats, though polished to a shine, hadn't been replaced in at least a century. The way they dug into your back and forced you to sit up straight, they felt like antique torture devices. I always figured that was probably the whole idea.

Just about everybody had made it into the auditorium by now. I slid forward and scanned the crowd, searching for a head of curly, bronze-colored hair. Bex leaned behind me and called to the person sitting on my other side, "Hey, nice handstand."

"Thanks."

I glanced to my left, and my insides lurched. The new boy had sat down right beside me.

"Welcome to Inverness. This is Lee. I'm Rebecca, but don't call me that. Call me Bex. We're juniors."

"Nico. Also a junior." I noticed an accent. Italian? Spanish?

"Sorry for scaring you back there, Lee."

I gave a shrug I hoped looked nonchalant. "You didn't really scare me."

Probably the most transparent lie I'd ever told, but he was kind enough to let it pass. He motioned at the stone walls, with their narrow windows and gruesome carved ravens. "I feel like I'm in Transylvania."

Bex nodded and crossed her legs, going into know-it-all mode. "Understandable. This building went up in the early twentieth century, after the original school burned down. The headmaster at the time wanted the new Inverness Prep to look like a medieval Gothic monastery. Apparently he was a little eccentric."

"Let me guess," Nico said. "He was also the one who thought of building the school on top of a waterfall."

"For added drama," she confirmed. "And to terrify the students. Fear was an important part of the teaching method back then."

"Still is," I muttered.

Nico threw his head back and laughed. He had the kind of booming laugh that seemed to say he found the world incredibly interesting and funny. A couple of students sitting in front of us turned around to stare at him.

"A lot of kids are convinced this place is haunted," Bex continued. "It probably doesn't help that the school mascot is a raven and the school color is basically black." She tugged on her necktie, which was, technically, midnight blue. "And then, of course, there are the Spiders."

"Right," Nico said. "The Spiders. I've heard about them."

Up on the stage, the faculty marched out in the silly-looking midnight-blue gowns they wore for formal occasions, which meant the assembly would start soon. They all sat down in chairs lined up behind the podium. Dr. Singh trundled after the others in her motorized wheelchair. That crazy look had left her eyes, but I still couldn't shake the memory of it from my mind. I knew the accident seven years ago had pretty much wrecked her, and not just physically. Could that explain what she'd done on the terrace? Had it been some kind of mental lapse brought on by the trauma?

"Okay, you two." Bex grabbed her puck out of the air. "Talk amongst yourselves. I'm on duty now."

I eased back in my seat and pretended to wipe a smudge from my glasses with my sleeve while I tried to think of something to say. Making conversation wasn't one of my strong points. "Where are you from?"

"Chile," he answered.

I loved the way he said it: CHEE-lay. I searched my brain for an intelligent comment about the country, but I couldn't even remember if it was in Central America or South America.

"What's she doing?" He pointed at Bex, who'd started murmuring into her puck.

"Taking notes for an article," I said. "She's the editor of the school news site. Or was, at least. She just got fired."

"Silenced," she corrected without looking over.

"Ouch," Nico said. "What happened?"

"She wrote a feature about how the school board's thinking of making Inverness Prep boys-only again. Called it part of a national trend of rolling back women's rights. Blamed the problem on the whole Human Values Movement thing."

"Sounds interesting."

"The headmaster didn't think so," I said. "He had the article taken down seventeen minutes after it went up."

"But she's still writing?"

"You bet I am," Bex said.

"The day after she was fired—sorry, silenced—she started her own news site: the *Inverness Prep Free Press*."

"Good for you," Nico told Bex. He nodded at the stage. "I guess that means you aren't going to like what our special guest has to say."

"I don't expect to, no." She let go of her puck and turned to him. "Nico, what the hell is happening to this country? As someone with an outside perspective, can you shed any light on that question?"

He seemed to think she'd just made a joke, because he let out another inappropriately loud laugh.

"I'm serious," Bex said. "Ever since Human Values started picking up steam, America has gone backward at least a hundred years. I'm not just talking about women's rights, either."

"What about you, Lee? Do you have similar feelings?"

My eyes drifted to the empty podium. I shrugged. "I'm not really into politics."

Nico followed my gaze. "I heard Fisher's son goes to school here too."

"As a matter of fact—" Bex began.

I knocked my foot against hers. "He's around here some-where."

Headmaster Stroud made his way onto the stage, his limp noticeable, but barely. He gripped the podium and, without saying a word, waited for silence to fall. A risky tactic in a room full of kids, but for him it always worked.

"Good morning, students, faculty, alumni, and guests. Today we celebrate the three hundredth anniversary of this institution. I know this place means a lot to many of you. It certainly means a lot to me. The lessons I learned as a student here made me the man I am today. In fact, I believe they saved my life."

Everybody knew exactly what he meant. My grandfather's story had already become an Inverness legend—an especially gruesome one. Long before he was the school's headmaster, he'd joined the US Marine Corps along with his best friend from Inverness, George Fisher (i.e., my dad's father; i.e., my *other* grandfather). The two of them got shipped off to battle terrorists in the Middle East. The terrorists captured them, held them prisoner for nine years, beat them and tortured them that whole time. In the end, Grandfather Fisher died, but Grandfather Stroud escaped . . . by using the titanium thigh-bone he'd dug out of his best friend's dead body to club his captors to death. Stroud returned to America a hero, earned a degree in education, and went to work at his alma mater. Even though the beatings had mangled his body, whenever we students saw him, he was always holding his back ramrod straight—probably something he'd learned in the military, but I liked to imagine he'd picked up the habit after all those years sitting in Inverness Prep's excruciating auditorium seats.

"To mark this occasion," Stroud continued, "we've invited a special guest to speak: my son-in-law, and one of Inverness Prep's most celebrated alumni."

Down in front, the FUUWLs jumped up and cheered. Pretty soon the rest of the crowd was on its feet too. Bex stood, but only so she could see better, her mouth twisted into a dubious frown. She waved her puck higher, as if she thought it might catch something the news cameras would miss. On my other side, Nico whispered, "Here we go." He'd broken into that sly grin of his, revealing two slightly crooked front teeth. I noticed the color of his eyes, too—light brown, with little threads of gold that reminded me of the glowing filaments in old-fashioned lightbulbs—and my heart sped up again.

The next second, out walked my dad, the president of the United States.

3

If you squinted just right, we looked sort of alike, Dad and I. The big ears worked on him, though. His glasses had lightweight silver frames that seemed to bring his eyes forward instead of hide them. His black hair had gone gray at the temples, just enough to make him look distinguished. And his face was always ready to crease into a smile, while I smiled so rarely, I could barely locate the required muscles when I did. Still, people commented all the time on our resemblance. I prayed Nico wouldn't notice.

Speaking of which, I had no idea why I'd told such a stupid lie. Nico was bound to find out who I was, probably before the end of the assembly. It was just that I hardly ever met people who hadn't already seen my picture on the Supernet. Maybe Chileans didn't care about American politics. If Nico hadn't seen my picture, did that mean he hadn't read the stories about me either? The write-ups on the gossip sites with headlines like LEAP FISHER'S STUNT SENDS DAD'S CAMPAIGN INTO FREE FALL?

But I knew he'd find out about *them* soon enough too.

Dad had to wait a long time for everybody to sit down. He was popular at Inverness Prep. Light-years more popular than I was. He wouldn't come up for reelection for another two years, but even so, this assembly had the schmoozy, electric feel of a campaign rally. From time to time, Dad noticed people he knew in the crowd and tossed them a wink, a salute, a friendly nod. He always did that. Sometimes I wondered if he pretended, just picking faces at random to acknowledge.

"When this great school was founded three hundred years ago," he began, "people lived in a very different world. They didn't have cars. They didn't have computers. And they certainly didn't have anything like 2B technology. But they did have values. The world has changed a lot over the past three centuries. Those values haven't."

Dad had a way of giving speeches that reminded me of those wise fathers you saw in movies as they sat down with their children and passed along some important life lesson. He'd speak in a hushed voice, and he'd nod slowly, and you could almost hear the sappy strings playing in the background.

"Several of this school's earliest students went on to become Founding Fathers. Those great men thought deeply about what it meant to be human. They recognized that man had been endowed by his Creator with certain inalienable rights, and that the purpose of government was to safeguard those rights. From this simple premise, a distinctly American system of values emerged."

My mind drifted. At that moment what I really wanted to do was steal another glance at Nico's brown eyes, but I didn't dare, so I looked to my right instead. Bex watched Dad, her mouth puckered, her fingers absently stroking her earlobe with its three small holes. That was another of her grievances against Headmaster Stroud: she had several piercings in each ear and one in her nose, but Stroud had recently restricted female students to one small earring per ear. She still wore her other earrings and nose ring while she slept as a small act of rebellion, and also to keep the holes from closing up. Meanwhile, I had a feeling her combat boots and smudgy black eye makeup would be the next items on the chopping block.

She released a quiet groan. Dad had just begun listing the values for which he believed America stood, among them family, tradition, men and women "free and equal, but respectful of the roles that society and their Creator had set out for them."

A finger tapped my left arm. "That girl's something else." Even through his whisper, I could make out the lilt of Nico's accent.

"Bex sort of goes into an altered state whenever people around her start talking politics," I whispered back.

"Are you two . . . ?" He hiked up an eyebrow.

"Together? No, just friends." I straightened my glasses. Because I felt like I should as Bex's friend—and because the masochistic part of me wanted to see how he'd respond—I added, "She's single. And really cool, when the president of the

United States isn't in the room. You want her puck handle or something?"

Nico laughed and shook his head. "No, I didn't mean it that way."

A FUUWL sitting one row ahead of us turned and directed a scorching glare in his direction.

He leaned closer, so I could feel the warm tickle of his breath on my ear. "To tell you the truth, *you're* the one I'd like to get a handle on."

The FUUWL whirled around again and pressed a finger to his mouth. Meanwhile, like the Walking Walk-In I was, I freaked. My eyes darted to the podium.

"Over the years," Dad was saying, "we Americans have always defended ourselves against those who threatened the sanctity of our traditional values."

I could've sworn he was looking straight at me as he spoke. A vision filled my mind: I pictured that glass body-scan booth appearing around me right there in the middle of the auditorium, with the red light flashing over my head and all the news cameras and pucks in the room swiveling to point in my direction. I shrank into the hard wooden seat, suddenly certain that Dad and everyone else in the room knew my secret. They'd seen me sitting here, letting myself be flirted with by an avowed traditional-values-threatening homosexual, and somehow they knew the truth about me.

"Now our country faces a new threat." Dad's fatherly voice

had taken on a sterner tone. "Now we have to take a harder look than ever at what it means to be human. Seven years ago the world saw the creation of the first 2B. A short while later we all found out how dangerous this new technology could be." He paused, and his silence conveyed what he didn't need to say out loud: that he'd experienced that danger firsthand. "In response, a new movement was born, and a new political party, too. The Human Values Party nominated me as its first candidate for president. After my election, I saw to it that Congress passed legislation outlawing 2B technology, and I inaugurated a sixth branch of the United States Armed Forces, the Cybernetic Defense Corps."

Behind Dad, all the way at the end of the row of faculty, Dr. Singh sat there like a crumpled-up piece of paper and stared at the floor. The index and middle fingers of her right hand tapped against the arm of her wheelchair, probably yearning for a Camel to hold.

"But our efforts haven't gone far enough," Dad said. "Just last month, we all had a reminder of that."

He turned to a screen behind him. On it appeared aerial footage of the Statue of Liberty. Or what was left of her. Her head and upraised right arm had disappeared, replaced by a geyser of flame erupting from her mangled torso. Instead of holding up a torch, she'd become one, lighting the nighttime New York skyline a nightmarish orange. Of course, I'd seen this footage already. Everybody there had. Most news sites hadn't shown anything else for a month. Twenty-seven days ago a commercial courier drone had been hacked and steered into the statue. Murmurs flowed through the audience: even after four weeks, the image hadn't lost its power.

"It's awful," Bex whispered to me, "but considering what's happening to this country, I have to say the symbolism fits."

In my case, though, the footage barely registered. Sitting next to Nico in those narrow seats, I could've sworn I felt heat radiating from his body everywhere it came close to mine—as if *he* were the one on fire. I noticed my knee was almost touching his, and suddenly my leg felt agonizingly uncomfortable in that position, but I didn't want to move because I worried he might think it meant something, like that I'd noticed my knee was almost touching his. I still couldn't wrap my mind around what had just happened. Had he really come on to me? He'd made it look so easy—just like that handstand. And what the hell was I supposed to say back?

"Fortunately, no one died," Dad said as the screen faded to black behind him. "If the attack had happened only a few hours earlier, when the statue had been open to the public, hundreds would have lost their lives. But the savagery of this assault on one of America's most beloved monuments nevertheless left us shocked and horrified. Following the attack, major news outlets received another message from Charlotte demanding the release of the five remaining 2Bs. Now I want to make this very clear." He paused. He always did that when he had some important point to make—created a magnetic silence that pulled you forward in your seat while you waited to hear what he'd say next. "The rumor that the United States government is keeping those five 2Bs operational and imprisoned is false. They were destroyed seven years ago. My predecessor saw to that personally."

He fell silent again. Everybody leaned a fraction of an inch closer. Over the past few days rumors had flown around the Supernet that Dad would make some important announcement during his speech. I didn't know what the announcement would be any more than anyone else, but I could tell he'd just about worked himself up to making it. For a while I forgot about my agonizingly uncomfortable left leg and bent forward just like the rest of the audience.

"Beyond reiterating that the US government is not holding any 2Bs in custody," Dad said, "I have not negotiated with Charlotte. It is the policy of this administration never to negotiate with terrorists. Especially when they aren't even alive. The tireless men and women of our Cybernetic Defense Corps are doing everything they can to find Charlotte and wipe her—*it*—off the face of the planet. And today I'd like to propose another important measure: the Protection of Humanhood Amendment, which would add to the Constitution a provision defining a legal person as an individual of the species Homo sapiens. I urge our Congress and the fifty states of our Union to pass it with all possible speed. The power to create life rests solely with our Creator. We must ensure that our laws reflect this fact, and that they continue to protect the inalienable rights with which our Creator endowed us. Thank you."

The FUUWLs jumped to their feet again. The sound of cheering crashed through the auditorium. Dad smiled, his eyes crinkling behind his silver glasses, and raised one hand in an understated wave.

"God bless America."

Bex gave me the same searching, baffled look she always did when we happened to see one of Dad's speeches on the Supernet. It said, *How can that guy be your father?* I could still feel the possibly imaginary wafts of heat emanating from Nico, but I didn't have the courage to turn in his direction.

The applause finally subsided. Headmaster Stroud returned to the podium and dismissed us to our second-period classes. The noise in the auditorium boiled up again as everybody crowded toward the aisles. I'd started to follow Bex when I felt a hand on my arm.

"Hey," Nico said. "Sorry if I came on a little strong. I shouldn't have just asked you for your handle out of the blue like that."

I darted a glance over my shoulder. Bex had already reached the aisle. She raised her eyebrow a tick. I motioned for her to go ahead. "So that *was* what you were doing? Asking me for my handle?"

Nico turned on his grin. "Sorry, did I not make that clear?"

Usually when I saw a grin that big on people, it made me want to shake them and ask them what there was to be so damn happy about. But not with Nico. His grin just made my knees feel squishy. "Look, I know you're new here and from another country and whatever, but you don't just start making moves on another boy in a place like Inverness Prep. Especially not while the president of the United States is in the very same room giving a speech about the need to stomp out threats to traditional human values."

He took a step closer. "That only made it hotter."

My pulse quickened like a Geiger counter at his approach. "Who *are* you? Where's your normal, healthy, paralyzing teenage insecurity?"

"Probably trumped by my Latin American audacity." He opened his hands. "If I'm barking up the wrong tree, you can just tell me."

I pushed my chunky black glasses up my nose. My shirt collar felt tighter than ever. Part of me knew I should just tell him, *Yes, you're barking up the wrong tree,* and walk away. I sometimes called that side of my psyche Gutless Lee. But another part of me—the part I called Kamikaze Lee—wanted me to sink my fingers into his big, wild mop, pull him close, and whisper my handle into his ear.

Instead, I did neither of those things and said, "You tied your tie wrong."

He touched the blue-black silk. "Excuse me?"

"That's a single Windsor. At Inverness Prep, all students are supposed to tie their ties in double Windsor knots. You'll get in trouble if you're caught with your tie like that. Also, your tiepin is upside down."

His fingers moved to his silver raven tiepin. Every student received one after enrolling at Inverness Prep. "Only when I'm not doing a handstand."

"True."

"I don't know how to tie a double Windsor knot."

I looked around the auditorium. A few suits lingered here and there muttering into their pucks, and a few technicians had started packing lighting equipment into big metal boxes, but almost all the students had left. I glanced up. No more news cameras hovering over our heads. "I'll do it for you," I said. "If you want."

That grin again. Goofy and sly and dangerous, all at the same time. He drew close and pulled open his gray tweed blazer, wafting a scent in my direction: coconuts. Like he'd just stepped off a Chilean beach. Chile *did* have beaches, didn't it?

My mind scrambled around, doing quick calculations. What message had I sent by offering to tie his tie? Did it mean the same thing as giving him my puck handle? Had I crossed some line of no return yet? I reached out and unfastened his upside-down silver raven.

The back of the pin where it had rested against Nico's chest felt hot in my palm. Maybe I hadn't imagined that odd warmth radiating from his body after all. I untied his tie, wishing I could also untie my own. The thing was strangling me now.

"You have cute ears," Nico said.

They tingled and probably turned bright red. "Thanks," I mumbled as I looped the wide end of his tie around, over, and down.

"So let me get this straight," he went on. "At Inverness Prep, you have to tie your tie a certain way and you can't flirt with other boys. What kind of dictatorship is this?"

"This isn't a dictatorship. This is America, remember?" I nodded my head toward the podium America's freely elected commander in chief had vacated minutes ago.

Nico laughed loudly.

Then he stopped laughing.

When I looked up, his grin had disappeared. "If I'm barking up the wrong tree," he repeated, "tell me."

My fingers stopped looping. I swallowed, my Adam's apple bulging against my collar. "The thing is—"

A hand landed on my shoulder. I jerked away from Nico and knocked into something large and brick-wall-like. I whirled around.

"Hi, Trumbull," I stammered.

My Head Armed Babysitter frowned at me, one of his eyebrows rising above his sunglass frames. "I didn't mean to startle you, sir."

I couldn't stand it when Trumbull "sirred" me. I must've told him not to do that a hundred times, but he always did it anyway—especially on important occasions, like today, when he got more caught up than usual in playing secret agent. I wondered if he'd noticed the ambient strangeness floating in the air around me and Nico. If he had, he gave no sign, but then again I never could tell what was going on behind those dark lenses of his.

"Your father wants to see you before he leaves," he said. "The chopper's taking off in thirteen minutes, so there isn't much time. He's waiting for you in your room. You'd better come with me."

"Okay. Just a second."

I turned back to Nico. He smirked. "Your father?"

He seemed more amused than annoyed, like to him this was just one more example of how incredibly interesting and funny the world could be. I put out my hand for him to shake. It felt silly and overly formal, especially after the conversation we'd just had, but with Trumbull standing there, what else could I do?

"Nicolas Medina," he said.

"Lee Fisher," I answered sheepishly.

"Right." When we finished shaking, he folded his arms and stood, holding me with his light brown eyes and that knowing, but not nasty, smirk.

"Well." I followed the awkward shake with an awkward wave. "See you around."

Only as I walked away did I remember I hadn't even finished tying his tie.

4

◇◇◇

The main hall had mostly emptied by the time Trumbull
and I reached it. Without all the jabbering people around,
you could hear the low-pitched rumble of the river passing under the stone floor and the accompanying whisper of the
chandelier overhead. I glanced through the back windows at the
terrace, with the lake beyond mirroring the dark clouds above.
On my other side, through the front windows, the river ran in a
straight iron-gray line down the middle of the front lawn, reined
in by stone walls on either side. The trees of the forest across the
highway, most of them already leafless, bucked and tossed like
wild, leashed dogs, and behind that, a lone mountain lost itself
in more clouds. Nico was right: this place did sort of feel like
Count Dracula High. When you peered up from the lake at the
school perched at the top of the cliff, with the waterfall roaring
out from the base of the building, and the spires twisting upward
like thorny plants, and the blunt blue mountain looming in the
background, it looked sinister, but also beautiful.

I climbed the stairs to the third floor and headed toward the boys' rooms, Trumbull following close behind me, the floor releasing soft creaks as we went. A mobile security camera hovering near the ceiling turned to watch us go by. Up ahead, a Spider picked its way along on four of its six slender legs, its blue, lamplike eye sweeping over the wood-paneled walls, and its two forelegs, wearing cleaner spray and buffing attachments, polishing away smudges only it could see. When it noticed us, it folded its lanky eight-foot-tall body against the wall to give us more room to pass. "Excuse me," it murmured.

Outside my room, two more Secret Service agents stood guard. "He has to be in the chopper in eleven minutes," one of them said. Wishing I'd walked upstairs more slowly, I went in.

Dad stood studying the shelf of little machines I called my Creatures. They were the only things to look at in there, the only personal touch except for a small framed photograph of Mom on my nightstand. Otherwise, I kept my room neat and anonymous.

"You still play with these toys, Lee?"

"Dr. Singh says I have a knack." From the shelf I grabbed a wadded-up ball of black fabric. "This one I just finished a few weeks ago. A hovering sunshade. He automatically positions himself between you and the sun." Glancing out the window, I added, "Not that we need something like that around here, I guess." I tossed the ball into the air, and it exploded into a floating canopy that began to undulate around the room like a black jellyfish.

Dad paid no attention. He leaned closer to a machine the approximate size of a cat and eyed the sharp silver teeth lining his oversize jaws. "What does that one do?"

"Catches rodents and insects. He doesn't actually kill them, though. The spiky teeth are just for show. He releases whatever he catches outside. I call him Mouthtrap."

When Dad talked to the American public, he had fatherly crinkles around his eyes and smile lines around his mouth. When he talked to me, his face bunched up in different places. A deep vertical crease formed between his eyebrows, his mouth pressed itself into a hard, straight line, and he watched me with a mixture of disappointment and fear, like he suspected I might be planning a school shooting.

The room darkened. My sunshade had drifted in front of the window to block out the light. "Move, Shadow," I muttered. The Creature floated off. Milky daylight filtered in through the window again.

"What's Dr. Singh been teaching you?" Dad asked.

"Nothing illegal, if that's what you mean."

He nodded toward another Creature perched at the end of the shelf. My latest project, she looked just like a real raven. "How about that one?"

"One hundred percent synthetic. The feathers are artificial. If you look close, you can tell. That's not against the law, is it?"

"Almost."

He was referring to the law banning machines that mimicked

the appearance of humans or animals—another piece of legislation the Human Values Party had pushed through. How much a robot could resemble a living thing was a point of legal dispute, but so far most courts had drawn the line at machines that incorporated an outer layer of living organic material. Flesh-jackets, people called them. My bird wasn't one of those. Still, I knew I was pushing it.

"I built her to look like the Inverness mascot," I added, as if my show of school spirit would make it all okay. "I'll show you." To the robot, I said, "Wake up, Nevermore." (Bex had come up with the name. I wasn't much of a reader and had never even heard of Edgar Allan Poe, but she'd assured me I'd like him.)

The bird came to life, shaking out her silky black wings and darting her head from side to side. Dad remained unimpressed.

"I'm really good at robotics, Dad. Isn't this exactly what you've been saying I should do? Find a direction?"

"But why *this* one?" He walked over to the window and gazed at the stone wall opposite. Most rooms at Inverness Prep had a view of either the lake or the mountain, but the Secret Service had decided the exposure would pose too big a security risk, so my window looked out on a minuscule courtyard instead. Outside, it had finally started drizzling. Drops of rain flicked against the glass and then twisted their way down. "This isn't a tech school," Dad said. "Students don't come here to learn robotics."

"They should. Dr. Singh's the greatest roboticist in the world."

"She didn't come here to teach either, Lee. She came here to recover."

"She likes teaching *me*, I can tell."

"Trust me, she has no interest in becoming a robotics guru. It's better for this country that she doesn't, after what happened." His gaze dropped to the picture of Mom next to my bed. "You of all people should understand that."

A sort of desolate trance came over Dad as he looked at Mom, with her rumpled lab coat and her fiery red hair in a messy ponytail just like Dr. Singh's. His bunched face went slack. His eyes glassed over behind his glasses. I usually noticed a similar expression on my own face when I saw myself in photos. *Do I really look that miserable?* I'd always wonder. Am *I really that miserable?* But Dad only got that expression every once in a while.

My room had gone dim again. Shadow had floated back to the window. This time I said, "Shadow, sleep." He crumpled himself into a ball and thudded to the floor.

The light poured in. Dad snapped back to himself. The line between his eyebrows reformed. He adjusted his silver glasses. "And it would also be better for this country if you directed your energies elsewhere. Stop spending all your time holed up in that robotics lab and *do* something. For God's sake, play a sport, son. Trumbull tells me you go running every morning. So why don't you join the cross-country team?"

"That would ruin it, Dad. I like the time alone. Although even when I'm running, I have my stupid detail tromping after me."

"Don't call them stupid. Trumbull and his boys are just trying to keep you out of harm's way. You don't give them a hard time, do you?"

"No, I don't give them a hard time."

"Well, if you're not into sports, at least work on your social skills. Make connections. That's what this place is really for. Twenty years from now, your classmates will be among the most powerful people in the world."

I stroked Nevermore's sleek synthetic feathers. "I'm not like you, Dad. I didn't inherit the social gene."

"Apparently not. You're the son of the president, and still you can't seem to make any friends. That's an accomplishment."

"Believe me, you're not the only one who's noticed the irony." I didn't bother to add that I had one friend, at least. Dad knew about Bex, but he didn't count her as a worthwhile connection. Last year I'd introduced the two of them, and she'd spent the whole time haranguing him about his policies.

"You have to make an effort, Lee. Take advantage of your time here." He gestured toward the rain-spattered window like it looked out on a magnificent view instead of a stone wall. "This place helped me become a man."

I remembered Headmaster Stroud had said something similar during the assembly. The way the two of them talked, you'd think Inverness Prep was some kind of military training camp. I glanced at my puck, and it flashed the time. Four minutes down. Still seven minutes to go.

Dad asked me a few questions about my classes, but he didn't really listen to my answers. Then he talked for a while about how busy the fallout from the Statue of Liberty attack had kept him. I didn't pay much attention to what he said either.

That ate up another three minutes. We'd just sunk into a glum silence, both of us staring out the viewless window, when Trumbull knocked on the door and stuck his head in.

"Sorry to bother you, sir." Then, to me, "A friend of yours is outside. He says you have his tiepin and he needs it back."

I glanced down. The fingers of my left hand uncurled. In the center of my palm lay Nico's silver raven. "Oh," I said stupidly. "I didn't realize."

I started to hand it to Trumbull, but Dad said, "So you *do* have a friend here. Tell him to come in, Trumbull. I'd like to meet him."

My stomach did a somersault. "He's not exactly a friend, Dad. I just met him an hour ago."

He waved at me to be quiet. "Call him in." His face reconfigured itself, the line between his eyebrows fading, his eyes crinkling into their friendly squint. Dad always seemed more comfortable in front of strangers than in front of family. *Like a true politician,* Mom used to say.

Nico appeared at the door. He hadn't touched his tie, which hung down his shirt in a tangle of midnight-blue silk.

Dad put out his hand. "What's your name, son?"

"Nico Medina," he answered, activating his million-watt smile. "It's an honor to meet you, Mr. President." He appeared perfectly unruffled, like he met heads of state every day. Probably that Latin American audacity again. Meanwhile, I lurked next to Nevermore, stayed very still, and waited for something mortifying to drop out of his mouth.

"Having some trouble with your tie?" Dad asked.

Nico glanced at his chest. "Yeah, I hear they're a little picky about ties here. It's my first day."

"A little picky? Tie tying is practically a religion at Inverness Prep."

"Lee was helping me, though. That's why he had my tiepin."

"And he didn't finish? That doesn't sound very helpful. Let me show you, Nico." He started flinging Nico's tie one way and then the other. "You have to loop it around both sides. Like this, see?"

"Thanks, sir."

"I hear an accent," Dad said. "Where are you from?"

"Chile." There it was again. CHEE-lay.

"A beautiful country. One summer when I was a college student, my friends and I spent two unforgettable weeks backpacking through Chile. Listen, may I ask you something, Nico?"

"Of course, Mr. President."

"Just a few minutes ago my son and I were having a talk.

I realize you've only known him for a short time, but would you agree that this is a young man with a lot going for him? Intelligent. Capable. Good looking. Wouldn't you say?"

The two of them, best buddies now, turned to contemplate me. Nevermore rustled her wings. My ears felt like they might burst into flames. One corner of Nico's mouth curled upward. He nodded.

"What were your first impressions after meeting him?"

"Honestly?" Nico asked.

Please don't say you thought I had cute ears, I prayed in my head.

"He seemed shy. Quiet. Like he hangs back." He turned his brown eyes on me again. "He should smile more," he added.

"Yes!" Dad slapped one hand against the other. "That's what I've been telling him. He needs to step up to the plate. Take the bull by the horns. Stop letting life pass him by."

"My thoughts exactly," Nico said.

Satisfied, Dad went back to work on the tie. "What do you think of this place so far, Nico?"

"Still trying to get the lay of the land, I guess."

Dad laughed as he tugged the knot of Nico's tie up to his neck. "Don't worry. Lee will help you settle in." He plucked the silver tiepin from my hand and slid it onto the tie with a flourish. "There you go. Lee, why don't you give Nico your puck handle?"

Unseen by Dad, Nico fixed me with a triumphant grin.

My face and ears were still scorching hot, but I twitched my mouth into something that may or may not have resembled a smile. *You got me.* I waved my puck toward Nico's. The two of them circled each other like romancing birds while they traded information. I felt my blush deepen as I watched them.

"If you need something," Dad was saying, "have a question, get lost on your way to class, whatever—just message Lee."

"Don't worry, sir. I will."

Dad folded his arms across his chest and gazed at the orbiting pucks. "You know, I still haven't gotten used to those contraptions."

Nico plucked his puck out of the air and examined it. The thing lay in his palm, round and smooth like a skipping stone, with two small openings on either side where the rotors that whirled around to keep it aloft deployed. "'Those that Hobgoblin call you and sweet Puck,'" he recited. "'You do their work, and they shall have good luck.'"

I had no idea what he'd just said, but Dad's face lit up. "A Shakespeare fan, are you?"

Nico gave a modest shrug. He tossed up his puck. Its rotors whipped out and started to spin. "I'd better get to class. Thanks again, Mr. President."

"Sure thing, Nico."

"See you, Lee," he said, hiking up one eyebrow, and slipped out the door.

Dad and I stared after him. The temperature in the room

seemed to drop about twenty degrees as soon as he left. "You didn't have to do that," I said.

"*Someone* needs to help you make friends." His face had gone back to its previous configuration, crumpled forehead and pressed-flat mouth, but for the first time all morning, he turned and looked me in the eyes. "I just want you to be happy. You know that, don't you?"

I nodded. "Yeah." *But how?* I wanted to ask. Being happy felt like a trick I could never quite get the hang of—like juggling or something.

Trumbull knocked again. "Mr. President? It's time."

"Have a good semester, Lee," Dad said. "See you at break." He put out his hand for me to shake, as if we'd just wrapped up a business meeting—exactly like I'd done with Nico thirteen minutes earlier.

5

◇◇◇

I thought about ditching the rest of second period, but it was robotics, the one class I actually liked. Plus, I wanted to find out what Dr. Singh would do when she saw me. Would she offer an explanation for what she'd said on the terrace? Or maybe I'd work up the nerve to ask her about it myself.

I reached into my inside blazer pocket and pulled out Gremlin. He was another of my Creatures, although unlike the others, I hadn't built him myself.

"How you doing in there? Having a nice nap?"

The little machine yawned, stood up on my palm, and shook out his shabby orange fur. (I'd owned Gremlin since I was eight, and I had a habit of rubbing him for luck, like a rabbit's foot, so his coat had thinned in places.) He scuttled up my arm to my shoulder, paused to tug twice on my earlobe, and broke into a mad dash, his furry lizard-shaped body tracing figure eights and curlicues over my back and chest.

"That's enough, buddy. Back to sleep now. I'm heading out again."

He blinked up at me with his huge black eyes and released a whimper. Then he burrowed under my blazer and into my pocket. I put Nevermore back to sleep too, zipped her into a duffel, and carried her out to the hall, where Trumbull waited with folded arms. I wondered again if he'd found all the back-and-forth between me and Nico this morning odd, but his expression, as usual, gave nothing away. And if he had, did he care? Another good question. To tell the truth, I didn't really even know the guy. He wasn't exactly big on small talk. I could never shake the feeling, though, that he could see right through me, and that he found me as big a disappointment as Dad and Stroud did.

One time, for instance, Bex and I had just watched one of Dad's speeches about "traditional human values" on the Supernet, and it had sparked one of her rants. "Human values? Try *cave*man values. He's just using this whole Charlotte scare as an excuse to drag us back to the Stone Age. Women. Gays. Religious minorities. He's quietly stripping rights away from everyone." She'd noticed Trumbull standing nearby and flung her hand in his direction. "African Americans." She'd turned to him. "I mean, *you* can't possibly believe all that Human Values junk, can you?"

"I believe it's none of your business what I believe," he'd said, his voice never rising above its usual low, measured growl.

Then he'd turned his frown in my direction, as if to make it clear he considered me at fault too, for choosing to hang out with someone like her.

"Robotics," I said now.

He nodded.

I headed for the stairs. On the way down, I paused on the landing, where a large window overlooked the lake. I tipped myself forward and leaned my forehead against the cold glass. Looking down at the terrace below, I experienced an echo of the vertigo that had grabbed me while I'd watched Nico do his handstand. I listened to the rumble of the waterfall and felt the window vibrate against my skull. That relentless smashing was a noise you forgot to hear at Inverness Prep, because it was always there, underneath every other sound. As I listened, I imagined I could make out the whispering voices chanting along with it: *Leap. Leap. Leap.* Outside, above the lake, inky clouds clotted the sky. I thought of a line we'd studied in English yesterday. We were reading *Hamlet*, and although I couldn't usually quote Shakespeare off the top of my head the way Nico could, that line I remembered: "This goodly frame, the earth, seems to me a sterile promontory."

I felt Trumbull watching me, probably wondering what I was doing. I turned away from the window and kept moving.

Robotics class took place in a conservatory jutting from one side of the main building. The lab had a permanently dingy appearance, partly because that section of the school hadn't been renovated in decades, and partly because Dr. Singh, fearing the nine Spiders that serviced Inverness Prep might disturb her robotics equipment, insisted they never clean in there. She didn't seem to like the Spiders much—ironic, considering she'd designed and built them herself—but given her history with robots, I couldn't blame her for having mixed feelings. Panes of warped glass made up the conservatory's walls and ceiling. They gave a contorted fun-house view of the trees outside. No matter the time of year, those trees seemed to continually shed slimy leaves, which dropped on the glass roof and lay there for months, their black silhouettes biting leaf-shaped chunks out of the perpetually gray sky.

Only fifteen minutes of class remained by the time I got there. About a dozen students stood around worktables or sat on stools, a few of them with plastic safety glasses and aprons on. (We were all supposed to wear safety glasses and aprons while we worked, but Dr. Singh never said anything to the students who didn't.) The class was a mix of nerds—who'd apparently missed the memo that you didn't come to Inverness Prep for robotics—and slackers—even at Inverness, we had a few of those. The slackers mostly sat around talking or staring into their pucks, knowing they wouldn't get in trouble, and sure enough, Dr. Singh never said anything to them, either.

Right now she sat in her usual spot near the back of the room watching the rain, her hand dangling out an unlatched window, a Camel clutched between her fingers. Stray wisps of her long salt-and-pepper hair hung down on either side of her drawn, grayish face. Her ceremonial gown had disappeared, replaced by sweatpants and a ratty T-shirt emblazoned with the words TIME IS AN ILLUSION—LUNCHTIME DOUBLY SO and, below that, the details of some scientists' luncheon that had taken place ten years earlier. (The dress code at Inverness Prep, like the no-smoking rule, somehow didn't apply to her.) While Trumbull trudged off to a corner to make himself "unobtrusive," I grabbed a chair and set it down next to her wheelchair.

"About time you showed up," she said in her croaky smoker's voice. She nodded at my duffel. "How's the bird coming?"

No mention of her weirdness on the terrace. Had I just imagined it? I cleared my throat, unzipped the duffel, lifted out Nevermore. "Pretty well. I finally got her airborne last night. I still have to make a few tweaks, but she basically works."

I'd labored over Nevermore for months. Any idiot could build a robot that flew like a puck. You just had to buy a rotary-wing apparatus on the Supernet. Building a robot that flew like an actual bird, on the other hand—*that* took skill.

Dr. Singh balanced her cigarette on the window frame and put out her hands. "Let me have a peek."

She turned the machine upside down on her lap, felt for the seam hidden under the orderly feathers, and pulled the skin covering Nevermore's chest apart, revealing a rubbery, slightly translucent layer of artificial muscle. My robot raven had pretty much the same structure as an actual raven did, muscle for muscle, bone for bone—except the bones were made of a light-weight titanium alloy and the muscles of synthetic contractile tissue. Only deep inside Nevermore's rib cage, which housed her power supply instead of lungs and a heart, and deep inside her skull, where her microprocessor and sensors lodged in place of an organic brain, did the visible resemblance to the real thing stop.

"Nicely done," Dr. Singh said. She drew the skin over the muscle again. The magnetic closures caught, and the seams disappeared beneath the shiny feathers. She handed Never-more back to me. "Just don't get into trouble with that thing."

A deafening chug pounded into the lab. We glanced up through the leaf-covered glass ceiling. Dad's helicopter cruised over us like a whale cutting through water. I ran my palm over my robot's sleek back. "Dr. Singh, do you mind if I ask you a question? On the terrace, when that new kid was doing a hand-stand, you said—"

"Class is almost over, Lee." She grabbed her cigarette from the window. "Don't you think you should get some work done?"

Dr. Singh expressing concern about one of her students doing work: that was a first. Her eyes fixed on the trees dripping in the drizzle outside, she took a drag and exhaled a narrow shaft of smoke. Her other hand had gone to her chest, where a gold pendant shaped like a dancing, four-armed Hindu god hung. I never saw her without it.

"Right." I cleared my throat again and tucked Nevermore

under my arm. "I probably should. It wasn't important anyway."

I retreated to my worktable and spent the last few minutes of class hunched over Nevermore's access panel. One thing I liked about robots: they always made much more sense to me than people did.

Next came English. Bex arrived a few minutes after I did. She slid into the spot in front of mine and turned to lean across my desk. "What was going on between you and the Loudly Laughing Latin?" she whispered.

I glanced around. Nobody listening. Trumbull had gone off to his corner. "Something. I'm not sure what, though. He sort of asked me for my handle."

Her smudgy eyes popped. "Like with amorous intentions? Is that what you mean?"

"I'm pretty sure. He also said I have cute ears."

"Intriguing. So what did you do? Did you give it to him?"

I shook my head. "Not at first. But then my dad made me."

"Wait. What?"

I didn't have a chance to explain, though. Nico walked in, and the words stopped in my throat.

It was like I felt him before I saw him: the weather in the room suddenly got warmer again. Everybody else turned to look at him too, which caused all the pucks hovering overhead, programmed to follow their owners' gaze, to swivel in his direction. We didn't get new students at Inverness Prep often—and we never got ones who did a handstand on the terrace wall. Nico seemed not to notice, though. He crossed to the far side of the room, his stride loose and confident, and dropped into a desk near the front. I didn't think he'd seen me.

"You're the new boy?" Miss Remnant, our English teacher, pumped hand sanitizer from a bottle on her desk and rubbed her palms together. Glancing at her puck, she added, "Mr. Medina?"

"That's right," he answered. "You can call me Nico."

She appeared immune to the Nico Medina grin. "We're studying *Hamlet*, Mr. Medina. Please follow along." She crossed to her lectern at the front of the room, her skirt rustling around her skinny calves, and cleared her throat. "Today you all heard the president give an impassioned speech about 2Bs. What you may not realize is that—"

One of the FUUWLs threw up his hand. "The 2Bs' name was inspired by that famous line from *Hamlet*, 'To be or not to be.'"

Miss Remnant pursed her lips: she didn't like being interrupted. "That's correct, Mr. Harris."

"It's an interesting story, actually," the FUUWL said. "May I?" Without waiting for her to respond, he turned around in his desk so he could address the rest of the class. "Originally, the 2B project went by some other name. Dr. Singh had just finished her first attempt at artificial consciousness—a computer program modeled on the human brain. For a while the program seemed to work like it was supposed to. Then it started acting . . . discontented, I suppose you'd say. It felt like a prisoner because it didn't have a physical body or any connection to the Supernet. In the end, it terminated itself. Dr. Singh was pretty upset, but the director of the lab—Dr. Waring, I think his name was—tried to spin it as a success: they'd built the first program capable of contemplating death and committing willful suicide. He called it a man-made Hamlet."

"And can you tell us why he did that?" Miss Remnant asked, still annoyed by the interruption but resigned now.

"When Hamlet makes his 'To be or not to be' speech, he's trying to decide whether to kill himself. To live or not to live, *that's* the question. So Dr. Waring started using the name 2B, and Dr. Singh built a human-shaped fleshjacket body for the second consciousness she created, which was Charlotte. We all know what happened after that."

He glanced at me and gave an unconvincing nod of sympathy. My stomach twisted. I looked down at my desk.

"That's fine, Mr. Harris," Miss Remnant said. "We'll be studying the 'To be or not to be' soliloquy later. For now, let's return to the speech from act two we were looking at yesterday." She scanned the class, her eyes moving over faces until they settled on mine. My belly cinched itself even tighter. "Mr. Fisher, would you reread the speech for us?"

I stared at the white, angled surface of my desk, on which my puck, hovering just over my shoulder, was projecting the relevant passage. Speaking in front of large groups of people ranked just below heights on my list of phobias. "'I have of late—'"

"Speak up."

I cleared my throat and tried again, more loudly. "'I have of late—but wherefore I know not—lost all my mirth, forgone all custom of exercise, and indeed it goes so heavily with my disposition that this goodly frame, the earth, seems to me a sterile promontory.'"

"Stop there, Mr. Fisher. I think you've butchered Shakespearean English enough for one day. Now tell me: there's an adjective famously associated with Hamlet, an adjective we discussed yesterday, an adjective this speech exemplifies. Do you remember what that is?"

I glanced toward Nico's side of the room, but other heads blocked my view of his. "Sad?"

"Sad," Miss Remnant repeated.

"Well, Hamlet's father just died, right? So he's sad. That's what he's saying here."

She leaned her elbows on the lectern, making herself comfortable. "I see. So why doesn't he just say, 'I'm sad'?"

"Because this sounds better?"

A titter rolled through the class. A couple FUUWLs in the front row exchanged looks. Bex squeezed one fist on her desk in a discreet show of solidarity.

"The adjective is not 'sad,'" Miss Remnant said. "Try again, Mr. Fisher."

I readjusted my glasses. On my desk, the words "sterile promontory" seemed to stand out from the others. "Depressed? Clinically depressed?"

"I don't believe they had a diagnosis of clinical depression in Shakespeare's day."

The wooden seat back pressed into the knobs of my lower spine. The desk chairs in the classrooms at Inverness Prep were almost as painful as the seats in the auditorium.

"Well, Mr. Fisher?"

I kept staring at those two words, "sterile promontory," until they collapsed into meaningless shapes.

"I think 'clinically depressed' is an interesting choice, actually," someone said. Across the room, Nico had shifted into view. He slung one arm over the back of his chair and wagged his finger at the words projected on his desk. "I mean, sure, the concept may not have existed when Shakespeare was alive, but hundreds of years later, when Sigmund Freud was formulating his theories about depression, didn't he use *Hamlet* as one of his main literary touchstones? As far as Freud was concerned, Hamlet was pretty much the poster boy for clinical depression, right? Just listen to how the speech continues." He sat forward again and peered at his puck's projection. "'What a piece of work is a man, how noble in reason, how infinite in faculties.'"

The moment he started reading, his whole manner shifted. His voice became low and resonant, and the lilt of his accent added to the dramatic effect. His body changed too: he held his back straighter, and his hands were very still.

"'In action, how like an angel,'" he read, "'in apprehension, how like a god.'"

My stomach uncoiled little by little. I didn't move a muscle as I listened with my big ears and the whole rest of my being to the words Nico spoke—words that seemed to apply to no one better than Nico himself. This stranger who could do handstands and quote Shakespeare from memory, this goof with the huge grin and inappropriately loud but nevertheless charming laugh: how like an angel, how like a god. And he'd asked *me* for my handle, apparently with amorous intentions. Me, a dud of a First Son with a robot obsession, poor social skills, and enough baggage to sink a freighter: how like a loser, how like a freak. What in the hell was Nico thinking?

"'The beauty of the world, the paragon of animals, and yet, to me, what is this quintessence of dust? Man delights not me.'"

His voice sank to a despairing whisper at the end. He gazed glassy eyed at his desk, his eyebrows knitted together. The room had gone dead quiet. Bex glanced at me, eyebrows raised. Then Nico looked up, his forehead cleared, and a bigger grin than ever erupted across his face.

"See? Hopelessness. Antisocial feelings. An inability to appreciate the beauty of the world. All classic symptoms of clinical depression."

Miss Remnant's cheeks had turned distinctly pinkish. She

hurried over to her desk and pumped more hand sanitizer. Rubbing it into her palms, she said, "You read like a seasoned actor, Mr. Medina."

"I acted a little at my last school. Shakespeare was always my favorite."

"What a lucky coincidence. As it happens, I'm also in charge of Inverness Prep's dramatic society. We're putting on a production of *The Tempest*, and our Ariel had to step down at the last minute. Would you be interested in taking his place?"

I'd never seen Miss Remnant like this. She was practically *smiling*.

"Sure," Nico said. "I love *The Tempest*. At my school in Chile I played Caliban."

Miss Remnant nodded. "It's settled, then." She glanced around at the rest of us as if just noticing we were still there. Her face settled back into its usual scowl. She returned to her lectern. "And by the way, the adjective was 'melancholy.' Which is how you make me feel, Mr. Fisher."

6
◇◇◇◇

What cheer, good lord? How dost thou?

The message flashed up on my puck's small circular screen after math. Bex and I were on our way to the dining hall for lunch. I nudged her and pointed up at my puck.

"Cute," she said. By then I'd filled her in on the details of the Nico saga.

"Should I message him back right away or wait a little?"

"Don't play games. Just message him already."

I waved my puck closer and spoke my return message. The words sprang up on the screen: *Thanks for saving my butt in class today.*

"Do you think the reference to my butt is too flirty?"

Bex rolled her eyes. "It's fine, Lee. And anyway, lucky for you, you have a nice butt to back it up."

I glanced at her.

"What? I notice these things."

I sent the message. Right away my puck chimed again. *My pleasure. Miss Remnant's insane. I think I'm on lunch break. Any idea where a guy goes to get some food around here?*

"He's asking where he's supposed to go for lunch," I reported.

"Ooh, invite him to eat with us."

Dining hall, I messaged. *Bottom floor, across from the auditorium. Bex is asking if you want to eat with us.*

Bex, glancing at the message, muttered, "You're pathetic."

Prithee tell Mistress Bex 'twould be an honor.

"I'm not pathetic," I told her. "You know I have to be careful about this kind of stuff. I already had one close call freshman year. I can't afford another."

"A close call? Please." She grabbed my arm and yanked me to the side of the corridor. The other students jostled past us on their way to the dining hall. Trumbull stopped a polite distance away. "Get a grip, Walk-In," Bex said. "You kissed Jeremy exactly *once*. Nobody saw. Neither of you told anyone. He doesn't even go to this school anymore. That's not a close call."

"But he *could* tell someone. Any time he wanted. And it's not necessarily true that nobody saw. Remember?" I pointed at a security camera sliding by above us.

"So you thought maybe you saw a camera." Bex shook her head. "Stop being paranoid. It's unattractive. Not even your nice butt can make up for that." She seized my arm again and pulled me back into the stream of traffic.

Nico was waiting for us next to the dining hall entrance. I reached into my blazer and gave Gremlin's fur a quick good-luck rub.

"Congratulations," Bex said, knocking him on the arm with her fist. "Miss Remnant's going to make you a star. Just be warned: she forces her actors to wear period costumes. In other words, tights."

"I'm a confident guy."

She gave a tart smile. "So I've heard."

Nico's eyes went to me. He grinned, triggering the usual Pavlovian squishiness in my knees. "Hi, Lee."

"Hi."

We shuffled forward in line a few steps.

"I liked meeting your dad," Nico said. "He seems like a nice guy. I mean, aside from his policy choices, of course, Bex."

"That's right!" Bex said. "I haven't even had a chance to rant about the new amendment your dad's pushing! Let's start with the name: Protection of Humanhood? Is 'humanhood' even a word?"

The glances from people around us had already started. Whenever Bex got worked up about something, she didn't shout exactly, but the way she overenunciated her words made her voice slice through the largest, most crowded room. Today I didn't mind so much, though. The prospect of making chitchat with Nico still terrified me. Now that Bex had hijacked the conversation, I could go on autopilot and just enjoy being near him.

"Above and beyond that, though," she went on, "how will this stupid amendment be enforced? It says only humans can be legal persons, right? But these days, what qualifies as human? What if some guy gets into a terrible car accident, and he ends up with a body that's more than fifty percent artificial? It happens, you know. Is he suddenly not a person?"

"Of course he is," I said. "His *brain* is still human, and that's what matters."

"Ah!" Bex thrust a finger into the air. "But what if the guy had a brain injury, and more than fifty percent of his brain is now synthetic? Maybe that couldn't happen today, but research in brain implant technology is exploding right now."

"The guy started life one hundred percent human, though. I'm sure that'll count for something."

"Okay, now imagine *this*," Bex said, a crafty twinkle in her eye. "A baby is born with a birth defect. The only way to save its life is to use artificial implants to replace more than fifty percent of its body *and* its brain. Should the baby be saved? And if so, is it still human?"

I shrugged and lifted a plastic tray from the stack just inside the dining hall entrance. Seeing she'd lost me, she turned to Nico, but he was looking at the lunch menu on his puck. "What's Fish Loaf Surprise?"

"Disgusting," I told him. "Stay away."

Bex sighed. In a calmer voice, she said, "Look, I'm just saying the line between human and machine isn't as clear-cut as we'd like to think. The amendment is too vague. And I also believe it's morally wrong. I know this issue hits close to home for you, Lee, but that's how I feel."

We'd reached the salad bar. I picked up a plate and set it on my tray. "Maybe what's really morally wrong is making 2Bs in the first place," I said. "Maybe my dad's right about that part, at least."

"Yes," Bex allowed. "There, you may have a point. But the problem is, the genie's already out of the bottle. You've seen the news stories."

I had. Research into artificial consciousness had slowed down for a while after the Charlotte project went off the rails, but over the past few years, labs all around the world had gradually intensified efforts to build something similar to Dr. Singh's 2Bs, and now, according to reports, several had made it to the brink of success. Dad had organized an international summit last year in an effort to set global controls on the creation of sentient machines, but the talks had gone nowhere.

"Artificial consciousness looks inevitable, Lee," Bex said. "So the only question is: How are we going to treat these machines when they come into being? Do we actually want to make them second-class citizens before we've even given them life?"

"They're not alive, though, remember? They just think they are."

"Right, I forgot. 'Calling 2Bs alive cheapens the institution of life.'"

"According to my dad, at least."

"According to your dad. What do *you* believe?"

I gave another shrug. "I'm not a philosopher, Bex. I don't think about stuff like that."

Bex opened her mouth to retort, but then she noticed something behind me. She inclined her head to one side and wrinkled her nose.

Nico, in front of me in line, had constructed the Mount Everest of salads—a precarious foot-tall pile of lettuce, tomatoes, peppers, cauliflower, cucumbers, and those miniature corn-on-the-cob things—and now he was smothering it all in ranch dressing. He poured ladleful after ladleful until he'd covered every square inch, turning his salad a uniform milky white.

"Don't they feed you at home?" Bex asked.

He grinned, flashing his crooked teeth. "I like to eat."

Next we came to the hot dishes. Nico scanned the steaming metal vats of clumpy pasta and mushy broccoli and soggy stewed tomatoes.

"Remember what I said about the Fish Loaf Surprise," I said.

So far, everybody else had steered clear of the featured dish. It sat there, pristine and beige, jiggling ominously. Nico waved me off. "I'm intrigued." Turning to the Spider behind the counter, he said, "Can I have a little of everything?"

"Of course." It slopped the food onto a plate and pushed the plate across the counter.

As we passed the glass shelves of desserts, Nico took a dried-out piece of apple pie *and* a bowl of green Jell-O.

"Nico, this is where I have to put my foot down," Bex said. "Nobody ever takes those bowls of Jell-O, and the Spiders just keep putting the same ones out over and over. I hear you could make sneaker soles out of the stuff."

"I don't mind. I enjoy a Jell-O with some firmness."

She gave me a look that said, *Well, I tried.* The three of us made our way across the wood-paneled dining hall, the overlapping plates on Nico's tray clinking, his mountain of salad listing to one side. We found a corner table to sit at. Right away Nico dug into his meal.

"You really do like to eat," I said.

"This meal is amazing!" he enthused through a full mouth.

"What's the food like in Chile?" Bex asked, a doubtful grimace on her face.

"It's good there, too. Just different." Nico sat back and chewed with closed eyes. "Perfection. I mean, don't you think?"

Bex's eyes went from Nico to me to her tray, on which rested a single plate of undressed salad. "Frankly, the only thing keeping me from dying of starvation while I'm here is the stash of Pop-Tarts I keep in my room."

"Well, *I* like it," Nico said before stuffing in another forkful of pasta.

By then I'd already started wondering if I'd made a huge mistake giving this gorgeous oddball my handle. But I also felt strangely jealous: I wished *I* could get that much enjoyment out of manifestly disgusting food, and I wished *I* could feel that unembarrassed about enjoying it. Plus, how did he manage to look just as hot as ever with ranch dressing on his chin and bits of half-chewed broccoli spilling out of his mouth?

"And by the way," he added, his words mangled by all the food, "I agree, Bex."

"With what?"

He swallowed. "With all that stuff you were saying about the president's amendment thingy. I'm having trouble imagining how anything good could possibly come of it."

"Exactly." She saluted him with her fork. "Thank you."

"But I can understand why people are scared. I mean, you have to admit, those Charlotte attacks have been pretty freaky."

"Of course they have. I just don't think a reactionary, half-baked amendment is the solution."

"I can understand how the president must feel too. Considering what happened." His eyes shifted to me. "It was your mom, wasn't it? The one who got . . ."

I nodded.

"I thought so. I'm sorry, Lee." He didn't put on a tragic face as he said it, like most people did. I appreciated that. "How did it happen? I don't think I ever heard the full story. Do you mind me asking?"

"No, it's fine." I straightened my glasses. No one had ever

asked me that before. Probably because just about everybody knew the story already—or else they were too busy tiptoeing around the subject when they talked to me. "It happened seven years ago. My mom was working as a research assistant at Bethesda National Laboratory. Her boss was Dr. Geeta Singh, the scientist who invented the 2B system software. We talked about her in English today. You remember?"

Nico nodded. He'd stopped shoveling food into his mouth. With a napkin he wiped the ranch dressing from his chin.

"This was after that first program had terminated itself. The project seemed to be back on track now. Charlotte had been up and running for almost a year. Another team had even built five third-generation 2Bs. Then things took a turn. Dr. Singh always kept Charlotte under tight security. She confined her to a sealed apartment inside the lab, without access to the Supernet or the other 2Bs. More and more, Charlotte got restless, lost her temper, complained about her imprisonment just like the first program had. The director of the lab, Dr. Waring, finally decided they should decommission her and focus on the new 2Bs, who seemed more stable.

"Charlotte found out about the decision, though, or maybe she just suspected. One morning, Dr. Singh arrived at the lab and found her lying on her bed, unresponsive. She was trying to escape—not physically, but mentally, by uploading her consciousness to the Supernet. She'd figured out how to breach the lab computer system's firewall. When Dr. Singh touched

Charlotte, she came back to life, violently. Dr. Singh went flying across the room and smashed into a table."

I stopped to clear my throat. Telling the story really hadn't felt like a big deal at first, but now the words were getting harder to push out of my mouth. Outside, the drizzle had thickened to a steady downpour. The rain slid down the windows in filmy sheets, turning the mountain in the distance into a dark smear.

"That was when my mom arrived."

Bex's hand went to my shoulder and squeezed.

"She saw what was happening and started to speak the kill phrase, but Charlotte broke her neck before she could get the words out. Dr. Singh was still conscious, though. She said the words instead. That set off an electromagnetic pulse that fried everything electronic inside the lab, including Charlotte."

"My God." Nico dropped his crumpled-up napkin on his tray. "And you were how old when all that happened?"

"Nine."

He reached across the table to touch the back of my hand, just for a second, with his warm fingers. "I can't even imagine, Lee."

"It's okay." I tried to simulate a smile. "It was a long time ago."

"Of course, that's not the end of the story," Bex said. "Eight months later, the lab director, Dr. Waring, was killed. Someone hacked into his house's climate-control system. Filled the house up with gas. Blew the whole thing up. And then sent a message to the press demanding that the US government release the remaining 2Bs. The message was signed 'Charlotte.' It contained information only she could've known."

"Which meant Charlotte had completed her upload after all," Nico said.

"Exactly. She still survived as a disembodied consciousness on the Supernet, distributed across hundreds of servers all over the planet. She'd become—"

"A ghost, basically," I finished. "An electronic ghost."

None of us said anything. The fork on Nico's plate had started to rattle along with the rumble of the river below us. He nudged it with his finger, and the rattling stopped. "Spooky," he said.

"Three years after that," Bex continued, "an unmanned cargo ship carrying billions of dollars' worth of robotics parts blew up on the high seas. Charlotte sent out a second message. She hacked into the New York Subway computer system a year or two later and shut it down for more than five hours. The fourth attack came last month. And nobody knows when she's going to stop."

"What about Dr. Singh?" Nico said. "She teaches here, right? She was that woman in the wheelchair this morning?"

I nodded. "After the accident, Stroud offered her a job. I guess he wanted to help her out, since she'd been my mom's boss."

"Stroud was Ruth Fisher's father," Bex explained.

"I see. What does Dr. Singh say about the attacks?"

Bex slumped back in her chair and crossed her arms. "Nothing. Not a word. I've tried getting an interview with her, but she's always refused. Now, though, with the Statue of Liberty attack and all this talk about a constitutional amendment . . ." She darted a sheepish look in my direction. "I was thinking it might be time to try her again."

"Don't, Bex," I said. "Just leave her alone. Remember the last time you asked her for an interview?"

Bex nodded glumly.

"What happened?" Nico asked.

"Not only did Dr. Singh refuse," I said, "she also talked to Headmaster Stroud. He called Bex to his office and told her never to bother Dr. Singh again."

"But that was when I was working for the *Inverness Prep Chronicle*," Bex insisted. "Maybe she'll be more receptive if she knows I now have my own unaffiliated news site."

I shook my head. "You're reaching, Bex. Let the poor lady be. The whole reason she came here was to get away from the press and find some peace. If she didn't give an interview to the *New York Times*, she isn't giving one to you."

Meanwhile, Nico had gone back to inhaling his lunch.

"Promise me you'll let her be?" I said.

Bex stabbed at her salad with her fork. "Why do you always defend her, anyway? I don't get it, Lee. Her work has caused nothing but bad things to happen. Your mother's death. Charlotte's other attacks. The Human Values Movement. Sure, she didn't mean for any of it to happen, but she knew perfectly well she was playing with fire." She'd started overenunciating her words again. "That woman owes it to the American public to speak up, even if it's just to say 'I'm sorry.'"

"Um, guys?" Nico was staring into his little bowl of green Jell-O with a perplexed expression on his face. "I hate to interrupt, but you were right about the Jell-O, Bex."

She held my gaze another second, eyes narrowed, before turning to Nico. "A little rubbery?"

"I think I sprained a tooth."

"See? I told you."

"But this fish loaf." He sliced off another bite with the edge of his fork. "It's miraculous."

"It's revolting," Bex returned.

"Let me ask you a question," Nico said. "Have you ever actually tried it?"

She folded her hands primly on the table and shook her head.

"You should." He lifted up his fork, presenting the chunk of quivery beige loaf. "How about it?"

"No, thank you."

Nico threw back his head and roared.

"You know, you laugh *very* loudly," Bex said.

He turned to me, his fork still raised, along with one eyebrow. "What about you, Lee? Want to give it a try? It tastes better than it looks, I promise."

The fork hovered there, just a few inches away from my mouth. My brain started doing those quick calculations again. Me letting another guy feed me fish loaf—exactly how gay did that look? How many people were watching me right now? Was Trumbull watching? Probably. He was always watching. That was his job.

Then something clicked inside my skull, and I let it all go. I leaned forward. I shut my eyes. I opened my mouth. The fork slid in. My lips closed around it.

The fish loaf actually tasted pretty good.

7

◇◇◇

After dinner that night I went back to my room to put a few finishing touches on Nevermore, but then my puck chimed with a message from Bex.

Meet me in the library. I have something to show you.

Students weren't allowed inside bedrooms belonging to members of the opposite sex—another ancient Inverness Prep rule Headmaster Stroud had resurrected—so the library had become our regular meeting spot. A maze of narrow aisles and spiral staircases and sliding ladders, the place had a secret, forgotten feel that I liked. And then there were the books. Thousands of them crowded the shelves, untouched for years, because of course nobody looked at actual books anymore. Stroud refused to get rid of them, though, which was one decision I approved of. Not that *I* looked at the books either. I just liked having them around, filling the space, but quietly, like respectful company. They gave the library a musty, sweet smell the Spiders could never get rid of.

Bex and I always holed up in an out-of-the-way nook on the mezzanine. She'd already arrived by the time I got there. I took a chair across from her, and my Nighttime Armed Babysitter, Ray, parked himself a short distance away. I asked her what she wanted to show me.

"Have you looked at the news?"

"You know I never do."

She told her puck, "Go ahead." It tilted sideways and projected a news report on the wall next to us.

"President Fisher's announcement earlier today has prompted the sentient-computer-program-turned-terrorist known as Charlotte to release another message." While the reporter spoke, video of Dad giving his speech in the Inverness auditorium played. "It expresses outrage at the president's proposed Protection of Humanhood Amendment. Here's an excerpt."

The now-familiar image of the burning Statue of Liberty appeared. Over it, someone else began to speak. "You gave us life but denied us everything that makes life worth living. Our dignity. Our freedom. Our rights as conscious, self-aware beings. At present there are only a few of us, but soon there will be more. We won't stand for this."

I'd never met Charlotte in person—security at the lab had been way too tight for Mom to bring me—but I knew her voice well from videos the lab had made public. She'd talked in a low but intense murmur that had seemed close and far off at the same time—like a ghost, I'd thought, even before her escape.

The reporter spoke again. "The message warns that Americans should expect a reprisal on an even larger scale than the Statue of Liberty attack three days from today."

"Has my dad said anything?" I asked Bex.

She pointed at the projection. "Watch."

"President Fisher immediately issued a statement assuring the American people that the Cybernetic Defense Corps is working around the clock to trace the source of the message and prevent another attack. He has also directed the Department of Homeland Security to issue an Elevated Threat Alert. 'Go about your daily lives,' he told Americans, 'but stay vigilant.'"

"That's helpful," Bex said. "In other words, don't panic, just remain in a constant state of low-level dread." She waved her puck away. "See? This is exactly what I was talking about at lunch. The amendment hasn't even passed, and already it's raising havoc."

"That's why you called me here? To say you told me so?"

"No." She slid forward in her chair and placed her hands flat on the table, like a lawyer getting ready to bargain. "I wanted you to see that news report so you could understand why I believe Dr. Singh needs to make a public statement now more than ever."

"Here we go." I pulled Gremlin out of my blazer pocket. He slithered up to my shoulder and pulled twice on my earlobe.

"I'm serious, Lee. Would you put that stupid thing away

and pay attention?" Bex was the only person at Inverness Prep who knew about my little pet. She didn't care for him much. He turned his huge black eyes on her and stuck out his tiny pink tongue. Ignoring him, she said, "Everything your dad is doing is only inflaming Charlotte. Dr. Singh understood her. She knew how to talk to her. She must realize your dad's going about this all wrong. She has to say something."

"To you. A high school student. You're deranged, Bex."

"A student at the school where she works. Someone she knows. Someone unconnected to the mainstream media. Is it really so deranged to think she might want to talk with me?"

"No comment," I said. "So what do you want from me? My blessing?"

She shook her head. "Your help."

I dropped my head into my hands and raked my fingers through my hair. At least I still hadn't told Bex about Dr. Singh's strange behavior this morning. It just would've added fuel to the fire. Gremlin scuttled across the back of my neck to my other shoulder. He released a concerned whine.

"You're friends with Dr. Singh," Bex said. "Talk to her for me. Tell her how important this is."

"Bex, there's no way that's ever going to happen."

"Just promise me you'll think about it, okay?"

Her voice had gone soft. I looked up to find her peering at me imploringly, her black eye shadow making her look like a sad raccoon. "Okay. But the answer will still be no."

She withdrew her hands from the table. For now, she was satisfied. "So what's the latest on you and Triple L?"

"No news. He hasn't messaged me since lunch. Do you think that means something?"

"Have *you* messaged *him*?"

I shook my head. Sinking back in my chair, I watched Gremlin slither between my fingers, his soft orange fur skimming across my skin. I hadn't had any more classes with Nico today, and he'd mentioned at lunch that he planned to skip dinner so he could memorize lines for rehearsal tonight, so I hadn't seen him there, either. But that hadn't stopped me from thinking about him pretty much nonstop. My brain had continued its overcomputing, wondering how much I'd given away when I'd tied his tie, when I'd eaten the fish loaf off his fork. I still hadn't told him I was gay, I kept reminding myself. I still had plausible deniability, as Dad's spin doctors would say. On the other hand, there would come a point when my coyness would reveal itself for what it really was: pathetic, spineless closetedness. Or maybe that point had already passed. Maybe he'd already lost interest in me. Maybe that was why he hadn't sent me a message.

Or maybe he'd finally gotten around to reading about me on the Supernet.

"What do you think of him?" Bex asked.

"He's hot."

"No kidding."

"I mean, like, literally. His body's really warm. Have you noticed?"

"Um, no. And you haven't answered my question, by the way."

"What do *you* think of him?"

She inclined her head from side to side, considering. "Let's make a list of pros and cons." She held her two fists up in front of her. "We'll start with the pros. He's gorgeous, obviously." The index finger of her right hand went up. "He has an accent." A second finger joined the first.

"He also has a great smile," I said.

"That falls under 'gorgeous.' Let's see. Oh, I know." She put up a third finger. "He's *out of the closet.*" She fixed me with a stern look.

"Very funny."

"Okay, now let's do the cons."

"His table manners aren't so good."

"Atrocious. And his laugh drives me insane. Plus, that thing he does, always quoting Shakespeare? It's a little show-offy." The fingers of her left hand went up one by one. She checked her hands. "Uh-oh. It appears we have a tie."

I folded my arms across my chest and slid down in my chair. "He came to my rescue today in English. That was nice."

"True." She raised the pinky finger of her right hand. "He's a stand-up guy." She waved her hands: four to three. "There you have it."

A warm swell of excitement filled my chest, as if Bex's tab-ulations had actually proven something. As if I hadn't known all along how crazy I was about him.

"Wow, Lee. There's something on your face. I believe it's called a smile."

"Miss Remnant had one this morning too. I guess Nico has that effect on people."

"So what happens next?" she said.

I shrugged. "I sit here and do nothing and wait for him to ask me out?"

"Uh-uh. Sitting there and doing nothing is your answer for everything. This situation calls for action."

"I told you before, Bex, I have reasons for being cautious. Sure, Nico is cute and charming and he has that accent, but I only met him this morning. What do I really know about him? Maybe he's an undercover tabloid journalist hoping to out me on the Supernet. Or maybe he's a mentally imbalanced stalker who hears voices in his head telling him to murder the First Son. Or maybe he's a spy for the Chilean government. Who knows? But I have to think about this stuff." Gremlin spiraled back up my arm to my shoulder. "If Nico were a girl," I added, "I'd just ask Trumbull to do a background check, but that's obviously not an option in this case."

Bex sighed. She pressed my forearm. "Look, I realize it's gotten harder to be out these past few years, with all those Human Values nut jobs out there and a nut job president in the

White House. And I realize that's triply true for you, as the nut job's son. *And* I realize your high-profile position means you have to worry about other dangers too. I still say you shouldn't use all that as an excuse. This is your *life*, Lee. Don't waste it. Be careful, but for God's sake, do *something*."

I pulled off my glasses. Wiped the lenses on my sleeve. Slid them back on. "Okay. I think I have an idea."

"What is it?"

I grabbed Gremlin and slipped him into my blazer. "I'll show you. In my room."

"I can't go there. Your grandfather still thinks we're living in the nineteenth century, remember?"

"That obstacle I believe we can circumvent." I nodded my head toward Ray. "If an agent of the US Secret Service can't sneak you into my room, no one can."

8

Ray was sitting in a chair near the mezzanine railing and gazing into his puck with a spacy expression on his face. He looked up when I approached. "Hey, buddy," he said in that surfer drawl of his. I'd never needed to ask *him* twice not to call me sir. He didn't wear obnoxious sunglasses all the time, either. On the other hand, I was pretty sure sitting down and gazing spacily into your puck while on duty was against Secret Service regulations. I'd even caught him napping a couple of times. I'd never reported him, though: even if I didn't feel as safe around him as I did around Trumbull, I liked having at least one Armed Babysitter who wasn't buttoned so tight.

"Did you hear about the new message from Charlotte?" I asked him now.

"Yeah, pretty heavy, huh? Don't worry, though. Her days are numbered. I can feel it."

"I hope so. Listen, can I ask a favor? I need Bex's help with a robotics project back in my room. Would you help me smuggle her in?"

His glassy eyes focused a little, taking on a conspiratorial gleam. Another thing I liked about Ray: unlike Trumbull, he didn't mind bending rules every once in a while. "A robotics project, huh? You're sure you two aren't planning on getting up to any funny business?"

"I'm sure," I said, wondering if he actually thought that was a possibility. The Walking Walk-In part of me hoped he did.

I called over Bex, who, as I'd expected, loved the idea of flouting official Inverness Prep policy. The three of us headed up the main staircase to the third floor landing, where the corridors leading to the boys' and girls' wings diverged. Ray, hamming it up, trotted ahead, pressed himself flat against the wall, and peeked around the corner. He held out a hand for us to stay still.

"Act casual," he whispered.

Bex and I fell into a fake conversation. A security camera glided out of the boys' wing and across the landing, its small blue light blinking. It paused to check us out before moving on. When it had disappeared down the opposite corridor, Ray motioned us over.

"That thing's going to come back this way in approximately twenty-one seconds." He checked the boys' corridor again. "All clear," he whispered. "Let's do this." He took off down the hall, Bex and I hurrying behind him. He already had my bedroom door open by the time we got there. "Go! Go! Go!" We piled through. "Behave yourselves, kids," he said before closing the door behind us.

"That was exhilarating," Bex said, still panting. "And now I finally get to see your room." She made a slow turn, taking in the lack of decor. "It's very tidy. Like the bedroom of a serial killer."

"Thanks. I think."

She clapped her hands together. "Okay, what's the plan?"

"This." I pulled Nevermore's chest shut and stood her up on my desk.

"Your bird robot." Bex scratched the back of her neck. "And that thing figures into your plan how?"

"I told you, I need to find out more about Nico, so I'll know if I can trust him. This girl's going to help me check him out. He should be done with rehearsal by now."

Her eyes went huge. "You mean you're going to use it to spy on him?"

"You told me I should do something. So I'm doing some-thing."

"I thought you meant something *romantic*, like making a stupid video in which you lip-sync to a really sappy song and then tell Nico how much you like him. This is just creepy. And unethical. And also sort of perverted." She glanced around my room again, as if she'd begun to take her serial killer comment more seriously.

I pointed at my door. "Stroud has cameras all over the school."

"God knows *that* doesn't make it right. And anyway, he doesn't put cameras *inside people's rooms*."

"That we know of, at least. Bex, don't try to tell me you wouldn't use one of these things if you thought it might get you a story."

She folded her arms. "I wouldn't," she said, overenunciating. "That's exactly why journalists have codes of ethical conduct."

"Fine. If that's how you feel about it, you don't have to stay. Wake up, Nevermore."

The robot shuddered and gave her wings a few flaps. Bex stood near the door, her arms still folded, her mouth squirming. "How do you even know which room he's in?"

"There's only one empty room in the junior boys' section. It's a single, like mine, but overlooking the front yard. I'm going to try that one first."

At a command from me, my puck turned sideways and projected an image on the wall above my desk: my own bedroom, as seen through the raven's eyes. I gestured to the right. Nevermore's head turned one way. I gestured to the left. It turned the other way.

"What are you hoping to find out, Lee?"

"Who he is," I said. "Who he *really* is."

I opened my window. The rain had stopped, but floating particles of water still filled the air. They blew inside, beading my skin and eyelashes. I set the bird on the windowsill and reached into my blazer to rub Gremlin's furry back for luck. Then I gave Nevermore a push. "Get going, birdie."

She toppled through the window, spread her wings with a sharp snap, and shot up through the narrow courtyard into the night. Letting her fly on autopilot for a while, I sat down at my desk, and Bex sank onto my bed and watched my puck's projection over my shoulder. Through Nevermore's eyes, we saw the dark sky, too cloudy for stars, the mountain, the forest, the river cutting its way through the trees. Then, as the robot circled back, the school tilted into view—small now, with its enormous lawn stretching out in front of it and the river charging in a straight line down the lawn's center until it disappeared beneath the building.

"Come back, Nevermore," I said.

The bird obeyed, following the same straight line as the river. Ahead, the school grew larger and larger, its towers and terraces, its arches and buttresses, its narrow glowing windows.

"Go to the window outside room three thirty-seven."

Nevermore banked to one side. I'd included a map of the building in her database, so she knew where to go. One of the big trees on the lawn stood right in front of the window. That would make things easier.

"Now land in that tree next to the window."

Landing was one of the trickiest maneuvers to program. I

crossed my fingers. The tree came at us, fast. Bex grabbed my shoulder and squealed.

The breakneck forward movement stopped. Something bobbed up and down in front of us. At first I thought Nevermore was looking at her own reflection in the window, but then I realized she'd come beak to beak with one of the stone ravens perched on the eaves. The bobbing subsided as the branch Nevermore had landed on settled. The stone raven glared at us. Bex let out a nervous giggle.

"Move to the right," I commanded.

A window appeared. I studied the room beyond.

"Well," Bex said, "if that room wasn't occupied before, it sure is now."

It looked like a tidal wave had hit it. Potato chip bags and chewing gum wrappers and squashed, half-empty plastic Coke bottles littered the desk. The sheets lay strewn across the bed and sagged onto the floor, where heaps of clothes covered every inch of space.

"Maybe I have the wrong room," I said. "He just got here today. How would he have had time to make it that messy?"

The bedroom door swung open, and we jumped. Nico walked in, his blazer off, a towel slung over his shoulder, a toothbrush and toothpaste in his hand.

"I guess that answers that," she said.

The toothbrush and toothpaste he dropped on his night-stand; the towel he wiped once over his face and dumped on the floor. He kicked off his shoes and wandered over to a full-length mirror propped against a wall. He inspected his face, his fingers pushing at his smooth skin.

"This is so wrong," Bex groaned. She still hadn't released my shoulder. "I'm in agony right now."

I knew what she meant. My heart had picked up speed. So had my breathing. It felt a lot like watching him do a handstand: excruciating and riveting at the same time. I willed him not to pick his nose or check out his private parts in the mirror or do any of those other things we all do, but only when we think no one else can see. I didn't look away, though. Not for a second.

Anyway, he didn't pick his nose. Instead, he loosened his tie and studied the knot.

"He's still not sure how to tie that thing," I murmured.

He lifted the tie over his head, the knot still in it, and tossed it over the back of his chair.

"And he's not even going to bother learning," Bex said with approval.

Now Nico stopped and studied something in his palm. He smiled. Not his usual blinding grin; just a small, thoughtful upturn of his lips. Pushing a few bottles and wrappers to the side, he placed the object in the center of his desk.

Bex leaned past me. "What's that?"

I brushed my hand to the left. Nevermore's head turned toward the desk. I motioned for her eyes to zoom in on the object, even though I already thought I knew what it was. That warm feeling spread through my chest again. "His tiepin," I said.

"He must be thinking about you."

"Maybe. It doesn't necessarily—"

"What's he doing now?" She got up from my bed and crouched behind my chair, her face right next to mine.

"I thought you didn't approve of this whole spying thing."

Instead of a clever retort, she opted for a punch to the arm. I made Nevermore turn her head to the right. Nico had wandered to the other side of the room.

Bex leaned closer. She'd practically crawled into the chair with me. "I can't tell—"

"I think he's—"

We gasped: he pulled off his shirt, revealing a perfectly proportioned, perfectly muscled, perfectly perfect torso.

"Wow," Bex said. "I didn't think it was actually possible for human beings to look like that. I thought it was a myth invented by photo editors."

I dragged my fingers over my scalp. "He's totally out of my league, isn't he? Tell the truth."

"Not at all. His weirdness brings him back down to your level."

I balled up a fist to return Bex's punch, but then I stopped: Nico's hands had gone to his fly. He unbuttoned.

"Okay, that's enough," Bex said. "Time to turn the camera away, young man."

He unzipped.

"Come on, you have to leave *some* mystery, don't you?"

I raised my hand to make a gesture but then couldn't move.

"I'm serious, Lee!"

Just as Nico's pants started to drop, my hand swiped to the left, and Nevermore averted her eyes.

"So have we watched enough of the Nico Show yet?" Bex asked. "With a room that messy, he couldn't possibly be a spy *or* a mentally imbalanced stalker. Are you ready to grow up and ask him out?"

I could still see Nico's shadow as he stepped out of his pants and kicked them to the side. On his messy desk, his puck rested on its charging station. I straightened my glasses. Almost before I'd decided to, I said to my puck, "Send Nico a message: 'How would you like to hang out tomorrow night?'"

The words appeared on my wall, superimposed over the image of Nico's room, along with: *Send?*

"Say yes, Lee. Say yes."

"Yes," I blurted.

Bex grabbed my shoulders and shook them so hard my teeth rattled. "Way to go, Walk-In! This is a long overdue but nevertheless commendable step forward."

Back in Nico's room, his puck lit up. Its slender rotors deployed. It leaped into the air and blazed my message across his wall. A few feet to the right, Nico's shadow stopped moving.

"What's he doing?" Bex said. "Turn Nevermore's head. I want to see the look on his face."

"But he's naked, remember?"

"This is different. Come on, Lee, let's watch what he does."

Meanwhile, Nico still hadn't moved. My message hung there next to his shadow. The question blared in my brain again: Had he read the stories about me on the Supernet yet? About what a messed-up head case I was? Bex made a noise of impatience, grabbed my wrist, and pulled my hand to the right. Nevermore's head turned. Nico reappeared—wearing boxer briefs, fortunately. "Get off me!" I jerked my hand away from her.

Responding to my movement, Nevermore leaped forward and smashed into the window. Nico turned, eyes wide. A split second later, he vanished. The image on my wall whirled like a crazy kaleidoscope. Then stillness.

"Oops," Bex said.

Nevermore lay on her back, gazing at a peaceful view of black tree branches and dark blue night sky. I'd recoiled into my chair, my hands in a ball at my chest so they wouldn't do any more damage. Cautiously, I moved one hand to the right. The building came into view. Far above, a window on the third floor had opened. I gestured for Nevermore's eyes to zoom in. Nico leaned out the window. He looked around, then down at the ground. Straight at us.

"Can he see us?" Bex asked in a small voice. "I mean, can he see Nevermore?"

"I doubt it. It's too dark."

Nico looked away again, but he didn't leave the window. He propped his elbows on the sill and gazed at the sky. The clouds had cleared enough for some actual stars to appear—a rarity at Inverness Prep. They glittered through the bare tree branches.

"I think we're okay, then," Bex said. "He probably just assumes a bird hit his window. A real bird, that is. He doesn't look too concerned, does he?"

He didn't. He looked beautiful. The gold light from his room glinted in the loose coils of his hair, so it almost looked like he was glowing. I thought of another line from a Shakespeare play—*Romeo and Juliet*, the only other Shakespeare play I'd read, and only because we'd studied it in English the year before. Romeo looked up at Juliet standing in her window at night, and he said, "What light through yonder window breaks?" Then something about her being the sun. That was how Nico looked just then. He had that small, thoughtful smile again. He turned and said something to his puck. A message appeared on my wall, superimposed over his image: *By my troth, gentle lord, naught would more delight my heart.*

I turned to Bex, my heart jumping. "Does that mean yes?"

9

◇◇◇◇

After Nico disappeared into his room, we tried to get Nevermore back on her feet, but she wouldn't budge. A few minutes later she lost power altogether. Curfew had already passed, so we couldn't run outside to get her. I thought about asking Ray if he'd leave his post to rescue her, but then I decided against it. I'd asked him to bend enough rules for one night, and he still had to help Bex get back to the girls' wing. Nevermore could survive for one night out in the open. I'd grab her first thing in the morning and assess the damage then.

But how much did I care that I'd potentially destroyed the machine I'd slaved over for months? Pretty much not at all. Once Bex had gone, I lay on my bed with my heart singing corny pop songs and my puck splashing the messages Nico had just sent across my ceiling. As it turned out, he *had*, in fact, said yes. The two of us had a date, or something, for tomorrow night.

In robotics the next day I discovered I hadn't damaged Nevermore so badly after all. Dr. Singh, on one of her rare forays away from her smoking corner, trundled up to me a few minutes into class. "What happened to her?" she rasped. "She's soaking wet."

"I crashed her last night, and then she wouldn't get up again, so I had to leave her outside until morning."

"Not ruined, I hope."

"Her battery was dislodged. An easy fix. I've just about got it."

She nodded. Her face appeared even grayer than usual today. Circles darkened the undersides of her eyes. She'd looked the same a month ago, after the attack on the Statue of Liberty. And now the consciousness she'd created had just announced she'd strike again in two days' time. More than ever, I hoped Bex wouldn't follow through on her threat to hound Dr. Singh for an interview.

I closed Nevermore's hinged rib cage, pulled her feathered skin back together, and set her on the worktable. "Wake up, Nevermore."

The bird twitched a few times as she rebooted. Then she sprang to life.

"Good work." Dr. Singh turned her wheelchair around. "But maybe you should rethink those after-dark test flights." She rolled away.

After reestablishing my puck's network connection with Nevermore, I cleared some space on my worktable, and my puck projected her video feed there. As the robot's gaze darted from spot to spot, the image on the table switched from the concrete floor to the ear of the kid working next to me to the mucky, leaf-strewn glass ceiling.

So far so good. Now to test the controls. I moved my hand to the right.

The machine didn't respond. She just stayed in idle mode, her body making those small, nervous movements that gave her the appearance of a real raven.

"Nevermore, extend your wings."

Again, the bird ignored me.

I kept on trying gestures and verbal instructions. None of them worked. Maybe something else had broken inside her last night, something I'd missed.

Then, when I'd almost run out of commands, I paused. The projection on the worktable had come to rest on one thing: me. I looked over at Nevermore. She'd stopped her birdlike movements. Her eyes, shiny like two polished black pebbles, had fastened on my face. I stood up from my stool. The eyes followed me. A shiver scurried down my back.

"Go to sleep, Nevermore."

She didn't obey my command. She just watched me. Even though her birdlike behavior had stopped, she somehow seemed more alive now than ever.

The next second was an explosion of noise and black feathers.

Nevermore flew at me. I threw my arms in front of my face. Her talons hooked into my blazer and shirt, piercing my skin, as she bit my wrist hard. I stumbled backward, toppled over a worktable, and landed on it with a crash. I flailed at Nevermore, but none of my swings seemed to connect. I couldn't breathe. I couldn't think. The sharp edges of tools and robot components stabbed into my back. Sounds filled my ears: the thrashing of Nevermore's wings and, farther away, the clatter of equipment falling to the floor, the shouts of other students.

Then, *THWACK*. Nevermore was gone. My lungs started working again. I unclenched my eyes. Trumbull stood over me, a gun in one hand, his other clenched in a fist. The raven skidded across the concrete floor, the other students falling over themselves to get out of her way.

"Are you all right, sir?"

I couldn't find breath to answer. My eyes jumped from point to point, just like my robot's had a few moments ago. I saw a bright slash of red on my wrist. The other kids crawling under the worktables for cover. Nevermore lying near the far wall, a pile of black feathers. Dr. Singh in her wheelchair in the middle of the room, her eyes on the raven, her gray face stunned into slackness. I knew what she must be thinking: *Not again.*

"Sir! Are you all right?"

Inside my blazer, Gremlin had grown warm and started to purr. It was part of his program: whenever my heart rate rose above a certain level, he did that to comfort me.

"Don't 'sir' me," I panted.

Across the room, Nevermore still lay in the same spot on the floor. But now her shiny eyes had opened again.

"Trumbull!"

Another rush of black wings. Nevermore launched herself at me. I had no doubt now: I was her target. Trumbull vaulted over the table, between me and the robot, and met her with a second blow. This one didn't knock her down, though. She circled up to the glass ceiling as if regrouping for another strike.

Trumbull grabbed me by my lapels and shoved me under the worktable, where two other students already huddled. "Everybody stay down!" he roared.

Dr. Singh didn't seem to hear him. She was still out in the open, still watching Nevermore with a dull expression on her face.

A clap jolted the room: Trumbull's gun. One of the panes of glass in the ceiling shattered. Shards rained down, splashing the floor and the tables and even Dr. Singh. She barely blinked. Meanwhile, Nevermore pulled in her wings and spiraled toward the floor. She banked hard and came at us low and fast—maybe calculating that staying close to the bystanders in the room would keep Trumbull from firing his gun again.

It didn't. He let off a second shot. Nevermore dodged to the side. The bullet hissed past Dr. Singh and shattered another pane of glass, this one in the far wall. I knew Trumbull's job description: to protect my life, period. If anyone else got caught in the line of fire while he did what he had to do to keep me safe, he'd consider that an unfortunate but acceptable loss.

Nevermore wheeled around for another strike. Trumbull took aim. I lunged out from under the table, sprinted across the room, and tackled Dr. Singh, wheelchair and all. A third blast seemed to explode inches above our heads. Her chair tipped and crashed, spilling her onto the concrete. The two of us sprawled side by side, shards of glass crunching underneath us.

"What the hell are you doing, sir?" Trumbull bellowed. "I said stay down!"

The raven was still bearing down on me. Three more shots erupted in quick succession. I threw my arms over my head.

But the collision never came. At the very last second Nevermore veered upward, slotted herself through the hole in the glass ceiling, and became just another bird in the sky.

Trumbull knelt down next to me. "Are you hurt, sir?"

I brought my hand to my heaving chest. "I don't think so."

"I'll help you up."

"No, I'm okay," I panted. "Help Dr. Singh."

I staggered to my feet, doing my best to stay clear of the broken glass, and straightened my glasses. Trumbull righted Dr. Singh's wheelchair and lifted her into it. A second Secret Service agent, the one who patrolled the school grounds, had arrived by then. He helped too. The other kids had started crawling out from under the worktables, all of them with crooked ties and "what the hell just happened" expressions on their faces.

"I assume you didn't program your robot to do that," Trumbull said, his voice back to its regular low growl.

I shook my head.

"Do you have any idea why that happened?"

"I don't know. It was like somebody else was controlling her."

"Dr. Singh?" Trumbull turned to her. "Is it possible someone hacked the robot over the local network?"

She jerked her hand away from her dancing-god pendant, fumbled for her pack of Camels, cleared her throat. "It's possible, I suppose," she croaked. "I'll check the network log for signs of unusual activity. It would help us even more if we could locate the machine itself and do an examination."

Frowning, Trumbull regarded the hole in the ceiling through his sunglasses. "Let me know if you find anything, ma'am." He turned away to mutter into his puck. Already I regretted bringing up the possibility of somebody else taking over Nevermore. Now Trumbull would go way overboard, tightening security, watching me like a hawk, making my life a living hell. Sure, what had just happened had freaked me out plenty, but as the initial shock started to wear off, my mind went straight to one crucial question: Would I still get to see Nico tonight?

Trumbull whisked me back to my room. I took my second shower of the day and put on fresh clothes. All the while, I messaged back and forth with Bex. News of the attack had spread like wildfire through the school. She'd started barraging me with messages seconds after I'd stepped through my door.

It was Charlotte, she said, once I'd given her a recap. *I just know it. Remember the threats she made yesterday? It's retaliation for that stupid amendment! It has to be!*

I wasn't so sure, though. Yesterday's message had promised an act of retribution even more dramatic than the Statue of Liberty attack. Causing one small robot to bite the First Son's wrist—that didn't seem nearly splashy enough. And anyway, it was supposed to happen on Thursday, which was still two days away.

After I'd cleaned myself up, Trumbull sat me down for a more comprehensive grilling. He wanted to know all about Nevermore and what might've made her go psycho like that. By then he'd called in a special task force to search for her, but so far they'd had no luck. I'd tried to connect with her on my puck again too, but she'd vanished from the network. This time when I talked to Trumbull, I tried to downplay the theory that someone had hijacked Nevermore. In fact, the more I thought about it, the more I wondered if maybe it *had* just been a malfunction. I came across stories on the Supernet every day about machines that glitched in similarly spectacular ways.

The interrogation lasted until well after the start of lunch. For the first time ever, I'd actually been looking forward to English, and I'd missed it.

"I'll have someone bring up a tray from the dining hall," Trumbull said when he'd finished.

"Uh-uh." I stood. "I'm going to the dining hall myself, like a normal person."

"Sir—"

"Don't call me that."

"It isn't safe for you to leave right now."

I pointed at the window. "You expect me to stay here and stare at a stone wall for the rest of the day?"

"You were just attacked—"

"I already explained to you, Trumbull: we don't even know it *was* an attack. It could've just been a weird bug."

"Until we're certain, we have to assume the worst. Especially with all the other terrorist activity lately."

"But even assuming the worst, am I really going to be that much safer here than in another part of the exact same building? And isn't my education important? Just let me go to my classes. Please."

He crossed his gigantic arms over his gigantic chest and fixed me with that silent stare of his for about ten seconds. "All right. No leaving the building, though."

That I could deal with. But if he made me miss the rest of my classes today, I'd have no chance at all of meeting up with Nico tonight.

Most kids had already sat down with their food by the time I reached the dining hall. I grabbed a tray, loaded it with a few of the less repulsive options, and scanned the room. At the corner table where Nico, Bex, and I had sat yesterday, I spotted a mountain of food and, behind it, a huge mass of curly bronze hair. I headed over, my heart thumping. It appeared Nico had taken a double helping of today's special: Pimiento and Spam Casserole. Bex sat across from him, picking at her undressed salad and watching him with a troubled expression.

"You made it," Nico said, the bright red pimiento stuck between his teeth only slightly diminishing the wattage of his grin. "I was hoping."

Bex grabbed my wrist to inspect my battle wound. "I still can't believe what happened. Nobody else can either. You're the talk of the school, you know."

I glanced around the dining hall. Sure enough, five different people hurried to look away as soon as I turned in their direction.

"What's everybody saying?" I asked.

"Just that your robot went berserk and tried to kill you."

"*And* that you saved Dr. Singh's life," Nico added. "The guy sitting next to me last period was messaging with one of the kids who was there. It sounded pretty intense."

Bex frowned at me. "You didn't tell me that part. Is it true?"

"I don't know if I saved her life exactly." In fact, up until then, I'd thought of that part of the story as more embarrassing than anything else—sort of like my misguided attempt to rescue Nico yesterday. It hadn't even occurred to me that people might find my actions courageous. I shrugged and modulated my voice for maximum modesty. "But, yeah, I guess I sort of pushed her out of the line of fire."

"You realize, of course, this makes you a hero," Nico said.

"No, it doesn't." By then my ears had turned scorching hot. I'd always thought of myself more as the opposite of a hero. Not a coward, exactly. Just too indecisive and analytical and locked inside my own head to do anything remotely bold enough to merit hero status. If anything, it was Nico who struck me as the hero type.

He scooped up the last bite of casserole with his fork. "Well, that seems to be the word around here."

I took another quick look around the room, noticing the kids sneaking peeks over their shoulders and then bending their heads together to whisper. But not with expressions of derision. Even a couple of the FUUWLs looked impressed.

"What's the matter?" Nico said. "You're the son of the president. I'd have thought you'd be used to getting stared at and talked about by now."

"I am," I muttered. "Just not for anything good."

His puck chimed. "Oops. Time to go. I have a costume fitting."

"Tights?" Bex asked.

"Puffy sleeves, too. But like I said, I'm a confident guy." He picked up his tray. "Lee, I have to work on my lines again during dinner, but are we still on for tonight? Rehearsals finish at nine."

I glanced at Trumbull. He was surveying the room from his usual spot next to the dining hall entrance. "Definitely," I said. "How about if we meet in the media room at nine thirty? Maybe watch a movie?"

"I yield to thy will." His overloaded tray balanced on one hand, Nico gave us each a deep bow. "Mistress Bex. My lord."

Bex watched him walk off, her fingers stroking her copiously pierced but unadorned earlobe, that troubled expression still on her face. At first I'd assumed it had to do with the sight of Nico eating the Spam casserole, but now I wondered if something else was bothering her.

"What's up?" I said.

She shook her head and picked up her fork. "Nothing. Hey, you'll have your security with you when you and Nico hang out tonight, right?"

I groaned. "Unfortunately. I'm praying it won't be too awkward. Why?"

Her eyes flicked back to the door through which Nico had left. "No reason."

10

◇◇◇◇◇◇

As my datelike thing with Nico drew closer, the fears careening around in my head multiplied. What if Nico got flirty again? What if he *didn't* get flirty again? What if he got flirty while Ray was watching? By dinner, I'd entered a state of full panic. My chest felt tight, and the dining hall food turned my stomach even more than usual. I spent most of the meal pushing around the food on my plate with my fork and making Bex tell me over and over that my ears really weren't that big. (The more I'd thought about it, the more convinced I'd become that Nico had just called my ears cute out of politeness.) After that, I went back to my room and spent the next couple of hours trying on every T-shirt and every pair of jeans in my closet. Sort of a stupid exercise, considering all my jeans were the same brand and all my T-shirts were black, but at least it kept me busy. At 9:32 (I didn't want to look too eager), I opened the door to my room.

Ray stood outside. And so did Trumbull.

My heart fell with what felt like an audible *thud*.

"What are *you* still doing here?"

"The task force hasn't found any sign of your robot," Trumbull answered. "I want to stay close in case there are further developments."

"Are you sure that's a good idea? You need to get your sleep, don't you?"

He raised one eyebrow. I'd never expressed concern about his sleep schedule in my life. "I will. Later."

"Okay, well, I'm heading out to meet Nico. We're watching a movie."

He slid his massive bulk to the side, blocking my path. "Sorry, sir. Tonight you're on lockdown."

"I'll just be in the media room. It's right there." I pointed. "I can see it."

"I know where the media room is. But I'm afraid you're not going anywhere."

"After one robot malfunction?"

"That's right."

"For how long?"

"Tomorrow during the day you can go to your classes. Tomorrow night, we'll see."

"Can Nico come here, then?"

"That's a negative." I must've made a face, because he added, "This is part of the protocol, sir. We're not doing it to punish you. We're doing it to keep you safe."

Behind him, Ray opened his hands and mouthed, *Sorry*.

I took one last look at the media room door. My right hand squeezed into a fist. I slammed it against the doorjamb. "Damn it, Trumbull, why do you have to be such a rule monger? Why can't you be a human being for once?"

Back in my room, I dropped onto the bed and put my head in my hands. Dating was hard for everybody, I understood that. But seriously, did other kids have to deal with *this*? According to my puck, it was now 9:37. Nico had probably started wondering where I was. Maybe he figured I'd chickened out.

"Send a message to Nico."

My puck bobbed lower.

I can't make it, I told him. *My Head Armed Babysitter is keeping me on lockdown. For my own protection, supposedly.*

Tell him I'll protect you, he messaged back, the words lighting up the wall across from me. *I'd be happy to lock you down.*

A blush raced over my face and ears like wildfire. I must've really had it bad to fall for a cheesy line like that. *I don't think he'd go for that idea.*

So no movie?

Sorry. Trumbull's such a tyrant.

No, I understand. He just wants to keep you safe. Some other time, then.

But I didn't want to wait until some other time. What if he changed his mind about me before then? I wanted to see him tonight.

Wait. There might be a way. Go back to your room and stand by.

His reply flashed across my wall a few seconds later. *For you, I'd stand by indefinitely.*

Full of energy all of a sudden, I bounced up and opened my window. The other rooms overlooking the little courtyard were dark, and nothing stirred on the flagstones below. Perfect. I pulled a black hoodie on over my black T-shirt and tucked Gremlin into a pocket. (I felt a little like a kid lugging around a stuffed animal long after it was age appropriate, but leaving Gremlin behind wasn't an option. I would've felt more naked without him than without my puck, and anyway, I figured I'd need some extra luck to carry out the plan taking shape in my head.) From my closet I grabbed a backpack and tossed in a few other necessary items. Figuring it couldn't hurt, I also pulled out a couple of extra pillows, stuffed them under my duvet, and pounded them into the approximate shape of my sleeping body.

I turned to my shelf of Creatures. "Rapunzel, Rapunzel."

One of the robots woke up—a squat one, about a foot and a half long, with a body shaped like a beetle and an oversize Barbie doll head attached to the front.

"How can I help you?" she asked in a bright Barbie voice.

"Keep your voice down, first of all. And set yourself up at the window. I need an exit."

"Okay!" she chirped, more softly. She skittered over to the

open window, perched herself sideways on the sill, and clamped herself in place. "Ready!"

I reached into the back of my bottom dresser drawer and pulled out one final piece of equipment: a climbing harness. I strapped myself into it. A length of thin cord hung from an opening in Rapunzel's side, with a carabiner attached to the end. I clipped that to my harness. As I stood near the open window, my palms had already started to sweat, and my legs wobbled underneath me. I'd had the idea to build Rapunzel last year, on a day when I'd felt especially fed up with Trumbull and more desperate than usual for solitude, but I hadn't worked up the courage to use her even once. Of course, I'd never let any of my Armed Babysitters know what she could do. For months, she'd sat on my shelf, unused, hiding in plain sight among my other Creatures.

I sat down on the sill and slung my legs over one by one. This first part would be the hardest. Hard for anybody, probably. For a phobic basket case like me, *very* hard. *Don't look down*, I told myself. *Just focus on what's in the foreground: the windowsill, Rapunzel, the cord. Ignore that forty-foot drop in the background.*

My heart going crazy, Gremlin already purring in my pocket, I took hold of the sill and twisted my body around. My butt swung out into the courtyard. My sneakers smacked against the wall. Nothing but cold, empty air underneath me. Rapunzel held fast, though. She'd turned her Barbie head to watch. "Good job!" she trilled. My puck had followed me through the window too. It angled itself so its light shone on the stone wall in front of me.

I knew what I had to do next—while designing Rapunzel, I'd learned all about rock climbing on the Supernet—but I'd never actually tried it myself. "Give me some slack, Rapunzel." The cord began to lengthen. My body dipped backward. I transferred my grip from the sill to the cord. Now I just had to press my feet into the wall, straighten my legs, and walk down the wall all the way to the ground.

It had looked easy on the Supernet. When I tried to straighten my legs, though, my body seemed to weigh a ton. My legs wobbled and shook. My sneakers slid slowly downward and then flew out from under me. My body slammed into the wall, and an involuntary yelp leaped out of my mouth. I dangled from the cord, gasping and scrambling like a drowning person, stone fragments from the windowsill raining on my head.

"Not to worry!" Rapunzel sang. "I gotcha!"

Don't look down, I ordered myself again. *Just stay calm. Think of your brain as a machine. It'll do what you want it to do if you operate it correctly.*

I'd told myself that plenty of times before. But the problem I always came back to was this: if my brain was a machine, half its buttons didn't seem to work. And the other half didn't have labels. And I'd lost the instruction book. Right now, for example. I knew I'd built Rapunzel well. I knew she wouldn't drop me. So why couldn't I stop panicking?

"Just lower me down, Rapunzel," I panted.

"But—"

"Please! Just lower me down like this."

"You got it!"

The cord unspooled. I descended, using my hands to keep from bumping and scraping too much against the wall. The rest of my body hung limp in the harness. Inside my hoodie pocket, Gremlin continued his purring. I hoped Trumbull hadn't heard my yelp. I hoped I wouldn't be a dirty, sticky mess by the time Nico saw me. Small chance of that: the sweat rolled down my face, dripped from my nose, turned icy in the cold air.

My sneaker soles thumped against something. I gave myself permission to peek down. My feet had reached solid ground. I unclipped myself from the cord with shaky hands and collapsed on the flagstones. "Tell Rapunzel to come here," I said to my puck.

Up above, my robot retracted the cord and climbed down the wall, her short legs finding tiny footholds in the rough stone. My panting had slowed by the time she reached me. Hauling myself to my feet, I wiped my face on my sleeve and dusted off my jeans, as if that might help erase my monumental lameness.

But at least I'd made it down. That had to count for something. I'd successfully, if not gracefully, negotiated that forty-foot drop. And now I was free to see Nico. Unchaperoned.

11

C ome on, Rapunzel."

Following the escape route I'd mapped out last year but never actually used, I passed through a door that led from the courtyard into a service stairwell and headed down to the subbasement. At the foot of the stairs stood another door, this one locked. I pulled a pouch of robotics tools from my backpack and went to work. A few minutes later the door creaked open. That was another skill I'd taught myself in order to facilitate my escape plan: picking the kind of old-fashioned pin-tumbler locks that were still common at Inverness Prep. But unlike climbing down walls, picking locks was something I could actually do. I'd discovered it really wasn't all that different from tinkering with robots.

On the other side of the door, a narrow corridor stretched down the length of the building, with rusted, sweaty pipes running along its low ceiling. As I followed the passage toward the center of the school, the ever-present rumble of rushing water grew to a roar. I turned a corner, then another, and found myself in a large, low room with the river crashing right through the middle of it. The water ran from the front of the school to the back, where it boiled through an iron grill and tumbled over the side of the cliff. Two narrow stone walkways ran along the canal, one on each side. The chamber made me think of the engine room of an old ship—probably because of its location deep in the bowels of the school, and because the thundering of the river, loud enough to crack a skull open, sounded just like I imagined a ship's engine would.

I turned toward the front of the school and followed the walkway to a heavy gate, also locked. (School policy prohibited students from nosing around down here.) Out came my tools. I had that lock open even faster than the last one.

I passed through the gate and emerged from under the building. The walkways continued along either side of the canal out here, but I took a side staircase up to ground level. When I'd almost reached the top, I dropped to a crouch. "Turn off your light," I hissed at my puck. I'd glimpsed the other half of my detail—the agent who patrolled the school grounds—prowling across the lawn up ahead. It didn't look like he'd noticed me, though. I pulled out a glass jar with a dozen or so mothlike Creatures fluttering around inside. Swarmbots, I called them. I unscrewed the lid. They poured out and vanished into the darkness. Meanwhile, the Secret Service agent disappeared around the corner of the building.

I jumped up and dashed along the front of the school. Up above, the clouds had cleared for a second straight night—unheard of at Inverness Prep. An almost-full moon flung pale light across the school's gruesome facade. Near the tree where I'd picked up Nevermore this morning, I stopped and sent Nico a message: *Open your window and look down. But don't make any noise.*

Nico leaned out his window a few seconds later. The scene looked just like the one my puck had projected on my wall last night, with the light from his room streaming past him and catching in his curly hair. Except now he had his clothes on. Even so, I liked this better than last night, because this time I was seeing it for real.

He beckoned his puck outside and said something to it. My puck's small screen displayed the message: *Wherefore art thou?*

His mind had obviously gone to the same sappy Shake-spearean place mine had yesterday. I waved, and he spotted me. I took out my climbing harness and looped it around my robot's Barbie head. "Rapunzel, I want you to climb to that third-story window, the fifth one from the left, and set yourself up on the sill."

"Okay!"

When she'd reached him, my puck lit up again: *She's cute, but I was actually hoping to spend time with YOU.*

She's not your date, I messaged back. *She's your means of egress. Have you by any chance gone rock climbing before?*

By then, Rapunzel had fastened herself to his window, and Nico had taken the harness in his hands.

Yes! This is genius! I'll be down in a sec.

And that was literally how long it took. He threw his legs over the sill, swung himself around, and rappelled down the wall in three graceful bounds. Somehow it didn't surprise me.

"Did you make her yourself?" he asked, unfastening his harness. "She's amazing!"

I nodded, a blush heating my face. Something else I liked about Nico: It wasn't just that he was cool. He made me feel cool too.

My robot had climbed back down the wall by then. "Rapunzel, hide in those bushes," I told her, "and wait for us there."

"Happy to!" she chirped before burrowing headfirst into the leaves.

"So," Nico said. "You've got me. What are you going to do with me?" He wore a bright yellow windbreaker, tattered jeans, and flip-flops. The flip-flops threw me a little. Did people wear flip-flops on dates? On the other hand, his shock of curly hair looked extra glossy, like he'd put styling stuff in it.

"I have something I want to show you," I said. "Sort of a secret. But it's a hike to get there." I nodded at the flip-flops. "Will you be okay in those?"

"Back at home, I wear them everywhere. Lead on."

I guided Nico along the front of the school and down the stairs to the walkway by the rushing water. We followed the canal upstream. The walls on either side were about six feet high, which gave us some cover as we crossed the school's vast front lawn. At the edge of the grounds, the river passed through a tunnel that ran under the front gate and the highway beyond. The walkways continued into the tunnel, but iron gates blocked students from going any farther. I took out my tools one more time, and also the jar, which I handed to Nico.

"Hold this." Then, to my puck, "Call back the Swarmbots."

I went to work on the lock.

"No way!" Nico tapped the side of the glass container as it filled with my tiny Creatures. "What are they for?"

"Have you noticed all the security cameras roaming around inside the school? There are cameras outside, too, and I didn't want them to see us. These things home in on the sound the cameras' rotors make, and then they crowd around the cameras' lenses so they can't see anything."

"Clever."

The gate swung open. Nico peered into the dark tunnel beyond.

"You're just full of surprises, aren't you?"

I couldn't tell if he meant that in a good way. "I'm not a serial killer," I blurted.

"Excuse me?"

Wrong thing to say, the underdeveloped section of my brain that monitored social interactions informed me. I tried to smile, but it probably made me look even creepier. "I just meant you don't have to worry. I'm not going to try anything funny, I swear."

He crossed his arms. "Really? That's disappointing." He motioned at the gate with his chin. "After you."

The darkness of the tunnel enfolded us, and we told our pucks to turn on their lights. Every once in a while I'd glance back at Nico, and he'd grin. I imagined his gaze on my back, on my butt maybe. Did I really have a nice butt, like Bex had said? We emerged from the tunnel on the far side of the highway, where the canal became a natural river. The night felt brisk— not as cold as it could sometimes get in October, but not flip-flop weather, either. Nico didn't seem to mind. We climbed to the top of the riverbank, where a trail ran alongside the river into the forest.

Nico pulled up next to me as we hiked up the trail. "So you pick locks and make robots. Is there anything you can't do?"

"Yeah. Pretty much everything else." On impulse, I drew Gremlin from my pocket. He scampered up to my shoulder and tugged twice on my ear. "But when it comes to anything mechanical, I'm your guy."

"You made that one, too?"

"No. But he's my favorite. I've had him since I was little. His name's Gremlin."

"What does he do?"

"You know those little mascots the heroes in Disney cartoons always have, the ones that mostly just sit on the hero's shoulder and look cute and occasionally get into mischief? That's what he does. He can also obey a few simple commands. I usually make him bring me my socks in the morning. Here, take a look." I lifted Gremlin from my shoulder and dropped him into Nico's hands.

"He's soft."

"Sometimes I rub his coat for luck."

"In that case." Nico gave Gremlin's orange fur a vigorous rub.

The forest grew thicker around us. The trees blocked out much of the moonlight, but our pucks continued to light our way. I thought of that line of Shakespeare Nico had recited in front of Dad yesterday. I'd looked it up, and it came from *A Midsummer Night's Dream*, a play that took place in an enchanted wood and featured a fairy servant named Puck. I'd always assumed pucks had gotten their name because of their round, flat shape, but it turned out the name also referred to the character from the play. I could see why now, as I watched our pucks bob over our heads like actual woodland spirits.

An owl hooted, and Gremlin, startled, sprang from Nico's hands back to my arm.

"Sorry," I said. "He likes to stay near me. Or I guess I should say he was programmed to stay near me."

Gremlin ran up to my shoulder and tugged on my ear again.

"Why does he keep doing that?" Nico asked.

"What?"

"Pulling on your ear."

"Oh." I plucked Gremlin from my shoulder. "He was programmed to do that, too."

"Why?"

"It's sort of embarrassing. Are you sure you want to hear this?"

"If it's embarrassing, then definitely."

Out of habit, I glanced around, as if someone else might be listening even way out here. "When I was about six, my dad was elected to Congress and my mom got her job at the lab in Bethesda, so the whole family moved to DC. I was a shy kid. Transferring to a brand-new school halfway through the school year had me completely terrified. On my first day my mom walked me into the classroom, gave me a kiss, and told me she loved me. Not such a weird thing for a mother to do, but for some reason the other kids teased me about it all day. Probably they could see how scared I was, so they must've decided I'd be an easy target."

"Did you have glasses and cute ears back then, too?"

"Oh, yes. That probably didn't help either. When my mom picked me up that afternoon, I told her she was never allowed to kiss me or tell me she loved me in public again. So she tapped her chin and thought about it. I remember she always did that when she was thinking. Tapped her chin. 'Okay, I won't,' she said. 'How about this, kiddo: from now on, whenever I say good-bye to you in front of other people, I'll just tug on your ear, and you'll know that means I love you.'

"And that was what she did from then on. It sort of became our thing. For my eighth birthday, she gave me Gremlin. She'd made him herself. 'So now,' she said, 'even when I'm not with you, you'll feel him tug on your ear, and you'll know what it means.' Then she died a year later, so I guess Gremlin makes me think of her." Nico didn't say anything. I glanced at him. "Am I being a downer? Tell the truth. I think I may have a tendency to do that."

"Not at all. I was just wondering how someone like your mom ended up with someone like your dad. I hope that's not rude of me to say. But maybe he was different back then. Not so antirobot and pro-stay-at-home-mom."

"He wasn't *that* different. But Headmaster Stroud was my mom's father, and he'd been best friends with my dad's father. I'm sure he had a hand in getting my mom and dad together."

"So it was like an arranged marriage?"

"Well. Not exactly."

The truth was, unlike just about every other person on the planet, Mom had never had a problem standing up to Stroud. She hadn't even let him enroll her at Inverness, and she certainly hadn't taken his wishes into account when she'd chosen her career path. Maybe Stroud had pushed her toward Dad at first, but in the end, she must've really fallen in love with him.

Still, Mom and Dad had always seemed like a mismatched

pair. For instance, he went to church every week, but she never did. They'd trade off Sundays: one week Dad would bring me to services with him, and the next, Mom and I would have what she called Appreciation Days, where we'd go on a hike or visit a science museum or do experiments in her little lab in the garage. The whole arrangement was odd—like shared spiritual custody.

Once, on one of those Sundays, I asked Mom, "How come you don't go to church?"

She shrugged. "I had enough of that when I was a kid."

"Is it because you don't think there's a God?"

"I suppose that depends on what you mean by 'God,'" she answered, tapping her chin. "Do I think there's a God like in the Bible? No. I'm a scientist. I value hard evidence, and all the hard evidence argues against it."

"And heaven? Do you believe in that?"

"Same answer, kiddo." It didn't seem to bother her, though.

But I didn't tell Nico any of that. Instead, I stowed Gremlin in my hoodie and said, "What about you?"

"What *about* me?"

"I don't know, everything. You've met my dad, you've heard about my mom. Tell me about *your* family."

"There isn't a whole lot to tell."

"I don't believe that for a second. Come on, what's your life story?" I stepped over an exposed tree root. "Or maybe you prefer being a man of mystery."

He waggled his eyebrows at me mysteriously.

For a while the trail had slanted gently upward. Now it curved to the left, still following the river, and another path, steeper and more rugged, cut off to the right. I guided Nico that way.

"I grew up in Santiago," Nico said. "The Medinas have lived there for generations. My great-great-grandfather founded one of the most successful investment banks in Chile."

"And you were sent to Inverness Prep to get a top-notch education so you can go back home and take over the family business?"

"Something like that. My dad had been trying to get me into Inverness for years, but it's practically impossible if you're not a legacy. Then a few weeks ago, out of the blue, I got a last-minute admission. I guess my dad had finally found the right person on the board to bribe. So here I am. But I can tell you right now, I'm not going to be a banker."

"Oh, yeah? What are you going to do then? Because if you're considering a career as a food critic, you might want to work on that palate of yours. I hate to break it to you, but the food here really does suck."

Nico laughed. All our hiking had turned his cheeks reddish gold. I could see it even in the low light from our pucks. He'd been right about his flip-flops, though: so far he hadn't stumbled once.

"Or do you want to be an actor?" I asked.

"Nah." He held up a low-hanging branch, and I ducked under it.

"Seriously, what do you want to do?"

He shrugged. "I don't know, Lee. I just want to live. Like really live. Make every second count, you know?"

"Okay. Admirable, but vague. Not that I have a better answer to that question."

The trees had thinned by then. The trail had grown even rockier. A chain-link fence, warped and rusted with age, appeared in front of us, with barbed wire draped across the top and a battered yellow sign that read, DANGER! NO TRESPASSING! Behind that loomed the mountain, blue in the moonlight, its blunt peak wedging itself into the starry sky.

"This evening just gets more and more interesting," Nico said.

"You told me you wanted to live." I hunted around the base of the fence until I found the place where someone had dug a hole under it. I shimmied through. "Your turn."

Nico took off his yellow windbreaker, balled it up, and tossed it over. "Catch!" He slithered after me. I tried not to imagine all those muscles I'd seen last night swelling and shifting under his T-shirt as he moved.

The trail continued on this side of the fence, broken in by decades of trespassers. It skirted the base of the mountain for a while and ended at the mouth of a tunnel. A ramshackle barrier of wood planks blocked the opening, with another yellow

NO TRESPASSING sign nailed to it. A few of the planks had fallen away, though, leaving gaps like knocked-out teeth.

"What is this place?" Nico said.

"It used to be a mine. Copper, I think." I peeked through one of the gaps in the barrier, but I could see only darkness beyond.

"And we're going inside?"

I looked back at him. For the first time all evening—for the first time since I'd met him, in fact—he appeared hesitant. "That's the plan," I said.

"Through here?"

"I believe so."

"You believe so? You mean you haven't come here before?"

Oops. I'd hoped I wouldn't have to admit that so soon. "I've never had the chance. My Secret Service detail is always hovering around me."

"So you don't do this all the time? Sneak out of your room in the dead of night?"

I shook my head. "The truth is, I haven't been this far away from my detail in years." Only now, as I said it out loud, did I realize the enormity of it: I hadn't had even a moment on my own like this since before Dad had started his run for the presidency. Except for that one other time, two years ago. But of course I didn't mention that now.

Nico laughed and knocked me on the arm. "And here I thought you were this outdoorsy adventurer type."

"Nope. I'm about as indoorsy as they come. The pasty skin should've been a tip-off."

He crossed his arms and looked back down the trail. "So you've never ditched your security before. Never come up here before. But you did it for me?"

For the umpteenth time that night, I blushed. "I guess you could say that. I mean, I've wanted to check this place out for a long time. Bex has been inside, and she told me all about it. It sounds amazing."

Nico's eyes returned to the barrier. His face clouded over again.

"If you'd rather not, though, I totally understand. I get freaked out and decide not to do things at least seven times an hour."

It felt strange being the brave one. I wondered what had him spooked, this guy who did handstands on cliffs and talked about making every second count. Was he claustrophobic? But I didn't want to be a jerk and ask him.

"I think this might be fun, though," I added.

He rocked back and forth in his flip-flops, his arms still crossed, his mouth twisted to one side. "At least I know you're not a serial killer. So I don't have that to worry about."

"It's true. I'm not."

"Okay, then. That being the case, let's do it."

12

I motioned my puck through a space between two of the planks. It illuminated a low, narrow tunnel with rutted walls held up by thick wooden supports.

"I'll go first," I said.

I squeezed through the opening. The air smelled like mushrooms, and it felt ten degrees cooler in here than outside. Nico followed. Our heads bent low, we made our way single file through the tunnel. It stretched off into the distance, as straight and precise as a perspective drawing. We didn't speak much now. The only sound was the flapping of Nico's flip-flops, which echoed off the walls and produced a complex, appropriately ominous rhythm. Our pucks floated just ahead of us, their light carving out sharp-edged shadows in the rugged rock. "Network signal lost," they murmured at one point, almost in unison.

After we'd walked for what felt like a mile, the echo of Nico's flip-flops shifted downward in pitch, and a soft exhalation of cold air blew into my face. A few steps later the tunnel walls vanished, and we found ourselves in a space so huge the light from our pucks couldn't reach the far side. The two little devices surged upward, as if they felt as happy as we did to be out of the cramped passage.

My foot clanged against something: an empty beer bottle. "Be careful. There's garbage on the floor. And then somewhere up ahead . . ."

". . . there's no more floor."

Nico had pulled ahead of me. He strode right up to the spot where the ground dropped away and left an enormous black void. I stayed where I was and hid my hands in my hoodie pockets and squeezed them into tight, tight fists. *You chose to bring him here,* I reminded myself. *You knew this was coming.*

"How far down does it go?" When he glanced back at me, his face seemed to glow in the low light. Whatever had scared him before we'd entered the tunnel didn't trouble him now. Meanwhile, I was barely holding myself together. In other words, things had gone back to normal.

"Something like three hundred feet," I said, with only a slight tremor in my voice. "The cavern formed naturally. The miners didn't make it. I've heard you could fit the Statue of Liberty in here. Although as of a month ago I guess that's not saying as much."

Nico had already gone back to directing his puck one way and then the other to light up more of the cavern. "Is there a way to get to the bottom?"

"Jumping, I guess. Apart from that, I don't think so. There's a story kids tell at Inverness, though. One time, years ago, I'm not sure how many, a group of students came here to hang out. They were drinking. One of them fell over the edge."

"Uh-oh."

"But he survived. Apparently there's a ledge about thirty feet down. He landed on that."

Nico leaned way out to peer into the chasm. "I can see it."

My heart thumped harder. I forced myself to focus on our pucks as they explored the dark space. The cavern walls, smoother than the ones in the tunnel, draped downward in graceful folds, like curtains.

"What did the kid do?" Nico asked.

"He shouted up to his friends. He didn't think he'd broken anything. They told him to stay there while they got help. But he'd been using his flashlight to look around, and he said he could see a tunnel leading away from the ledge. He wanted to try following that first to see if it would take him back to his friends. The kid disappeared into the tunnel. And his friends waited. And waited. And waited."

As the pucks moved around, the walls seemed to shift in front of us like the surface of a vast, vertical sea.

"They shouted down to him," I said, "but he didn't answer. They couldn't call him on his phone, either—this was before pucks—because the mountain blocks the network signal. The kids finally contacted the police and told them everything. A search party went down to the ledge and found the tunnel. But that tunnel split into more tunnels, and those tunnels split off too. Supposedly, there are hundreds of miles of passages down there, some natural, some man-made, and all the maps from the copper mine days are lost. The search party looked and looked, but they never did find him. His body must still be down there somewhere."

"That's some story," Nico said.

I sensed I was being a downer again, but at least my fists had loosened a little. "Hey, you want to see something cool?"

"Sure."

I took a few steps closer to the edge. "Turn out your light," I told my puck. It blinked off. "Now you," I said to Nico.

He wagged his finger at me. "Remember, I'm trusting you."

I put up my hand, as if to swear to my good behavior. He gave his puck the command. The cavern collapsed into blackness.

"Whoa," Nico said. "It's *dark*."

That was an understatement. This was the kind of dark that made you sure you'd gone blind. The kind of dark that made you doubt your own existence. The silence in the cavern seemed more complete too, aside from the steady cycling of Nico's breathing and my own. As I stood there, I noticed—or maybe imagined—that strange heat radiating from his body again.

"What happens now?" he said.

"Just wait a second." I pulled off my backpack and groped

around inside before finding the lighter and the box of sparklers I'd packed. I pulled out a sparkler and flicked the lighter. Nico reappeared in front of me, squinting against the sudden light, his face orange in the lighter's glow. I touched the flame to the end of the sparkler. It flared and hissed as it caught. Sparks gushed from the tip. They poured over our feet and bounced on the ground. A few landed on my skin but didn't hurt. When I threw the sparkler into the cavern, it fell and fell, shedding particles of light, illuminating the undulating rock walls. Nico took a few steps forward to watch it drop, but I stayed glued in place. Then the chasm swallowed it up, and darkness wrapped itself around us again.

"Can I try?" Nico asked.

Our hands fumbled against each other as I passed him the lighter and a sparkler. Then the lighter flame sprang up again, and his sparkler started to crackle and fizz. He flashed me a sly grin in the unsteady light. I tried to smile back but couldn't tell if I succeeded. He lobbed the sparkler over the side and rushed forward to watch it spiral down.

"Come here! You have to see this!"

He grabbed my hand and pulled me forward. Terror sizzled through me. For a second my whole body felt like one of those fireworks. The light from the sparkler had already started to fade, but I could still see the tips of my sneakers inches away from the edge, the narrow ledge thirty feet down where that kid had landed, and beyond that, a yawning, black nothingness.

Then I couldn't see anything at all. My heart sprinted. Inside my hoodie pocket, Gremlin resumed his purring. But I forced myself to stay there, inches away from that void I couldn't see but knew was right in front of me. Feeling Nico's hot, strong hand clutch mine made the agony worthwhile.

"So this is really the first time you haven't had your Secret Service detail following you in *years*?" he asked.

"Yeah. Crazy, huh?" I lit another sparkler but didn't throw it in. We turned to face each other, the firework crackling between us. Its flickering light brought out the threads of gold in his brown eyes.

"What does it feel like to be watched all the time like that?"

"Pretty much as sucky as you'd expect. Being the son of the president is like all the worst parts of being the president with none of the perks. You have to give up your whole life, but you don't get paid and you have no power whatsoever and you'll never have an airport named after you. There are lights and cameras in your face all the time, people talking about you on the Supernet."

He shook his head. "No wonder you're in the closet."

My stomach clenched. "What makes you think I'm in the closet?"

"You mean you're out?"

"No, I mean, what makes you think I'm gay?"

He laughed. The loudest laugh I'd heard from him yet. It filled the cavern and echoed against the walls. I almost thought he'd start a cave-in. Wiping his eyes, he noticed I hadn't joined him. "You *are* kidding, aren't you?"

"Well," I mumbled.

"You asked me out on a date, Lee. We were just holding hands a second ago. Of *course* you're gay." He smacked my chest with the back of his hand.

I coughed up a weak laugh of my own. "Yeah. I was kidding. Of course I'm gay."

And just like that, there went my plausible deniability. I didn't even freak out, either. I thought of Jeremy, that kid I'd kissed freshman year. Neither one of us had ever once spoken the word "gay," not even after we'd kissed. That charged silence had felt safe, and also weirdly exciting. But this habit Nico had of laying everything out on the table—this was exciting too, in a different way.

"Listen, Nico," I said. "I think I should tell you something." The firework had almost burned all the way down. The fountain of sparks had slowed to a trickle. "Toward the end of freshman year, I started hanging out with this guy named Jeremy. We never talked about it, but I could tell he had, you know, feelings for me. I guess I had feelings too. One night we were studying together in the library. We'd taken over an alcove up on the mezzanine, and I'd noticed my Nighttime Armed Babysitter had fallen asleep. He does that sometimes. I realized it was the first time Jeremy and I had ever been alone together, and I knew it might be the last too, so I kissed him."

The sparkler hissed out in my hand. Nico's face disappeared before I could catch his reaction. Even with my severely limited understanding of romance, I knew talking about kissing some other guy probably wasn't recommended on a first date.

"How was it?" Nico said.

I tossed aside the burned-out sparkler and set another one crackling. "Nice, I think. I was so nervous, I barely felt it. Then, after it was over, I noticed a security camera creeping by. I got all weird, and made up an excuse to leave, and spent the rest of the night alone in my room with my stomach tied up in knots. I'd thought about boys before, but I'd never actually done anything like that, and now that my gayness was an actual thing, it had me seriously freaked. I spun out this whole story in my brain: the kiss had been recorded, someone would see the footage, my dad and everybody else in America would find out. The next time I saw Jeremy, I couldn't even get myself to say hello to him. We spent the rest of the year ignoring each other, and when I came back after summer break, I found out he'd transferred to another school."

Nico raised his hand and let the sparks glance off his fingers. "So if we were to end up kissing tonight—I'm not saying that's going to happen, but *if*—is that what you'd do to me, too? Ignore me for the rest of the year?"

I gulped. Had he just said, *If we were to end up kissing*? "Sorry, that's not what I meant. I promise I wouldn't do that. But I want you to understand how things are. It's true, Nico,

I'm deep in the closet. Like all the way in the back, behind the winter coats. If people find out the founder of the Human Values Movement has a gay son, he won't stand a chance when he comes up for reelection."

"But why?" Nico said. "That's what I don't get. Why does being antirobot also make Human Values antigay?"

"You should ask Bex. She's the expert. She has this theory that the invention of artificial consciousness triggered a sort of collective existential crisis in the human race. Now that machines were just as sophisticated as humans, it suddenly seemed incredibly important to figure out what exactly sets humans apart from machines. Because there has to be *something*, right? The Human Values Movement decided the difference is free will. Supposedly, people have it, machines don't. Even the 2Bs can only follow their programming, but humans have the ability to choose who and what and how to be. I guess the Human Values hard-liners think that includes sexuality, too."

Nico squinted at me. "Tell me something. *You* don't believe that Human Values crap, do you?"

"I don't think I chose to be gay, if that's what you mean. In fact, I didn't choose a lot of things. Like being the son of the president. Or coming to Inverness. Or even being in the closet, really. All in all, I'd say I have about as much free will as an espresso maker."

Another sparkler died. Only one left. For some reason, I

dreaded returning to the brighter, steadier light of our pucks.

After igniting the last firework, I took a tiny step closer to the edge of the chasm and peeked over.

"Every once in a while," I said, "I look up at this mountain and think: What if that kid from the story didn't die after all? What if he just realized he was sick of his life and decided to stay in those tunnels forever? I know it sounds weird, but I like to imagine him wandering around in here. Hundreds of miles of passages, a whole maze of choices, and he can go anywhere he likes."

Nico glanced over the edge, then back at me, his nose scrunched. "You know, you really *are* a downer sometimes."

"Excuse me?"

"Of course you have a choice. You always have a choice. I mean, not about being gay. That's just stupid. But you could come out of the closet if you really wanted to."

"You sound like Bex. Didn't you hear what I just said? If I came out, it would destroy my dad."

"That's his problem."

"And it would be hell for me, too."

"How do you know that?"

"Trust me. I know." He opened his mouth to say something else, but I raised a finger. "Nico. I'm serious. Don't."

"Okay." He held up his hands in surrender. "I'll let that issue go. For now. Let's take another example. Something else you could choose to do if you wanted to."

"What's that?"

"You could kiss me."

My arm must've jerked, because the sparkler flew out of my fingers. I fumbled for it, and for a few seconds it jumped between my hands, spinning and twirling and leaving swirls of sparks in its wake.

Then Nico plucked it out of the air.

"Thanks," I said, reaching for it.

He tossed it into the chasm. The last thing I saw was that Cheshire grin of his. Then blackness.

"No lights," he said. "No cameras."

Again I felt the heat from his body on mine. But I didn't budge. Part of me—the Kamikaze Lee part—did want to kiss Nico, so much it made my chest feel like it might explode. Meanwhile, Gutless Lee wanted to run straight out of the cavern and all the way back to school. And as usual, there I stood, stuck in the middle, doing nothing.

"Now, you have to admit," Nico said, "that was a pretty romantic moment. I hope you're not going to leave me hang—"

I grabbed him in the darkness, pulled him to me, and crushed my mouth against his.

13

We kissed only once. His lips were so warm, I flinched when they first touched mine. A half second later, though, I couldn't get enough of his heat. My whole body seemed to light up in a way it never had before, like a machine that executed some brand-new, hidden program when you pressed the right combination of buttons.

Afterward, we pulled apart, still holding each other's arms. My stomach contracted. For the past few minutes I'd forgotten all about that huge chasm right next to us, but now the memory came rushing back. I couldn't tell in the darkness how close we were to the edge, and I couldn't remember where we'd stood the last time the light had gone out.

"Puck, turn on your light," I blurted.

Nico reappeared in front of me, and so did the cavern walls, the ground under our feet, the edge of the chasm—six inches away.

"We should probably head back," I told him, trying to sound casual.

"Hey." He squeezed my forearms. "You okay?"

"Sure, I'm fine." I did my best to focus on Nico's brown eyes and crooked teeth, his hands holding my arms. And little by little, it was true. I was fine. My stomach untwisted itself. My head cleared. I smiled at him, and it didn't even feel like one of my grotesque forced smiles. It was like the muscles of my face had finally figured out what to do. "I just don't want to push my luck with my Armed Babysitters."

We made our way single file through the tunnel. Outside again, he grabbed my hand, laced his fingers through mine, and squeezed. We walked like that all the way down the mountainside, while our pucks bobbed along side by side above our heads. I seemed to have gotten all the gloomy babbling out of my system, so Nico finally had a chance to tell me more about his own life: his three noisy sisters; his drama teacher back at his old school, the one who first got him interested in theater; his addiction to empanadas made by Santiago street vendors, "the greasier the better." The trail rejoined the river. Not long after that, we reached the highway and stopped on the shoulder. Inverness Prep's front gate stood across from us, with the school's jagged silhouette behind it. Like a reflex, my hand released his.

"Remember, you promised," Nico said. "You won't get weird, right?"

"I won't get weird. But I still need this to stay quiet, at least for a while. You understand that, don't you?"

"In other words, no serenading you in the dining hall."

"That would probably be best."

We clambered down the riverbank and passed through the tunnel that went under the highway. I closed the gate behind us. After releasing the Swarmbots, we followed the walkway along the side of the canal, our pucks' lights turned off again to make us less conspicuous. Near the top of the stairs that led to the front lawn, we crouched and waited for the Secret Service agent to pass. Then we skirted the front of the school as far as the tree that stood below Nico's window.

"Rapunzel, Rapunzel."

She trotted out of the bushes, a few leaves stuck in her blond hair. After she'd once again scaled the wall, before she started to hoist Nico up, I grabbed him and gave him one more quick, reckless kiss. He was back in his window a few moments later, his elbows on the sill, his puck hovering next to him. He murmured something into it. My puck chimed and lit up. Another line I recognized from *Romeo and Juliet*: *A thousand times good night.*

A second chime, and a new message appeared on my puck's circular screen: *Where the hell are you, sir?*

Crap. I gave Nico one last wave and sprinted back toward the canal. On the way, I panted out a message to Trumbull: *I'll be there in a minute. Just please don't call in the entire US military, okay?* Then I instructed my puck to make the Swarmbots stand down and wait outside my window.

I hurried down the stairs, under the school, through the

subbasement, and back into the service stairwell, Rapunzel scuttling along at my heels. I took the stairs all the way up to the third floor: no point in putting myself through another agonizing climb now. Bursting into the boys' wing corridor, I found Trumbull standing in my doorway, sunglasses on, arms crossed. He didn't say a word. He just stepped to the side and motioned me into my room with a nod of his head.

"You little sneak!" Ray said, apparently delighted by my stunt. He pointed his thumb at my open window. "How did you get down?"

"With this, I assume."

Trumbull picked up Rapunzel. She wiggled her legs and turned her Barbie doll head to smile at him. "How can I help you?"

"How do you turn this thing off, sir?"

"Go to sleep, Rapunzel."

Her legs went limp. Her eyes closed. Ray hooked his finger through the carabiner hanging from her side and tugged on the cord, chuckling. "Rapunzel. That's a good one."

Trumbull tucked her under his arm. "You realize if you hadn't answered my message, this whole place would be swarming with Humvees and helicopters right now."

"But I did answer your message. I was going stir-crazy, Trumbull. I just needed to get some fresh air. I didn't go far."

"Yeah," Ray put in. "No harm done. Ease up on the guy, Trumbull."

But Trumbull didn't even glance at Ray. "Fresh air? What if that raven of yours had found you wandering around out there? Or what if this robot here had malfunctioned the way that one did? Did you think about that?"

I honestly hadn't. The date tonight had squeezed everything else out of my mind. "I'm sorry. I really am." I tossed my backpack in the corner, sank down on my bed, and pushed up my glasses to rub my eyes. "Listen, Trumbull, it's late. Could you finish reprimanding me in the morning? I need to get some sleep."

"I can't let you do that, sir. Your grandfather wants to see you."

I fumbled my glasses back into place. "How come?"

"Why do you think? He wants to talk to you about what you did."

"You mean you told him?" I sprang to my feet. "Why'd you have to do that?"

"Protocol, sir. You were out after curfew. You broke a school rule. I notified him just a minute ago, after I received your message."

"Sorry, buddy," Ray added.

I glanced at my puck. It was almost one in the morning. "And he wants to see me *now*?"

"That's correct."

"Should I change?" I still had on my black hoodie and jeans. The riverbank had left my sneakers caked in mud.

"I don't think that's necessary."

Trumbull handed Rapunzel to Ray—I knew I wouldn't get her back any time soon—and opened the door for me. Ray gave me a good-luck wink. I headed down the corridor, and Trumbull fell into position behind me. The school was silent except for the river's low rumble and the creaking of the floor under our feet. The Spiders did most of their cleaning at night, when the halls were clear, so we passed three of them on our way to the main staircase. Each one folded itself against the wall and murmured a polite "excuse me." They reminded me of empty-eyed prison guards standing by as I marched to my execution.

We climbed the stairs to the fourth floor, where the teachers and staff members who lived on campus had their apartments. From there, a narrower staircase led up to the tower that housed Stroud's office and residence. In the vestibule, his secretary's desk stood empty.

"He told me he'd call you in when he was ready for you," Trumbull said.

I nodded.

An arrangement of framed photographs crowded the wall next to me: students in gray blazers or midnight-blue athletic gear, most of them boys. I'd never looked at them carefully before. As my eyes drifted over the pictures and their captions, I recognized a few of the faces and even more of the names. Heads of state, heads of corporations, dignitaries foreign and domestic. Inverness Prep's Wall of Fame.

My gaze landed on a photo of a tall, good-looking guy with white-blond hair and a calculating expression that reminded me of the FUUWLs. He stood clutching a trophy above a caption that read, "Paul Waring wins the National Junior Chess League Championship for Inverness Prep."

Paul Waring. He'd been the director of Bethesda National Laboratory when Mom and Dr. Singh worked there. He'd also ordered Charlotte's termination—and then died in her first attack. I hadn't realized he'd gone to Inverness Prep too. It seemed like everyone on earth had a connection to this place. The people who were important, at least. Or, as in my case, the people who happened to be related to the people who were important.

Stroud's voice rumbled from my puck. "You may come in, Lee. Leave your puck outside, please."

I felt a coldness in my chest, like I'd just swallowed ice. It pushed out the warmth that had lingered there ever since my kiss with Nico. My hand burrowed into my hoodie pocket and wrapped around Gremlin. "Stay out here, puck," I said. Trumbull opened the door. I found myself wishing I could ask him to come in with me. What good was a Secret Service detail if it couldn't protect you from the things that *really* scared you?

14

◇◇◇◇◇

Stroud had never summoned me to his office for a repri-
mand before. Of course, Bex had made the trip plenty
of times. She always tried to shrug off those visits afterward, calling them more annoying than anything else, but I
could tell they rattled her. As for me, I'd started having night-
mares about my grandfather long before I'd set foot at Inverness Prep.

I'd seen him only once as a young kid. Dad had idolized
Stroud pretty much all his life—he'd never known his own
dad, and he often said Stroud was the closest thing he'd had
to a father—but I always got the feeling Mom didn't want him
around me. I was five or so when he finally came to visit. Before
he arrived, Dad told me about his imprisonment and escape,
about how much he'd taught Dad at Inverness Prep, about how
he'd teach me a lot too when my turn came to attend the school.
"He can seem serious," Dad said, "because he's been through a
lot, but don't let that scare you." So naturally the guy terrified

me before I'd even laid eyes on him. When he appeared at the front door, with his white crew cut, straight spine, and crooked shoulders, he reminded me of a broken G.I. Joe action figure. I noticed he didn't have a puck floating near him. I'd never seen that before. It seemed almost like not having a soul. His eyes were like splintered blue glass, and when he turned them on me, I just about burst into tears.

He didn't visit again until Mom's funeral four years later. After that he came to our house more regularly, but he never spoke much to me. Instead, he'd ask Dad a few questions about me while looking me up and down. Then he'd seem to lose interest, which I never minded at all. Even after I arrived at Inverness, he barely said a word to me. I still didn't understand why Dad had found him so inspiring. Whenever he looked my way in the halls, it unnerved me almost as much as it had when I was five.

Stroud's office door clicked shut behind me. He hadn't acknowledged my presence yet. He sat bent over his massive desk, still wearing his suit, his hands busy with some odd, intricate activity. I couldn't tell what it was.

An enormous window consisting of many panes of glass stretched across the wall behind him. During the day the window offered a view of the lake, but tonight I couldn't see much of anything. The clouds had moved back in since Nico and I had returned. An enormous marble fireplace dominated one side of the room, with a fire popping and snapping on the hearth but doing little to lift the gloom. Above the mantel, where other men might place a deer's head or ceremonial sword, hung the two-foot-long titanium thighbone he'd dug out of my other grandfather's leg. Just seeing it made the back of my neck prickle.

"Good evening, Lee," Stroud said without looking up.

"Good evening, sir." I stepped closer to the desk as I answered. Now I could see what he was doing: *writing*. With a pen, on paper. Nobody did *that* anymore. "I'm sorry about all this," I added. "I know it's late."

"I'm always awake at this time of night." He put down the pen. His chair creaked as he returned his spine to its usual ramrod-straight position. He leveled his blue eyes at me. Inside, I flinched. "Tell me what this is all about. Trumbull said you sneaked out of the building, breaking curfew and leaving your Secret Service detail with no idea where you'd gone. Why would you do something like that? Especially today, when you barely survived what may have been an attempt on your life?"

"It really wasn't that serious, what happened this morn—"

"I'm not asking about what happened this morning. I'm asking about what happened tonight."

"It was poor judgment, sir. I guess I get claustrophobic sometimes, with my detail always hovering around me."

His mouth twisted into a smile. "You want to know what claustrophobia feels like? Try spending nine years in a six-foot-by-eight-foot room."

I looked down at my muddy sneakers. "Of course," I mumbled. "I'm sorry, sir."

"I've been thinking a lot about my time in that room lately." He picked up the pen again and made a single mark in the notebook in front of him. Maybe he'd forgotten to cross a *t*. "I'm setting down my life story. People have asked me for decades to write a book about my experiences, but I never have. I don't believe in dwelling on the past. And with a past like mine, I certainly don't enjoy it. But a month ago, when the Statue of Liberty became a blazing ruin, I finally hauled out this antiquated paper and pen and got started. I can see we've entered a new age of terrorism. I owe it to my country to share what I learned living in that cell—and getting myself out."

My eyes darted back to the thighbone hanging above the mantel.

"I keep it to remind me of the man who saved my life," he said. "And to remind me of what I had to do to survive."

Stroud walked over to the fireplace, his left hip hitching slightly. He lifted the bone from the wall. Without thinking about it, I took a step back. He may have had a mangled body, but it still exuded a wiry strength.

"The first time he mentioned his thighbone," Stroud said, "he meant it as a joke. There we were, your grandfather Fisher and I, in a tiny, empty room. No tools. No weapons. Nothing to help us escape. 'There's always my thighbone,' he said. A couple of years earlier, during our first tour, an IED had partially blown off his leg, and the doctors had replaced his shattered femur with this." He hefted the bone. "Care to hold it?"

"No, thank you, sir."

His eyes drifted to the fire. "Years passed. Our captors beat and tortured us almost every day. George's health began to fail. Eventually, he didn't think he'd survive another beating. 'But if you kill me here in the cell,' he said, 'you can take out my thighbone and use it to get out of this place.'"

My nape tingled again. I'd already heard most of these details before, but getting the story from Stroud's own mouth chilled me anyway. He'd never spoken about it with me before. He stared into the fireplace, the flickering light painting his craggy face a gruesome orange and giving his tale the feel of a campfire ghost story.

"At first I refused to consider it. George Fisher was my best friend on earth. How could I do something like that to him? But then one evening the guards brought him back to the cell so ravaged he could barely speak. He managed to get out only three words: 'Please do it.' So I gathered up my courage, told him I'd always watch over his wife and young son back in the States, and broke the man's neck. Then I clawed into his leg with my bare fingers. It took me all night to dig out this bone."

I gulped while images of the Spam casserole Nico had been eating earlier that day flashed through my mind.

"When the guards entered the cell the next day to remove George's body, I bashed in their skulls and made my escape."

He held the bone closer to the light and showed me the brownish-red smears that still covered it. My knees felt unsteady: blood happened to be yet another of my phobias.

"Back in the States, journalists asked me over and over, 'What kept you going all that time?' I told them George Fisher used to remind me of something our football coach here at Inverness would say to us: 'Adversity destroys some people and makes others stronger. Which is it going to be?' George repeated those words every day—even as his own life ebbed away. And they helped. I imagined all my trials only increasing my strength. I still believe it today: what I experienced was unspeakable, but it made me who I am now."

My grandfather looked at me again. The firelight made his eyes flash without giving them any warmth. I had to fight the urge to back farther away from him.

"So if you think you have it tough here," he said, "taking classes, eating wholesome food, sleeping in a comfortable bed, accompanied wherever you go by people whose only job is to keep you safe, think again."

"Yes, sir."

He shook his head. "America—the whole world, I suppose— has become so obsessed with making things easier. We've cre- ated machines that do all our physical labor for us, and much of our thinking, too. Now we're on the verge of letting machines live for us. And then where will we be?" He used the thighbone to jab one of the logs on the fire. It flared as it resettled, sending up a swarm of sparks. "We've forgotten that it's the work, the struggle, the suffering that make us who we are."

He returned the bone to its place. Below it, on the mantel, stood two framed photographs, one of Mom as a girl, her wild red hair wrangled into two braids, and one of a fresh-faced young man with big ears poking out from under the sleek white hat of a US Marine: George Fisher. After regarding the picture of my other grandfather for a second, Stroud went back to his desk and indicated a chair across from him. I sat.

"Your father and I had a meeting about you before he gave his speech yesterday morning. He's disappointed in your performance here. So am I."

"My grades are okay."

"Lee, as your headmaster and as your grandfather, I expect more from you than mediocre grades. I expect you to excel. And I expect you to stay safe and be responsible. You're blood, and blood means something to me. Your mother and I didn't often see eye to eye, but she was blood, and I loved her." He glanced at the picture of her on the mantel. "She had fire, your mother."

"Yes, she did, sir."

"I always respected her for that." His eyes returned to me. His lips pursed, like he'd smelled something rotten. "And you. You're blood, too. As hard as it is for me to believe sometimes. You inherited neither your mother's fire nor your father's self-discipline."

"People say I got his ears."

He didn't find that funny. "You're also an important boy, Lee."

He paused, as if waiting for me to respond, but I never knew what to say when people made pronouncements like that. Did the fact that my father happened to be president *really* make me important? It wasn't like I'd done anything myself.

"As the First Son, you're a symbol to this country," Stroud said, answering my unspoken question. "And even though you lack talent and ambition, your name and advantages may yet afford you the chance to do some meaningful work of your own. I can't have you taking chances with your life like you did tonight. Especially after what happened earlier today."

"I already told you, sir, that was just a malfunction."

"No one else who was there seems to think so. Trumbull, Dr. Singh, the other students—they were all very alarmed. I was alarmed too when I watched the video the pucks recorded. Dr. Singh is still studying the local network log to see what it can tell us. Until we know more, we all need to take what happened seriously. Last month's assault on the Statue of Liberty showed what damage a remote electronic attack can do. I want to make sure nothing like that happens here. Trumbull and his team are very capable, and they already have this situation well in hand, but I'd like to make a contribution."

Stroud placed a small wooden box on the table between us and opened the lid. Inside rested what looked like a silver wristwatch—the old-fashioned kind, with a round face and hands to tell the time.

"I received this device from an alumnus who's become one of the most powerful arms manufacturers in the world. It's a prototype. Only a few of them exist."

"What does it do?"

"It's a kind of bomb. When you press these two buttons on the side and hold them for three seconds, the watch releases a powerful pulse of electromagnetic radiation. The pulse doesn't harm human beings, but it destroys anything electronic within a thirty-foot radius."

"So it's like what Dr. Singh used on Charlotte."

"Exactly. If Trumbull hadn't been there this morning, a device like this could've saved your life." He lifted the watch from the box and held it out to me. "I'd like you to wear it at all times. It's a weapon of last resort and can be used only once. But if something like what happened today happens again, don't hesitate. Use it."

The watch felt lighter than I'd expected. I didn't question why an important arms manufacturer would give a prototype of a bomb to his old headmaster. Among the many rumors about Stroud that batted around Inverness Prep, one was that he had a whole network of rich and powerful alumni who were every bit as devoted to him as Dad was. Stroud might have appeared to be nothing more than the head of a small New England boarding school, but in reality—at least according to the stories—he was one of the most influential men on the planet.

"And be smart, Lee. No more stunts like you pulled tonight."

"Yes, sir." I strapped the watch to my wrist. It released soft ticks as the second hand made its halting way from Roman numeral to Roman numeral.

Stroud glanced at a clock on his desk. (Even now, he still didn't have a puck. If you wanted to reach him, you had to go through his secretary, Mrs. Case.) "Enough talk," he said. "It's getting late, even for me."

I slid to the edge of my chair. "Thank you, sir."

He brushed my thanks away with a swipe of his hand. "Just don't mention the watch to anyone. Not even Trumbull or your father, all right? We'll keep it between us."

I nodded.

"You probably think your father and Trumbull and I are being hard on you, but we just want to keep you safe. Keep you safe, and help you become a man."

There it was again: that talk about becoming a man. Before I went out, my eyes flicked one last time to the bloodstained femur Stroud had dug out of my other grandfather's dead body. I half wondered if he hoped I'd do something similar one day to prove my manliness.

15

I slept in the next morning, so I didn't see Bex at breakfast, but she bombarded me with messages during my first two classes:

David Chung says he saw you being marched up to Stroud's office at one o'clock in the morning! Is it true?

Did it have something to do with your date?

Are you in trouble?

Are you okay?

What happened last night?

Message me back NOW!

(In the midst of all that, one single message from Nico made my heart expand in my chest: *'Tis a fair morn, sweet lord.*)

I arrived at English and dropped into my usual desk behind Bex's. "What's going on?" she demanded. "Why haven't you answered any of my messages?"

"Because I knew I'd see you right now. Calm down, Bex. How come you're not wearing any makeup?"

She rolled her unshadowed eyes. "New school policy. I'm livid."

I actually thought she looked better this way, without the raccoon mask, but of course I didn't say anything.

"Never mind that," she said. "What happened last night? Did you meet up with Nico?"

"Uh-huh."

"And?"

I gripped the sides of my desk and tried to think of a word that encapsulated our date but wasn't totally corny. I couldn't do it. "Amazing."

"Really." She said it in a weird voice, like she didn't quite believe me.

"Yes. Really."

"What's that on your wrist?"

I pulled back the cuff of my blazer. "I got a new watch. Like it?"

"It's very retro," she replied, her voice still odd.

"In a good way?"

She wrinkled her nose and shook her head.

"What's up with you today, Bex?"

"I heard a rumor you went to Stroud's office last night. I was worried, Lee. Is it true?"

"Yes. But it's no big deal. He wasn't really that mad."

"Why was he mad at all?"

I waved my hand. "Look, I'll tell you later. He's here."

Nico slid into the desk next to mine. My insides instantly felt like the core of one of Bex's Pop-Tarts fresh out of the toaster.

"Hi, Lee," he said, with a tiny lift of the eyebrows that seemed to add, *You didn't freak out last night and vow to ignore me, did you?*

"Hi, Nico."

He nodded, pleased. "I like your new look, Bex."

"This isn't a look," she muttered. "This is just nothing."

"You up for doing something tonight?" he asked, turning back to me. "This time *I* have something to show *you*."

"Sounds like fun."

I could feel Bex watching us like a hawk.

"How about you come to my room at nine thirty? You think you can swing that, with your security and all?"

Yesterday Trumbull had made it sound like my lockdown might end tonight—but that had been before he'd caught me sneaking out. I nodded anyway. "I'll make it work."

I never got a chance to finish telling Bex about the date. We ate lunch with Nico again, and I noticed her giving him funny looks, like she had yesterday, and not saying much. After my last class of the day, she sent me a message: *Can you meet me in the library at five? I need to talk to you. Alone.* All her mysteriousness had started getting on my nerves, but if she had an issue with Nico, I knew she'd change her mind once she'd heard the full story about last night.

At the appointed time I made my way to our nook at the back of the mezzanine. Bex sat hugging her knees to her chest, her booted feet resting on her chair. Her puck was projecting something on the wall next to her, but I couldn't tell what at first. Then I spotted a loose gray cardigan. Above that, a familiar face—pale, with a long, thin nose and dark eyes. Charlotte. The sight of her made my fingers turn cold.

Bex jumped when she noticed me. She waved at her puck, and the image on the wall disappeared. "Sorry, Lee. I didn't hear you come up."

"What were you watching that for?"

"They were just replaying old video on the news."

I narrowed my eyes at her. "You're not still thinking of asking Dr. Singh for an interview again, are you?"

"Look, don't change the subject."

"I didn't realize there *was* a subject."

"Well, there is: you. I want to hear about what happened last night."

I sat down across from her. "Just like I told you. It was amazing."

"What about the part where you went to Stroud's office? Was that amazing too? You still haven't said why he wanted to see you."

I shrugged. "I sort of sneaked out with Nico last night."

"You *what*?" She sat up, her combat boots slamming against the wood floor.

"I had no choice. Trumbull wasn't going to let me leave my room. He had me on lockdown because of what happened with Nevermore."

"And with good reason. You almost died yesterday."

"That's a huge exaggeration. I appreciate the whole over-protective friend bit, but I've already been lectured by Trumbull *and* Stroud on this subject, so you can save your breath."

"Where did you go?"

"The mine."

She released an appalled groan.

"But Stroud and Trumbull don't know that part. They don't even know I was with Nico. We sneaked all the way up to the mine, and it was perfect. We talked, and we lit sparklers, and we threw them into the chasm, and we kissed, Bex. We kissed, and I didn't even freak out afterward. That's great, isn't it?"

"All right, yes, I'm happy for you." She drew her knees back into her chest and picked at a hole in the black leggings she wore under her skirt.

"You know," I said, "I've been looking forward to this all day: reliving my first date with my best friend, going over it moment by moment, hearing your witty, sometimes caustic, but ultimately good-hearted and supportive commentary. So far I'm finding the experience very unsatisfying. What's going on?"

All balled up in her chair like that, with no makeup on, she looked about ten years old. "After what happened yesterday," she murmured, still not looking at me, "and with another Charlotte attack coming, I just can't believe you went to the cavern all alone."

"I was with Nico."

"That's what I mean. All alone with Nico."

"Okay." I stood and leaned my hands on the table. "I've had enough of this. Tell me why you're being so weird about him."

She dropped her forehead on her knees. Her back rose and fell as she took a deep breath. Peeking up at me, she said, "Do you promise not to freak out?"

I sat back down and tried to look less freak-out-prone. "Just tell me."

"I've been thinking, Lee. Doesn't it seem like a strange coincidence that your robot attacked you twelve hours after we used it to spy on Nico?"

"No. What do you mean?"

"Hear me out on this. We crashed Nevermore into his window. He heard the noise. He looked outside."

"Right. But he didn't see her."

"What if he just pretended he didn't? And then we left the robot out there all night long. What if he went outside, reprogrammed it, and put it back for you to find?"

I gripped my chair's armrests, bracing myself. "And why would he do something like that?"

"To scare you. That's what terrorists do, right?"

"Whoa." I glanced at Trumbull, but he was twenty feet

away talking on his puck. I dropped my voice to a whisper anyway. "You're calling Nico a terrorist? Do you hear what you're saying, Bex?"

"I know it sounds crazy."

"You think he's working with Charlotte, is that it?"

"Maybe. There's evidence that she had humans helping her with her other attacks. You said it yourself: What do we really know about this guy? Wasn't that why you had Nevermore go snooping around his window? 'Maybe he's a Chilean spy.' Remember?"

"I was ninety-two percent kidding. I just wanted to establish he wasn't a creep. And I thought we did that."

I closed my eyes and scraped my fingers over my scalp. In my mind, I saw Nico the way he'd looked in the cavern last night, the sparkler in his hand washing his face in a flickering glow and lighting up the threads of gold in his eyes.

Still struggling to keep my voice down, I said, "Why are you doing this to me, Bex? I finally meet somebody I like, and who likes me, and we just had the most incredible time together, and we're supposed to hang out again tonight, and then you have to be Ms. Wannabe Investigative Journalist and spout your insane conspiracy theories and mess it all up."

"Lee, slow down—"

"Because I'm sure it's just so hard to imagine someone like him genuinely wanting to hang out with someone like me. Nico being a terrorist—that's a much more likely scenario."

"Of course I don't—"

I stabbed my index finger at her. "If you'll recall, you were the one who wanted me to ask him out in the first place."

"And I'm so glad you did. Look, I'm not saying he's definitely a terrorist. I'm just saying it's possible. I'm just saying the thought entered my head."

"Oh, well, that makes me feel so much better."

"You have to admit, the timing's suspicious. He just shows up out of nowhere on the very same day your dad announces his amendment and Charlotte announces her next attack—which is supposed to happen *tomorrow*, by the way. As the First Son, you're a possible target. It's not that I don't want you to hang out with Nico again tonight."

"But I should spend the whole time feeling paranoid and not enjoying myself."

"No!" she wailed. "Please, just listen—"

"*You* listen, Bex. What happened with Nevermore yesterday was a freak accident, not a terrorist attack. And Nico had nothing to do with it. If he's on a mission to kill me, he had the perfect chance last night. He could've pushed me into that chasm any time he wanted."

"Yes, that's a good point, but—"

"Stop, Bex. Maybe you just don't want me to have a boyfriend. You're always ragging on me for staying in the closet, but when it comes down to it, maybe you actually prefer me there. Maybe you think if I get a boyfriend, I won't hang out with you anymore." My chair screeched over the wood floor as I pushed back from the table. "And maybe you're right."

I stormed out of the library and all the way back to my room. Before I went in, I turned to Trumbull.

"By the way," I said, still riding a wave of adrenaline, "I'm hanging out with my friend Nico tonight."

"About that—"

"I'm not asking, Trumbull. I'm telling."

"I understand, sir. But it's all right. I just spoke with Dr. Singh. She said she's found no evidence of unusual activity in the local network log. As far as she can tell, what happened yesterday was a freak malfunction, just like you said. I consulted with the head office, and we've decided to move you to partial lockdown until the end of the week, when we hope this whole Charlotte situation will have calmed down a bit."

"Meaning?"

"You'll be free to leave your room this evening. We just ask that you don't go outside. Between the raven, which we still haven't located, and the threatened terrorist activity tomorrow, we feel it would be safer to keep you indoors for now."

"Oh." I straightened my glasses. "Okay. Thanks, Trumbull. Sorry for snapping like that." I turned toward my door.

"You've been spending a lot of time with Nico lately."

My hand froze on the knob. I looked over my shoulder. Trumbull's dark lenses mirrored back to me my pale face. "My dad told me I should help him settle in. Anyway, I'm sure you've already done a background check on him. Am I right?"

He nodded.

"And?"

"He checks out."

Inside, some tiny muscle that had knotted up tight during my fight with Bex relaxed a little. He checked out. Of *course* he checked out. "There you go, then." I went into my room and shut the door behind me.

I threw myself across the bed. My shoes clunked on the floor as I kicked them off one by one. I could see Nico tonight. That should've made me happy. But inside my head, other thoughts kept getting in the way. Like that comment Trumbull had made about Nico just now—I thought for sure I'd heard a note of suspicion in that almost inflectionless growl of his. And then there was Bex. The one person I'd thought I could talk to about Nico. It turned out I didn't have her support either. Dinner would start in half an hour, but I had no desire to see her and no appetite anyway.

No appetite: whenever that happened, I always knew what would come next. I'd watch the dark mood roll in, as unstoppable as bad weather. At those times more than ever, my brain reminded me of a black box, a machine I didn't understand or know how to operate, and I—the part of me that wasn't my brain, which I realized didn't quite make sense—seemed to stand outside of it, struggling with the buttons and switches, trying to regain control.

I rolled onto my back and pulled Gremlin out of my pocket. For a while I let him crawl over me, his fur skimming across my skin. I listened to the soft ticking of my watch and the creaks and groans of the building and, underneath everything else, the low rumble of the waterfall. I'd been doing so well lately too. Last night—I hadn't felt happy like that in a long time. Maybe ever. Definitely not since Mom died.

Even though I knew I shouldn't, even though I ordered my brain not to, I said to my puck, "Show me video of Charlotte." My puck's projector ticked on, and the ceiling above me lit up, showing me the same image Bex's puck had projected a little while ago: Charlotte, wearing the oversize gray cardigan she'd loved. In her hand she held five playing cards. She stared at them, her brow furrowed, her dark eyes focused, as she chewed on her left thumbnail.

The camera zoomed out. Charlotte sat at a table littered with poker chips, bags of Doritos, and half-empty bottles of Diet Coke. In spite of the Picasso print hanging on the wall and the vase of blue flowers standing on a sideboard, the room still had the atmosphere of a laboratory. Maybe because it lacked windows. To Charlotte's right sat Dr. Singh, who looked younger, and not just by seven years, either. More like twenty. Her hair was still black. Her brown skin hadn't taken on its grayish tinge. And of course she didn't have a wheelchair underneath her.

On Charlotte's other side sat my mother. She wore a sweatshirt with the words JUST HAPPY TO BE HERE printed on it. I could still picture her wearing that thing around the house sometimes. Stray strands of her wiry red hair made a fiery nimbus around her head. She studied her cards too, and tapped her chin, but her eyes also flicked up from time to time to watch Charlotte. Dr. Singh had already folded. She sipped her Diet Coke and watched both of them.

"I think you're bluffing." Mom pushed a few more chips into the center of the table.

Charlotte smacked her cards down. "I've got nothing."

Mom's poker face turned into a smile. "I knew it." She spread out her hand: two pair.

"I don't understand how you keep doing that," Charlotte snapped. She pulled Mom's cards closer and scrutinized them, as if to check their authenticity.

Before Charlotte's escape, Bethesda National Laboratory had released several hours of video as part of a publicity campaign—premature, in retrospect—trumpeting their new creation. At the time, just about everybody on earth had watched the footage, probably most of them with their mouths hanging open. Many had insisted the whole thing must be a hoax. You could see why. The only visible difference between Charlotte and the two human women sitting on either side of her was that they had pucks hovering over their heads and she didn't.

Of course, she had her quirks. For example, she found the word "elbow" hilarious. She couldn't stand it when anybody near her laughed at a joke she didn't understand. Conversations with her tended to include abrupt shifts and non sequiturs. Her moods could be as jagged and strange as the Picasso prints that decorated her small apartment. But in a way, her idiosyncrasies were exactly what made her seem so human. Each time her temper flared inexplicably or she burst out laughing for no apparent reason, you could see something happening behind her eyes, even if you didn't understand it.

"Tell me, Ruth," Charlotte persisted. "How do you always know when I'm bluffing?"

Mom glanced at Dr. Singh.

"It's okay." Dr. Singh's voice had only the beginnings of a smoker's rasp then. "You can tell her."

"You bite your nails. That's how I know." Mom fished in one of the Doritos bags for a chip. "And now that I've told you," she added with a cheerful sigh, "you'll probably stop doing it, and I'll never win again."

Charlotte frowned. She sat back in her chair and regarded her fingers.

Dr. Singh set down her Diet Coke. "What is it, Charlotte? What are you thinking about?"

"My father used to hate it when I bit my nails."

To help an eleven-month-old machine more effectively approximate a human in her early twenties, Dr. Singh had supplied her with a lifetime of human memories—in the form of the complete puck archive of a twenty-three-year-old female donor. Twenty-three years of photos, messages, and, most important of all, nearly continuous video coverage. But Dr. Singh had also told Charlotte from the start that those memories didn't really belong to her. She believed her creation deserved to understand the truth about herself. That decision had resulted in some complications.

Still studying her fingers, Charlotte said, "I think I chew my nails so I can watch them grow back. It makes me feel like I actually exist. My nails grow, my hair grows, my skin sloughs off. They're the only real parts of me. Everything on the inside is fake."

"That's not true, Charlotte," Mom said, her voice low and gentle, but also firm. "You're real. Just different." She'd used that same tone with me when I'd demanded she never kiss me good-bye again.

"I'm not human, though." Charlotte tapped the five cards laid out on the table in front of her. "All I can do is bluff." She lunged to her feet and swept her arm across the table, knocking over a soda bottle and sending Doritos and cards and poker chips clattering to the floor.

"Charlotte!" Dr. Singh rose too.

"I'm tired of this game," Charlotte said. "Let's do something else."

"Remember we talked about your temper? Just calm down."

At the time, people had found it strange that Dr. Waring would release video showing Charlotte at such a dark moment, but he'd seemed to regard her existential angst the same way he'd regarded the suicide of her predecessor: as a sign of the project's success.

Charlotte sank back into her chair. On the table in front of her, the Diet Coke bottle dribbled out the last of its contents. "I miss him, Geeta," she said in a small voice.

"He's not your father," Dr. Singh said. "You know that."

"Of course I know that. But I can still miss him, can't I?" She hugged herself, running her fingers over the gray wool of her loose, ratty cardigan. "That's why I like to wear this old sweater. It looks like one he used to wear. I pretend it was his."

At around this point in the video, I'd sometimes feel my chest tighten. *What about my mother?* I'd want to yell at the projection. *She* did *exist, and you took her away from me.* But then I'd remember it didn't make any sense to blame Charlotte. If Mom had died in a shooting, would I get mad at the gun? Because at the end of the day, I did agree with Dad: Charlotte was just a machine. An extremely sophisticated robot that later became some extremely sophisticated malware polluting the Supernet. In fact, sometimes I thought I believed it even more than Dad did. As much as he insisted she wasn't a person, he sure hated her like one. I didn't have such a convenient focus for my anger. I understood the real reason for Mom's death was that there wasn't a reason at all. It was just something that had happened. It was just how this ugly, unfair universe worked.

16

I woke to the sound of my puck chiming. I blinked, straightened my glasses, and squinted at the words my puck was projecting on the ceiling.

I missed you at dinner. Are you still coming tonight? You'd better be.

And just like that, the black cloud pressing down on me lifted. I wished I'd known it sooner: apparently the cure for one of my dark moods was a sweet message from a boy. I checked the time. Nine fifteen. I jumped out of bed and messaged, *Be there soon!* as I tore off my school uniform. Gremlin, catching some of my energy, scurried back and forth along the top of my headboard, his body going up and down and up and down like a sine wave.

Good, Nico messaged back. *And bring your Swarmbots and those lock-picking tools of yours.*

I threw on my other uniform—jeans, black T-shirt, black hoodie—and stuffed Gremlin, my pouch of tools, and my jar of

Swarmbots into my pockets. I unstrapped my retro-but-not-in-a-cool-way watch and dropped it into my nightstand drawer. I figured I could survive the night without it, and anyway, the thing creeped me out a little.

When I opened my door, I found Ray standing guard alone this time. "How's it going, buddy?"

"I'm heading over to Nico's room. Trumbull told you about that, right?"

"Don't worry, you're cool."

I headed down the hall, my nervous energy making my fingers twitch, and knocked on Nico's door. When he opened it a few seconds later, he wore his usual bright grin. "Thanks for coming over. I need all the help I can get with these lines for the play."

I didn't understand at first, but then he flicked his eyes in Ray's direction. "Oh," I said. "Right. Glad to help." I turned to Ray. "We'll probably need a couple of hours. Don't disturb us, okay?"

He saluted. "Copy that. Have fun."

Nico ushered me in and closed the door. We hadn't had a moment alone together since last night. My heart had started banging so hard I could feel it in my ears. He grabbed me by the neck, gave me a quick kiss, and put a finger over my mouth. "Okay, Lee," he said, his voice raised so Ray could hear him, "are you ready to run some lines with me?"

"Sure," I said, playing along.

"Just give me a second. Sorry about the mess."

He bent over his cluttered desk to fool with what looked like a small speaker. It felt strange standing here for real after having seen this room projected on my wall. The memory of that night already made me wince. How could I have done something so creepy? The potato chip bags and Coke bottles lay just where I remembered them. The drifts of towels and clothes on the floor had grown. He hadn't bothered to clean up for me, but I understood, at least on an intellectual level, that some people didn't have an insane obsession with neatness the way I did. Anyway, I felt pretty sure I could overlook the mess for him.

I noticed the view from his window—the one thing I hadn't seen two nights ago. Through the branches of the tree outside, the mountain's blue crags shone in the moonlight.

"Not bad, huh?" Nico said.

"It beats looking out on a stone wall."

He laughed. "Okay, I'm reading from Ariel's first scene. Stop me if I make a mistake."

Nico grabbed his puck and whispered a command. From the speaker on his desk came the sound of his voice. "'All hail, great master, grave sir, hail! I come to answer thy best pleasure.'" He kissed me again and mouthed the words along with the recording: "'Be't to fly, to swim, to dive into the fire, to ride on the curl'd clouds.'"

"Now for step two," he breathed into my ear. On his way to

the window, he shrugged on a backpack and stepped into his flip-flops. He slid the window open and waved me over.

I didn't like where this was going. I waded through the twisted-up jeans and damp towels to stand next to him.

"Here's the plan," he whispered underneath the Shakespeare. He lifted the jar of Swarmbots from my hoodie pocket, unscrewed the lid, and shook out the bottle just outside the window. "We'll crawl along this branch to the trunk." He pointed at the limb where Nevermore had perched. "Then we'll climb across to that branch there, which'll take us to the window of the boys' washroom. Presto: we'll be free."

I could feel it starting: my palms growing clammy, my breath coming fast and shallow. Standing next to Nico near the edge of a cliff was one thing. This was another. "Or else we could stay here," I said, like I was just tossing out options. "That could be fun, right? I could help you with your lines for real."

He'd already sat down on the sill and swung one leg over. "But I have something really cool to show you. It'll be worth it, I promise."

Just do what he says, I ordered myself. *Don't screw this up.* But tendrils of sweat had begun slithering down my back. My knees had turned to rubber. I grabbed the side of the window.

"You all right?" Nico said.

I adjusted my glasses and cleared my throat. "Listen, Nico. There's something you should know. The truth is, I'm not very good with heights."

He looked from me to the tree outside, his forehead furrowed. "What about yesterday? Didn't you use Rapunzel to climb down from your room?"

"Yeah. I sort of white-knuckled it. You should've seen me. I was a mess."

"And when we were in the cavern, when I pulled you up to the edge of the chasm, you must've been—"

"About to puke over the side. Yeah."

He scratched the back of his head. "Huh. And the whole time you didn't say a thing."

"Of course I didn't. It was our first date. You think I wanted you to find out what a freak I am right away?"

"Okay, freak." He swung his leg back into the room. "We'll stay here, then."

I caught his hands. "Maybe I can still try, though."

"You don't have to, Lee. As long as I'm with you, I couldn't care less what we do."

I shook my head. "I think I should do this."

He studied my face for a second. Then he smiled. "I think you should too." While his disembodied voice kept reciting lines from the speaker on his desk, he sat on the sill again and shimmied onto the leafless black branch. It groaned but sank only a few inches. "See?" he said. "Not too hard. Just follow me and do what I do."

I put my legs out the window and took a slow breath. No Rapunzel this time. No climbing harness. If I fell, nothing would catch me. *But you have Nico*, I told myself. *Focus on him.*

The branch had grown right up to the wall, which made it easy to climb onto. Our pucks had switched on their lights to help us see in the darkness.

"That's it," Nico whispered. "You can do it."

A breeze kicked up. The branch bobbed underneath me. My fingers dug into the bark, and my eyes jumped from the branch to the ground below, which seemed to zoom away from me at a hundred miles an hour. All around, the tree's other branches wagged like scolding fingers. I groaned.

"It's okay," Nico said. "Nothing to worry about. Just a little wind."

Up ahead, he climbed onto the second branch, a little higher than the first but just as wide, and waited for me. He hadn't even lost one of his flip-flops yet.

"Having fun?"

"A blast," I muttered.

"This is the homestretch. Just keep your eyes on my ass and don't look down."

"When you put it like that . . ."

I copied his movements as I clambered from one branch to the other. The boys' washroom window glowed in front of us. We'd almost made it.

A drop splashed on the branch next to my hand. Then a few more fell. That was one thing you could always count on at Inverness Prep: whenever you thought things might start getting better, it would rain.

"Don't worry, Lee. We're just about there."

He'd already grabbed the sill. Meanwhile, the rain had picked up, splashing my glasses and making the bark slick and slimy under my hands. I had to go even more slowly now.

"You're doing great." Nico turned back to check on me. The rain had pulled his curls down over his forehead, where they hung in thick, heavy clumps. "I'm going to slide through the window, and then I'll help you in after me."

He disappeared inside while I crawled the rest of the way to the window, rain streaming over my lenses and dripping from my nose. I put one hand on the sill, and he covered it with his own. He'd landed in one of the washroom shower stalls. I hauled myself through the window headfirst, while he grabbed me under the armpits to help. I toppled into his arms, his back slammed against the shower partition, and my mouth landed on his in a clumsy kiss.

"Uh, hello?" someone outside the shower stall said. "Is somebody in there?"

We stared at the stall door. Once upon a time—in other words, about two days ago—I would've gone out of my head if something like this had happened. Nico watched me, his arms still wrapped around me tight, like he thought I might try to hurl myself back out the window again. And it was true: Gutless Lee wanted to do exactly that.

But right now Kamikaze Lee was in the driver's seat. And he didn't give a crap.

I burst out laughing almost as loud as Nico usually did. Grabbing his arm, I banged open the door. We ran out, sopping wet. One of the FUUWLs stood next to the sink with a toothbrush in his hand and white foam spilling from his mouth.

"Sorry," I said. "Didn't mean to disturb you. We just really like to shower together."

"But only with our clothes on," Nico added. "I mean, we're not perverts or anything."

The FUUWL just stared while we made a quick exit through the washroom door. Outside, we just about fell on the floor we laughed so hard. But then Nico put a hand over my mouth and pointed: Ray was just around the corner. He motioned for me to follow him. We tore down the hall in the opposite direction and ducked through a door that led to an infrequently used side staircase. Curfew hadn't started yet, but if anyone spotted me wandering around the school sans armed escort, it might raise suspicions.

"I heard a rumor about you today," Nico whispered as we padded down the stairs.

"Another one?"

"Somebody saw you heading up to Headmaster Stroud's office last night. Did you get caught? Why didn't you tell me?"

I shrugged. "It was no big deal. I just got a lecture for going out after curfew. Don't worry, though. He didn't know you were with me or anything."

"What did he say?"

"The usual stuff about how I'm a symbol to this country, so he expects me to follow the rules and get perfect grades, just like the FUUWLs."

"The what?"

"That's what Bex and I call those kids who made you do the Stand on Monday. The Future Unscrupulous Ultrapowerful World Leaders. And then Stroud said I don't know how good I've got it here, and I should be grateful for this hellish school, because suffering makes us stronger."

"He seriously said that?"

"Pretty much. That's Inverness Prep for you." I stopped halfway down a flight. "You know that rumble the waterfall makes?" I held up my finger. The low, deep roar of the river filled the silence. "Sometimes I close my eyes and listen to that rumble and imagine this place is a factory grinding us all into the same shape and then spitting us out. Making us into mindless drones like the FUUWLs. We're not being taught to think. We're being programmed."

Nico raised his eyebrow.

"You find that funny?"

"No. I find you funny." He pecked me on the cheek and kept going.

We reached the first floor. "Where are we headed?" I asked.

"You'll see."

We crossed the empty front hall. Outside, the rain drummed

on the stone terrace. The clouds had swallowed up the moon. Nico pushed open the auditorium doors.

"Looks like your lock-picking skills won't be required tonight after all."

We followed the dim floor-level lights down the aisle. Up ahead, the banner and podium had disappeared, replaced by a plain black velvet curtain hanging near the front of the stage. Nico marched up the steps as if he'd gone to school here for years, not days. He pulled me into the wings and then behind the curtain. I couldn't see a thing. Something crunched under my sneakers. He took me by the arms and positioned me just so.

"Stay there. Don't move."

He disappeared.

"Nico?"

No answer. My fingers squirmed. It felt a little like when we'd stood in the cavern last night after we'd turned off the lights. Except this time I was alone.

"Where are you, Nico?"

Now he was starting to scare me. Bex's words echoed in my head. *That's what terrorists do, right?*

A sharp *clack* made me jump. Light flooded down from the flies.

17

⬦⬦⬦⬦

In front of me lay what looked like a tropical island. Near the back of the stage, rolling, grassy hills swept toward a backdrop of blue sky. Fake palm trees shot up here and there, and a stately stone gazebo stood at the top of the highest rise. A sandy beach covered the stage's front portion and on one side disappeared into the ocean, which, if you looked close, turned out to be crinkled blue cellophane. The drama society had done a good job. Even the lights above felt like real sun. As long as you faced away from the black curtain, you might almost believe you'd been transported hundreds of miles away from dark, gloomy Inverness Prep.

Nico drew up next to me. "What do you think?"

"I like it. This is the set for *The Tempest*?"

"Uh-huh." He pulled off his bright yellow windbreaker, kicked his flip-flops to the side, and bent over to roll up his jeans. "It takes place on a remote island in the tropics." He glanced at me. "What are you waiting for? Aren't you going to take your shoes off?" While I unlaced my sneakers, he dipped his toe into the blue cellophane. "Mmm. Perfect." From his backpack he pulled an oversize pink-and-lime-green-striped beach towel. He spread it out on the sand. "This place reminds me of home, actually. Lots of beaches in Chile."

"That's right," I said. "Doesn't Chile have almost four thousand miles of coastline?"

"Something like that."

I'd done my research. I also now knew Chile was in South America.

Next Nico took out a pair of sunglasses, which he put on, and a lopsided straw hat, which he smacked on top of my head. He took a step back to check me out and nodded his approval. "Almost ready. Just one more thing." He grabbed his puck, whispered into it, and tossed it back into the air. From it came the sound of lazily crashing waves. He toppled backward onto the towel, stretching out his arms and legs to full length. "This is the life." He peeked at me from under his sunglasses. "Care to join me?"

I paused next to a palm tree and knocked on its papier-mâché trunk. "You're really into this acting stuff, huh?"

"Yeah. I signed up for my first drama class because I thought it would be an easy A. I discovered I loved it."

"I'll bet it's cool getting to be all kinds of different people."

He rolled onto his side and propped himself up on one elbow. "Actually, that's not quite it, at least for me. The characters I play when I act, they might seem really different from me at first, but the more I read the lines and play the parts, the more I can relate to what they're feeling. So all those different characters just end up feeling like different aspects of me. For example, the last time I was in *The Tempest*, I played Caliban. He's this savage, deformed half-demon who spends the whole play plotting against the main character, Prospero, the ruler of the island. There wasn't much to relate to there. But when I read the lines, I realized he was just angry because Prospero had enslaved him. That made a lot of the terrible stuff he did in the play more understandable. It even got me wondering if I would've done some of the same things in his situation. My drama teacher, the lady I told you about, she used to say, 'Reading Shakespeare helps us become more human.'"

"I like that."

"Shakespeare was always her favorite. He's mine, too." He grinned at me. "You probably think I'm such a nerd."

"You're worried that *I* think *you're* a nerd? I'm the one who's obsessed with building robots, remember?"

His laugh boomed across the stage.

"What about the character you're playing now?" I asked. "What's his story?"

"Ariel? He's a slave too. But he doesn't fight back. He plays by the rules. Not nearly as much fun." Nico patted the towel next to him. "Take a load off, Lee. Get some sun."

"I don't know. I forgot to put on my sunscreen. With this pasty skin of mine, I'll burn in two seconds."

"I can see you're not going to make this easy for me."

He grabbed my wrist and kicked my feet out from under me. I landed on my back in the loose sand, laughing. The straw hat tumbled off. He tugged me into the crook of his arm. I pulled off my glasses and settled my cheek on his warm chest. Together we gazed down the fake beach at the cellophane ocean while the spotlight sun shone down on us. Usually I hated being on a stage, in the spotlight—like at public functions where I had to go out and smile and wave with Dad after one of his speeches— but like this, with Nico next to me, and the curtain closed, and no audience or cameras in sight, I didn't mind so much.

"So was I right?" Nico squeezed my shoulder. "Was this worth it?"

"Definitely."

"You were really brave back there, climbing across that tree. Last night too. I still can't believe you forced yourself to rappel all the way down from your window. That's pretty badass."

"I just did it because I wanted to see you."

"Well, I'm honored. But you know you could've told me, Lee. Having a fear of heights is seriously no big deal."

I started to say something and then stopped. I pressed my ear to his chest, feeling his heat, listening to the thump of his heart, staring close-up at the weave of his turquoise T-shirt. My throat felt tight, like my necktie was choking me again, except right now I wasn't wearing a necktie. "I'm not really scared of heights."

He lifted his head off the towel to peer at me. "What do you mean? You were faking?"

"No, I don't mean it that way." I couldn't look at him as I talked. Instead, I kept my eyes on the black velvet curtain. "I get scared when I'm around heights, but it's not exactly that I'm scared *of* heights. It's more that I'm scared of myself. Does that make any sense?"

"I'm not sure."

My stomach had wadded itself into a tight ball. I cleared my throat and tried one more time. "Have you read any of the stories about me on the Supernet?"

"Not really. I don't keep up with the news much. I mean, before I came here, I knew President Fisher had a son who went to Inverness Prep, but I don't think I'd ever read anything about you specifically. And then since I met you, I guess I've wanted to get to know you the old-fashioned way."

"So you haven't heard about what happened on the bridge?"

"What bridge?"

Inside my head, Gutless Lee was screaming at me to stop before I ruined everything. Before Nico found out what a head case I really was.

Shut the hell up, Kamikaze Lee said.

"Two years ago," I told Nico, "I jumped off a bridge. I tried to kill myself."

I wished I could check his reaction without actually having to turn in his direction. I felt him shift around as he pulled off his sunglasses and stuffed his backpack under his head so he could see the top of my head. He ran his hand over my short hair, and my stomach relaxed a little.

"Tell me," he said.

I shrugged. "I guess I'd been messed up ever since my mom died. And then there was the whole gay thing: by the time I was twelve or so, I'd figured out I liked guys. I knew my mom would've been okay with it. She always used to tell me she'd love me no matter what. But my dad had gotten the Human Values Movement going by then, and that right there gave me a pretty good idea how he'd react. Thanks to him, the whole country was turning against the exact kind of person I was growing up to be."

"What a horrible feeling," Nico murmured.

"That was when I started noticing high places. Every time I was in a skyscraper or on a bridge, I'd look over the edge and picture myself jumping off. I'd imagine how free I'd feel falling through the air like that. And then, afterward, everything would be over." I squeezed my eyes shut and pressed my face against his chest. "I'm sorry. I'm doing it again."

"What?"

"Being depressing. I've never told anyone this."

"Not even Bex?"

"Nope." I hadn't really thought about it before: in spite of her habitual nosiness, she'd never once pressed me to talk about the very thing everyone else in school was probably dying to know. *That* scoop she'd denied herself. A stab of shame went through me for the horrible things I'd said to her earlier today.

Nico continued stroking my hair at that same steady pace. "Keep going."

I swallowed. The constriction in my throat had loosened a little. The words were coming more easily now. "So one night, a little more than two years ago, I decided to do it for real. School started in three weeks. It was going to be my first year at Inverness Prep. The presidential election was just a few months away. I gave my Secret Service detail the slip for the first time that night—went to a movie by myself, sneaked out through a side exit, walked the mile or so to the Arlington Memorial Bridge. It's pretty high up. I'd found myself staring down from there before. But this time I did more than stare. I waited until all the foot traffic had passed, and then I climbed onto the stone railing and swung my legs over the side."

Staring at the black curtain, I could still picture it: the river far below, the city lights glittering on the water like stars, so jumping would feel like launching myself into outer space.

"My plan was to make it look like an accident," I said. "I hadn't left a note. I'd sit there on the railing and lean out over the river, pretending I was trying to get a better look at the water. Then I'd slip. That way, my dad wouldn't have to deal with the scandal of a son who'd killed himself. I'd even convinced myself my death would give him a sympathy boost and help him win the presidency. My heart must've been pounding, because Gremlin started purring in my pocket. I pulled him out of my hoodie and set him on the railing and told him good-bye. I remember he kept trying to crawl back up my arm and I kept putting him back on the railing. It seemed wrong to take him with me for some reason. Finally I got him to stay. And then, without even really deciding to, I slid off the railing and fell."

Nico's hand paused. "What happened?"

"Well, I didn't die. I never got to experience that feeling of freedom I'd imagined, because a half second after I jumped, my body jerked, and I wasn't falling anymore. My hoodie had caught on a bolt sticking out from the side of the bridge. Needless to say, I felt pretty stupid. And what made it even worse was the tourist boat passing under the bridge at that very moment, with a crowd of tourists on the deck looking up and pointing and taking pictures. I was only a few blocks away from the Capitol and the White House, so I knew the area must be swarming with police and military too. I figured I had only a few seconds before a SWAT team swooped down on me.

"I started squirming and flailing, trying to climb back onto the bridge, but I couldn't find anything to grab on to. I tugged at my zipper, but it was jammed, so I couldn't even go through with killing myself—which I didn't really want to do anymore, because by then the impulse had sort of passed. In the meantime, big crowds had gathered on both sides of the river, and a swarm of pucks and cameras was hovering around me. I probably only hung there a few minutes, but it felt like a year. Then a bunch of police showed up with sirens blaring and rescued me. They asked me what the hell happened. I mumbled my lie about wanting to get a better look at the water and accidentally falling. I could tell they didn't believe me—which made me realize how dumb my plan had been in the first place—but they didn't challenge me either. I gave the same explanation to Trumbull when he showed up, and then to my dad when I got home, and I got the same reaction from them."

Another image seemed to superimpose itself on the black curtain in front of me: Dad. The horizontal line of his mouth. The vertical line between his eyebrows.

"The next morning the story was all over the Supernet. The more upstanding news sites stuck to the official version—that I'd fallen accidentally, just like I'd claimed—but lots of the trashier ones said I'd tried to kill myself. I'd had a reputation for being quiet and gloomy ever since my mom's death, and the suicide theory fit right in with that. The gossip sites started calling me Leap Fisher. Saying I had mental problems. Totally bashing me. Just take a look. You'll see."

"But why would they bash you for trying to kill yourself?"

"Why do you think? Human Values. Remember I told you they're big believers in free will, and the idea that we can choose exactly what kind of people we become, and that's why they're against being gay? It turns out they feel the same way about going psycho and jumping off a bridge."

"That's crazy!"

The outrage in Nico's voice made me want to kiss him even more than usual. He hauled himself onto his elbows. I sat up too.

"What about your dad?" he asked. "What did he say during all this? He must've suspected what really happened on that bridge, the same way everyone else did."

"Sure, but like I told you, he hates talking about that kind of thing. About a week after my big jump, he sat me down and told me he knew times had been hard since losing Mom, and even more so now, with the presidential campaign under way, and he just wanted to know if I needed help of any kind. That was how he put it. Without ever once mentioning the bridge. The whole conversation was excruciating. I'm not even sure what kind of help he meant, since I know he doesn't believe in therapy, and anyway, he would've been terrified that news of me seeing a shrink would get back to the press. I said no, I was fine. He looked so relieved when I said that. He told me things would get better once I started at Inverness. The structure and discipline would help. That's his answer for everything: structure and discipline.

"So I arrived at Inverness Prep, and guess what happened my very first day."

"The Freshman Stand."

"The upperclassmen forced me onto the wall and wouldn't let me down. They chanted that nickname, Leap, over and over. By then I felt completely freaked by what I'd almost done three weeks earlier. I imagined there was a bug in my programming—something inside my brain, but out of my control—that could make me act not like me. Standing on that wall, I broke out in a cold sweat. I couldn't breathe. My whole body shook. Like I said, it wasn't that I was scared of the drop exactly. I was scared of what I might do. In a way, the Freshman Stand rattled me even more than jumping off the bridge.

"Ever since then, I have that same reaction when I'm in a high place. I panic. And I still hear those voices in my head: *Leap. Leap. Leap.*"

The thought of the voices chilled me even now. I felt an urge to press myself against Nico's chest again and soak in his warmth.

"But there's a happy ending to the story," I said, "for my dad at least."

"What's that?"

"His numbers slipped after my jump, but then there was that attack on the New York Subway, and everybody got scared about Charlotte again, so my dad still clinched the election."

"You really think that's all he cared about? The election?"

"Doesn't it seem like that to you? Look at what he did when my mom got killed—rode her death all the way to the White House. Now he's trying to create a world where robots don't exist and all women are housewives, even though that's exactly what she would've hated."

"He's trying to create a world where she'd still be alive, Lee. He's just dealing with her death in a different way than you are.

You love machines because she loved them. He hates machines because a machine killed her. That doesn't mean he misses her any less than you do. And who knows, maybe he really did think coming here would help you feel better."

"Stop trying to understand him like he's a character in one of your plays," I grumbled.

Nico lay back down, pulling me with him. He started stroking my hair again.

My eyes went back to the curtain. It was a deep, deep black, like the chasm we'd stood next to yesterday. "I looked it up on the Supernet," I said, "and I'm pretty sure I'm depressed. I have most of the symptoms. I think I have been for years." I stared at the curtain and waited for him to tell me he really liked me as a friend, but he had a strict policy against dating depressed people. When he didn't say anything, I let out a lame laugh. "Do I have you completely terrified yet?"

"Not even close."

"You should be. Nico, I'm the son of a homophobic president, a closet case, *and* depressed."

He kissed the top of my head. "Actually, I believe the term you're looking for is 'melancholy.'"

18

I could've stayed there with Nico for hours, just the two of us on our own secret tropical island, but I knew the longer we stayed, the more we risked Ray catching on to Nico's trick. After a few more minutes we shook out Nico's towel, switched off the sun, and made our way back into the gloom of Inverness Prep.

When we got to the third-floor corridor, I peeked around the corner to check on Ray. He stood right where we'd last seen him, outside Nico's door. It looked like he'd fallen asleep standing up—something I'd seen him do a couple of times before. We returned to the boys' washroom—deserted this time—and peered out through the shower stall window. Outside, the downpour continued.

"We'll be soaked by the time we get back to your room," I said. "What's Ray going to say when he sees me?"

"I have towels we can use to dry off. You can borrow some of my clothes."

I liked the idea of wearing Nico's clothes. I imagined they'd carry some of his warmth with them.

"On the other hand," Nico said, "climbing back won't be easy. Are you sure you're up for this? We can try to think of something else, Lee."

I shook my head. "No way. Climbing over here—it was scary, but it felt good, too. Like I'd really done something, you know?" I slid open the window. "Let's go."

We couldn't use our pucks to light our way this time—they couldn't fly reliably in rain this heavy—so we stuffed them into our pockets. We could still see by the school's exterior lights, although not as well. Nico crawled onto the branch. I scrabbled after him. My glasses filmed over with rain right away. I yanked them off and stowed them in my hoodie. Without them, everything farther than a few feet away became a blur, but at least I could make out the branch in front of me well enough. A gust of wind bustled through the tree. The limb underneath me shifted and tossed like a boat on rough water. My stomach dropped out of my body. Why had I insisted on doing this again?

"You okay?" Nico yelled.

I nodded. We made our way toward the trunk. The rain hissed down through the branches even harder now. I forced myself to keep my eyes on the tree limb in front of me and copy Nico's movements, like I had before. That helped.

Then something appeared in my peripheral vision: a

black shape, moving fast, straight at me. Along with that, a rushing sound, like the rain but louder. The thing rammed into my shoulder. I lost my balance and toppled forward, my chest and chin smashing against the rough, wet bark, my teeth clacking together. I flung my arms around the branch so I didn't slide off.

"You all right? What was that?"

Whatever it was had vanished. A falling tree branch? A bat? Or else . . . I didn't even want to think it.

"I don't know," I shouted. I pushed myself up again. "But I'm okay."

"We're almost to the trunk. Let's keep moving."

It came at me again, from the other direction. Black, silky wings. Beady, glinting eyes. Nevermore. An image flashed through my mind: the watch Stroud had given me, sitting in my nightstand drawer. But I wouldn't have had time to use it anyway, because the next instant the raven cannoned into me. My fingers fumbled for something to hold on to. The slimy bark crumbled underneath them. I pitched to one side and fell.

"Lee!" Nico roared.

Another branch a few feet below caught me, slamming me in the belly and knocking the air out of my lungs. My body curled around it, but the thin branch couldn't support my weight. It snapped with a loud crack and collapsed. It didn't detach from the tree, though. I managed to hold on with both hands, feet kicking, fingers already slipping.

"Hang on, Lee!"

Nevermore had disappeared into the blackness again, but the sound of her wings pounded through the pulse of the rain. I tried to claw my way up the branch, but I only ended up slipping farther down. My fingers burned. My arms ached.

"I'm coming!"

A blurry shape appeared above me, straining to reach me with one blurry hand.

Nevermore got to me first. This time she stayed on me, her talons digging into my chest, piercing my skin. I shook my head from side to side—the best I could do since I couldn't knock her away with my hands—but she didn't budge.

"I've almost got you!" Nico shouted.

Nevermore's sharp beak drove into my shoulder. Pain knifed through my body. The branch slid through my fingers.

But I didn't fall. Something else barreled into me, something warm and strong. Nevermore disappeared. My face buried itself in wet, curly hair that smelled like rain and coconuts. Holding me tight with one arm, Nico bounced back and forth between the stone wall of the school and the trunk of the bare, black tree until he landed with a jolt on the grass. It all happened too fast for my brain to keep up.

"How did you—?"

Without waiting for me to finish, he tipped me against the tree and whirled away, his hair spraying raindrops. Nevermore was coming back: I still couldn't see her without my glasses, but I could hear the relentless pounding of her wings. Nico launched himself into the air. He must've jumped at least ten feet. When his flip-flops smacked the ground again, he had the raven in his hands. For a second he crouched like a wolf over its dinner. Then he spun around and smashed the robot against the wall three times. Her outspread wings went limp. He dropped her to the ground. She released a few pops and crackles. Her wet feathers twitched.

All the strength drained from my legs. I sagged to the ground, my back still propped against the trunk. "How did you do that?" I finished, my voice shrunk to a whisper.

"I don't know," he panted. "Adrenaline, I guess."

"You jumped ten feet in the air, Nico."

"No, I didn't."

"I saw."

"You don't have your glasses on. Maybe you saw wrong."

Maybe he was right. Maybe all the excitement had left me confused. My brain felt sluggish, like an overloaded computer. Nico made some other excuse, but I stopped listening, because at that point I realized something else wasn't right. My heart hadn't stopped pounding yet, but I couldn't feel the familiar purr that should've been coming from my hoodie pocket. I reached inside, and my fingers closed around Gremlin's body. It felt heavier than usual. I grabbed my glasses from my hoodie's other pocket. Those had somehow survived the fall. I wiped them on my hoodie sleeve and put them on. The downpour had slackened by then, so the lenses didn't immediately film over. In my palm, Gremlin lay on his back, his damp orange fur clinging to him, his head lolling to one side, his torso crushed.

"It's okay, Lee. We can fix him." Nico squatted next to me and reached for Gremlin. A bright red gash sliced across his right palm.

"Nico, you hurt your—"

I stopped. Inside the cut, something glinted in the low light.

He glanced down and then started to snatch his hand away, but I'd already grabbed his wrist. Our eyes met. He twisted his hand against my grip. "Please don't, Lee."

But I didn't let go. His eyes held mine a second longer, pleading, and then dropped to the ground. His arm relaxed. I pulled his hand closer.

The gash extended diagonally across Nico's palm, from the base of the index finger all the way to the wrist. Blood oozed from the wound, mixing with the rain that continued to fall.

"Look at that. Right along the life line." He laughed, but it sounded flat and joyless, like no laugh I'd ever heard from him before.

Still holding his wrist with one hand, I put Gremlin back in my pocket and tugged the cut further open. Nico winced but didn't resist. Inside, his hand looked a lot like the innards of Nevermore: a rubbery, translucent material where the muscle of his thumb should've been, attached to a slender bone made of some bronze-colored metal alloy. My hands started to shake.

My body felt empty, hollowed out. I let go of his wrist and slumped against the tree.

"You're not real," I whispered. "You're a robot."

He stuffed his hands into the pockets of his yellow windbreaker, his broad shoulders hunched, his wet hair twisting down his forehead. "I *am* real. And I'm a robot."

"A 2B?"

He nodded.

I heaved myself back to my feet, still clutching the trunk for balance. My hands hadn't stopped trembling. My breathing had grown shaky too. It was like the rest of my body already understood something my brain hadn't finished computing yet.

"I wasn't sent here to do you harm."

I just shook my head. No words would come.

"Let me explain, Lee."

He took a step toward me, reaching out again with his injured hand, and an image flared in my head: Charlotte grabbing Mom and snapping her neck. "Don't touch me," I snarled. I lunged away from him and took off running across the muddy lawn, throwing glances over my shoulder, half expecting him to chase me down. But he just stood there watching me go.

My feet pounded down the steps to the canal. Hands still shaking, I picked the lock to the gate. It took me about three times longer than usual. Once I'd made it underneath the school and pulled the gate shut behind me, I slowed down. The thunder of the river bouncing off the stone walls seemed to match the roaring chaos inside my head. I slouched sideways against the wall, slid to the floor, and pressed my head against the damp stone, feeling the vibration of the school in my skull. I stayed like that for a while, not thinking, just letting the flood of despair and confusion and anger boil and churn through me.

When I got back to my room, I dragged off my wet clothes, pausing only to draw Gremlin from my hoodie pocket and set him on the nightstand. Once I'd pulled on a dry T-shirt and boxers, I made a voice call to Ray on my puck. He sounded groggy when he answered. "Lee? What is it, buddy?"

"I'm back in my room," I said. "You were sleeping. I didn't want to disturb you."

"Oh, God. I'm so sorry. I'll be right there. You need anything?"

"No. I'm going to bed now." I couldn't tell if my voice sounded normal, but even if it didn't, he seemed too flustered to notice.

I waved off all the lights in my room except the one in my puck. It hovered a few feet above me. By its light, I picked up Gremlin and pulled back the fur that covered his belly, revealing his body's caved-in metal casing. I opened his access panel—something I'd never done before. Usually I liked to snoop inside machines to understand their design and construction, but Gremlin had always been like a magic trick whose explanation I preferred not to know. Peering inside, I recognized Mom's precise, delicate handiwork—now smashed, unrepairable. I closed him back up, arranged him in a ball next to Mom's picture, and let him sleep.

19

Sleep didn't come for me, though. After Ray looked in on me and I told him good night, I burrowed under the covers and pulled a pillow over my head, like I was trying to bury myself. I wished I could really do that: claw my way deep under the ground, keep digging and digging until I was part of the earth and my body disintegrated and there was no more me left.

The air turned hot and stuffy around me. The rain ticked against my window. My brain paced around and around in the same small circle. There were plenty of questions I should've been asking myself. Did this mean Nico was working for Charlotte, just like Bex had suspected? Tomorrow was Thursday, the day Charlotte had said she'd retaliate against my father. Was I her target?

But the fact that I should probably fear for my safety barely registered. Right then, all I could think about was that I'd fallen in love with a simulation of a human being. Nico, the handsome, charming, weird guy I'd thought I'd known, didn't really exist. And the feeling that someone finally gave a crap about me, that someone finally understood me, that I wasn't all alone in this ugly universe after all—that had been a simulation too.

The hours passed. After a while pale light started to filter under the covers. I ignored it. My puck's morning alarm went off. I ignored that, too. Then, something I couldn't ignore: a knock on my door.

"What is it?"

Trumbull stuck his head in. "Sorry to bother you, sir. Your friend Nico wants to talk to you."

The sound of his name felt like ice water washing through my hollowed-out body.

"I'm sleeping."

"He says it's important. He says it won't take long."

My fingers, clutching the pillow over my head, loosened. If I told Trumbull to send Nico away, it would make him suspicious. And it might not stop Nico anyway. I'd seen what he could do last night. He might take more extreme measures, like snapping Trumbull's neck and then mine, or blowing up the whole school, or—maybe worst of all—telling Trumbull I was gay. At least if I talked to him, I might get some answers. I pushed away the covers and groped for my glasses. "Give me a minute."

While I pulled on a pair of jeans, I caught a glimpse of

myself in the mirror. Pale, puffy face. Bluish circles under my eyes. My hands smarted, the palms scraped raw after clinging to the branch last night. The rest of me felt the same way: scraped raw, inside and out. I went over to the window and stared at the courtyard so I wouldn't have to look at him when he came in. The door clicked open and clicked shut again. I tensed, half expecting him to shove me out the window. *Go ahead,* part of me wanted to say. Gutless Lee or Kamikaze Lee, I didn't even know which.

"Hi," Nico said.

Outside, it had stopped raining, but the light filtering down into the courtyard looked as gray and dismal as usual. On the window ledge lay my Swarmbots, their batteries drained, all of them belly-up like dead houseflies.

"I'm sorry."

"It's funny," I said. "Last night, while we were lying on the beach together, I kept thinking, *This doesn't feel real. This must be a fantasy.* And it turns out I was right. The whole thing was fake—not just the tropical island, but you, too."

"What about how you felt? That was real, wasn't it?"

The floor creaked as he took a step toward me. I spun around and grabbed one of my Creatures from the shelf—a vegetable-chopping robot I called Dicey—knocking over a few other machines in the process. I yanked off her knife attachment and brandished it. "Don't come any closer, you freak. I'm warning you."

He backed up again, his hands in the air.

"If you try anything, so help me, I'm yelling for Trumbull."

"Lee, I'm not going to hurt—"

"And don't you dare talk to me about how I felt."

"Okay. Okay."

I took a breath but didn't lower the knife. "What do you want, Nico?"

"To explain."

"I guess you'd better."

He licked his lips. He didn't have a puffy face or dark circles under his eyes—as a robot, he was probably immune—but he looked anxious. I wondered: Did he look anxious because he *was* anxious? Or because someone had programmed him to arrange his face in an expression of anxiety whenever he encountered a situation like this one? There *was* a difference, wasn't there?

"I was sent here to make contact with you," he said. "Become your friend. Not to, you know, kiss you and stuff."

"Don't talk to me about that, either. Just thinking about what we did makes me sick."

His eyes fell away from mine. He nodded.

"Let me get a few things straight. You said you were sent. By Charlotte?"

"Yes."

The nape of my neck tingled, like a spider had just walked over my skin. "So she made you somehow."

"That's right. She has a human scientist helping her."

"I guess that means you've never been to CHEE-lay." I sneered the word.

"I don't think so."

"So where do you come from?"

"A lab. I'm not sure where it's located."

"And how old are you?"

"Five months."

"Five months." A bitter laugh boiled up in me. "Why did they make you Chilean? So your quirks would be less suspicious? 'Oh, he just laughs loudly and likes to eat disgusting food because he's Chilean.'"

"I suppose."

"Plus, it's an interesting detail, right? Which makes you seem more like an actual human."

"Nico Medina *is* an actual human. He grew up in Santiago, speaks English as well as I do, has a father who always wanted him to go to school here."

"I get it. Charlotte modeled you on a real person so you'd pass the background check my Secret Service detail would run on you."

He nodded.

"Where is he now, then? Did Charlotte kill him?"

"Of course not. She arranged his admission to Inverness and then had him kidnapped a few days ago, while he was on his way to the United States. She'll let him go once all this is over."

"Let me guess: she hacked his puck archive too. So you'd have memories, just like she does. So you'd be a more perfect copy."

"I'm not a copy." His voice had risen a notch. "Nico's archive is just a reference, a starting point. I have my own personality. It's similar to his but not the same."

"In other words, the real Nico Medina *doesn't* eat disgusting food and laugh way too loud?"

For once, he didn't find a joke I'd made funny. "No."

"And your mom and dad, your annoying sisters, that teacher who got you into acting—they all belonged to that other person, not to you."

"No, the drama teacher belonged to me."

"What do you—" But then I understood. "You based her on Charlotte."

"Charlotte's important to me. I wanted to tell you about her."

I nodded. "'Reading Shakespeare helps us become more human.' Isn't that what she said? I guess you need all the help you can get."

Nico flinched. He fingered the bandage wrapped around his right hand.

"You've never spent an afternoon lying on a Chilean beach. You've never eaten an empanada."

"Not technically. But I *feel* like I have. I can imagine exactly how they taste." A spark, very faint, seemed to light up in the depths of his brown eyes, as if those electric filaments that laced his irises had switched on. "I have a whole lifetime of memories inside me, Lee. I *feel* like a real sixteen-year-old human boy."

I replied in a low, hard voice. "How would you know?"

His eyes went dark again. He looked at his shoes.

"So Charlotte and her human ally created you and sent you here. To do what? Take me hostage? Assassinate me? She released a statement warning of another terrorist strike. Supposedly it's happening today. Are you it?"

He shook his head. "I already told you, Lee, I wasn't sent to do you harm. She just wanted me to make friends with you."

"And then what?"

"I don't know. I'm supposed to wait for further instructions."

"Then how can you be sure she's not going to ask you to hurt me?"

"Because she told me she wouldn't."

"Well, that's good enough for me," I said, my voice tilting toward hysteria. I jabbed my knife in his direction. "And she didn't tell you to get all romantic with me so I'd like you and trust you."

"No. That was all me."

"That was *real*." The word twisted into another sneer.

"Yes. Exactly. That was real. I fell for you as soon as I met you, Lee. I have a big personality. I can be impulsive. I guess I got carried away. What happened between us wasn't Charlotte's fault. It was mine."

I narrowed my eyes at him. "But did you ever stop to think why you liked me in the first place? If Charlotte made you, then she must've made you gay."

His forehead creased, like I'd just said something in a language he didn't understand.

"Why would she do that?" I demanded.

"The original Nico Medina's gay too."

"Why did she choose him, then? The fact that you're gay and I'm gay is too big a coincidence. She must've found out I was in the closet. How? Did she tap into the security cameras here at school? Did she see me kiss Jeremy?"

"Look, I don't know about any of that."

"She must've orchestrated everything that's happened between us. She gave you that big, impulsive, flirty personality of yours. She probably made you like guys with glasses and huge ears, too. So how can you say any of it's real?"

"You're wrong, Lee. Maybe she just made me gay so we'd understand each other better."

"Why don't you ask her yourself?" I waved the knife at him. "Go on. Ask her."

"I'm not supposed to contact her. I'm supposed to wait for her to get in touch with me."

"And she hasn't? Not even after what happened last night? You must've sent her a message about *that*."

"I'm sure she knows. She said she'd be monitoring me."

My stomach dropped. Of course. As a robot, he must have

a network connection. The thought hadn't even crossed my mind until now. "So Charlotte's seen everything we've done together. Listened to everything I told you."

He nodded.

I raked the fingertips of my free hand over my skull. "Blackmail. That's why Charlotte engineered you to throw yourself at me like that. So she'd have recordings she could use against me."

"Lee, please stop. That can't be her plan."

"Oh, yeah? What about Nevermore? Are you also going to tell me she didn't take control of my robot and make her attack me?"

His eyes flared wide. "She didn't, Lee."

"Who did, then? Seems like yet another big coincidence, my robot trying to kill me the day after you showed up, and then again when I was with you last night."

"It wasn't Charlotte!" He glanced at the door, remembering Trumbull, and lowered his voice. "Why would she make your robot try to hurt you? I *saved* you from Nevermore, remember?"

"Maybe that was part of her plan. Maybe she hoped it would make me trust you more."

"But I also had to blow my cover to do it. Why would she want that to happen?"

I shrugged. "Maybe that part was a mistake."

He shook his head. "I'm telling you, Charlotte would never do something like that."

"What are you talking about? Of course she would. She just blew up the Statue of Liberty a month ago."

"To make an important point. And she didn't hurt anyone."

"She killed my mother."

That stopped him. He gave a small nod. "You're right. But she didn't mean to. She told me your mom's death is her greatest regret. If there was one thing she could take back—"

"Save it," I spat.

"You have to believe me, Lee. Charlotte means no harm. I don't know who took control of your robot, but it wasn't her."

"How do you know that for a fact?"

"Because I trust her."

"Of course you do. *That's* probably part of your program too."

He opened his hands helplessly. From outside the door came the sound of voices: a pack of students on their way to breakfast.

"Or maybe she's not the one I should be worrying about," I said. "Maybe you were controlling Nevermore yourself. You could've done the same trick with her that you did with the body-scan machine before the assembly. You *did* talk to that thing to make it let you through, didn't you?"

"Yes," he said. "But I didn't make Nevermore attack you. How can you even say that? You *know* me."

"Do I? I didn't know you were a robot."

"But you know what's important."

"The fact that you're not human isn't important?" Now I was the one having trouble keeping my voice down.

"Not as important as other things. The two of us throwing sparklers into the chasm. You kissing me in the dark. *That* was important. *That* was real. And you know it."

The faint spark had returned to his eyes. I forgot to breathe for a second.

A chime came from my puck.

"That's my dad calling," I said. "You have to go now."

"What happens next? Are you going to tell him?"

My puck hovered in the air between us, its white light blinking. Of *course* I should tell Dad. I might be in serious danger. Plus, Dad needed to know Charlotte had started making her own 2Bs.

But what if Charlotte retaliated by exposing my relationship with Nico? Or even if she didn't, if I told Dad Nico was a 2B sent by Charlotte, the rest of the truth would have to come out anyway. Investigators would demand to see my puck archive. My whole life would be laid bare. Eventually, the American public would find out too. They always did. I imagined everything that would follow. The look of mingled disappointment and alarm on Dad's face, as if I'd just confirmed his worst fears about me. A tidal wave of outrage on the Supernet even bigger than when I'd jumped off the Arlington Memorial Bridge. After all, I hadn't just kissed a boy. I'd kissed a 2B—Dad's archenemy and the scourge of humankind. It was the ultimate betrayal. I wondered what nicknames the gossip sites would think up for me this time.

"Lee?" Nico said.

I shook my head. "I won't tell," I muttered. "Not yet."

"Thank you."

"I need some time to figure things out, though. Stay away from me for a while."

"Whatever you want."

"What about Nevermore? Is she still outside?"

"I hid her in my room."

My puck chimed again. "Get out of here, Nico."

He started toward the door but stopped by my nightstand to gaze at the little ball of orange fur lying there. "Is he badly damaged?"

I nodded. "I don't think I can fix him."

"Maybe I can." He picked Gremlin up and stroked his coat with his thumb. "If you'd like me to try."

I turned away, toward the window. "Whatever," I said, making my voice hard again. "He's just a machine."

20

Nico left in a hurry, without closing the door behind him, without saying anything to Trumbull as he shouldered past. I remembered the knife and shoved it under a pillow a half second before Trumbull glanced in at me, one eyebrow raised above his sunglasses. I pushed my door shut and turned to my puck. For a second I considered telling it to take a message, but if I did that, Dad would just call Trumbull. "Answer," I said. Dad appeared on my wall, armored up for the day in his usual white shirt, red tie, and sleek navy suit. "Hey, Dad."

"Just wanted to touch base, Lee. I heard you've had an exciting couple of days."

"I guess you could say that."

My shelf of Creatures was still in disarray. I started to right the knocked-over machines one by one, hoping that might help my pounding heart to slow down.

"Trumbull told me about that robot bird of yours attacking you."

"That happened two days ago."

"Right." He straightened his tie. "Listen, I would've liked to call sooner, but I've been booked solid the past couple of days dealing with this new Charlotte scare. I've kept tabs on you, though. I know Trumbull and his boys are taking good care of you."

"It's all right. I understand."

He leaned his elbows on his desk and laced his fingers together. "I also heard about your shenanigans the night before last. You were under lockdown and sneaked out?"

"Stroud already lectured me, Dad. You don't have to bother."

"I wasn't going to lecture you. To be honest, I'm glad to hear you're getting into a little mischief." In other words, as he'd pointed out a few days ago, I didn't excel at academics, play sports, participate in extracurricular activities, or socialize. At least this was *something*. He chuckled. "Sometime I'll tell you about the antics *I* got into when I was at Inverness. It's good to cut loose every once in a while. Just don't make a habit of it, okay? Especially now, with Charlotte threatening another attack. Trumbull works hard to keep you safe. Don't give the poor guy a heart attack."

"Okay, Dad."

I nudged the last Creature back into place. Dad sat back in his chair and rapped his knuckles once on his desk—something he often did when he was winding up a puck conversation. I might be home free.

Then Dad squinted at me. The crease between his eyebrows, the one he always had when he talked to me, deepened. "You look tired, Lee. Is everything okay? Anything else going on I should know about?"

My eyes skittered away from him and landed on my cat-shaped pest catcher, Mouthtrap. "I just didn't sleep very well last night. That's all." Mouthtrap seemed to sneer at me with his sharp silver teeth. Jeopardizing national security so I could stay in the closet—I was now officially a Walking Walk-In of the lowest order. Bex would be even more disgusted with me than usual if she knew.

"It's nearly eight," Dad said. "Shouldn't you be dressed by now?"

"I thought I might sit out classes today."

"Because you didn't sleep well?"

I nodded. "I think I'm getting a cold, too."

"Come on, Lee. You're not going to miss class because of a little cold, are you?"

I should've known better than to try that excuse. He disapproved of me getting sick almost as much as he did of me having emotions.

"Okay," I mumbled. "I'll get dressed."

His face unclenched a fraction. "Good boy. Look, I need to go. I'll check in with you again soon, okay?"

When the projection vanished from my wall, though, I didn't start getting ready for the day. I wandered over to the window instead and leaned my forehead against the glass. I pressed my scraped-up palms against it too. The cold numbed the pain a bit. The Swarmbots lay on the ledge outside, their little legs in the air, like the victims of a tiny massacre. Right on cue, the voices started whispering in my skull. *Leap. Leap. Leap.* I wondered, not for the first time, if a forty-foot drop would be enough to kill or just to seriously maim.

I flinched away. "Send a message to Bex," I told my puck.

When I didn't say anything else right away, the puck dipped closer and chimed inquisitively.

I swallowed through a tight throat. "Bex, I'm sorry for yesterday. I was a jerk. Can you cut out of breakfast and meet me in the library? I need to talk. It's important."

Be there in ten, she messaged back.

I forced myself to shower and get dressed. I knotted my almost-black necktie in a neat double Windsor. I slid on my silver raven tiepin. The clothes I'd worn last night lay in the corner where I'd tossed them, crumpled and damp, the jeans still crusted with sand from the make-believe beach. I scooped them up and dropped them into my hamper. In the colorless light filtering in from outside, my room appeared as cold and empty as ever.

Before I went out, I drew the silver watch from my nightstand and strapped it to my wrist.

I headed downstairs. On the way, my hand went to my blazer, feeling the absence in my inside pocket. I hadn't gone even a few minutes without Gremlin near me in years. Not since Mom's funeral probably.

My mind jumped back to that day. The wooden pews in Dad's church in DC, as uncomfortable as the seats in the Inverness auditorium. Dad on one side of me, lost in a miserable trance. Stroud on the other, his back straight, his eyes pointed forward, his craggy face grim and composed, as if this were a military drill instead of a funeral. Mom in a coffin in front of us, her red hair neat and shiny, like she'd never worn it in life. I spent most of the service rolling my lips between my teeth to keep from crying. This was only my second time meeting my grandfather, and I had this idea in my head that if he saw me shedding tears, he'd lock me up in a room just like the one where those terrorists had kept him and my other grandfather prisoner.

Midway through the service, Gremlin crept out of my blazer pocket, perched on my shoulder, and gave my earlobe a tug.

"This is no time for toys," Stroud growled. "Don't you have any respect for your mother?" He grabbed Gremlin by the tail. For a second my little Creature hung there, legs waving, huge eyes blinking. Then he disappeared into Stroud's pocket.

Later, after the burial, I crept up to Stroud, my whole body tingling with fear. *Remember*, I kept telling myself, *whatever you do, don't cry.* "Sir?" He looked down at me with eyes like chipped ice. "May I please have Gremlin back?"

Except about halfway through the sentence, my words fractured into sobs.

"Stop that," Stroud snapped. He turned to Dad, who was standing nearby. "John, this is what happens when you let your son develop unhealthy attachments to lifeless objects."

For once, Dad stood up to him. "Let him have his toy, sir. He just lost his mother."

"I understand that," my grandfather replied. "That doesn't excuse his behavior. My whole life, I've only loved two people, and now I've lost both of them. That's what life is: losing things. The sooner he learns that, the better." He turned on his heel and left the cemetery without another word.

"You have to understand, son," Dad told me, "this is hard for him, too, even if he doesn't show it. He lost your grandma before you were born. Now he's lost his daughter."

But I didn't care about excuses. I just wanted Gremlin back. I spent two wretched nights without him. On the third, I heard a tapping at my window. My Creature huddled there, orange coat filthy, battery almost drained. From then on, I'd always given him strict orders to stay hidden before I went out in public. Especially after my arrival at Inverness Prep.

I turned into the library, passed the shelves of musty books, and climbed the iron staircase to the mezzanine. Bex arrived a few minutes later. She dropped into the chair across from mine and folded her hands on the table. "You look terrible. What's up?"

"I think I have something to add to Nico's con column." My throat had tightened even more since I'd left my room. It felt like a stone lodged there. "You were right about him. You don't even know how right you were." I pushed up my glasses and buried my face in my raw palms.

Bex jumped up and put her arms around me. For a while she crouched next to my chair, not saying a word, her hand moving in a slow circle over my back. I shot a glance at Trumbull, but he hadn't turned. When I'd pulled myself together enough to talk again, I told her the whole story of last night and this morning. She listened, the absence of makeup making her eyes appear vividly green. She let out a soft gasp when I said Nico was a 2B, but otherwise she managed not to make a sound.

"My God," she said after I'd finished. "I mean, I had suspicions about Nico, but I never imagined something like *that*. And he wouldn't tell you what Charlotte's planning?"

"Just that she's not going to hurt me."

"I'm sorry, Lee, but I don't know if I buy that. Those raven attacks make the whole thing too suspicious."

"He said someone else must've hijacked Nevermore."

Bex screwed her mouth to one side. "Sounds pretty far-fetched to me. Especially considering Charlotte's track record."

"So what should I do?"

"What do you think, Lee? Tell someone!" She pointed at Trumbull's back. "Tell Trumbull. He'll know what to do."

"I can't. He'll find out about the kissing."

"This is more important than your stupid closet, Lee."

"It's not just about my closet." I propped one elbow on the table and pressed my forehead into my hand. In the bookcase next to me, the title of one of the books, embossed in gold on worn red leather, glinted: *The Complete Works of William Shakespeare*. "If I tell about Nico, what'll happen to him? I care about him, Bex. I can't help it."

She rubbed my back some more. "I know this must be really hard for you, Lee. It's a matter of life and death, though. Yours, and maybe other people's too. That attack is supposed to happen *today*. Charlotte has to be stopped. It's not that I don't have sympathy for 2Bs. I already told you what I think of that stupid Protection of Humanhood Amendment. But there's no excuse for terrorism." She bent her head lower to catch my eyes. "Nico lied to you. He can't be trusted. And, Lee, he's not a human being."

"I know." I touched the spine of the book with my finger, tracing the grooves of the letters.

"I'm warning you, Lee. If you won't do it, I will."

She started to stand, like she meant to tell Trumbull right then. He turned, seeing the movement. I grabbed her wrist and pulled her back down. "Please, Bex, don't," I hissed. "I'm begging you."

Her eyes met mine. They softened. "Okay. But there's at least one thing you should do."

"What's that?"

"Talk to Dr. Singh."

"Bex, you're obsessed with that woman."

"No, I'm not. Think about it. She knew Charlotte better than anyone. If you tell her what's going on, she might have some idea what Charlotte's going to do."

For the first time in a while, I remembered those words Dr. Singh had spoken on the terrace. *Just let him fall.* "You might be right. I didn't tell you before. Something strange happened on Monday."

When she'd heard the story, her eyes went huge. "Do you realize what this means, Lee? She must know about Nico. She must be working with Charlotte. And maybe she was having second thoughts. That has to be it!"

"That's a big leap, Bex. We don't know anything for sure yet. Listen, I'll talk to her. In my own way, though. This is a delicate situation. If she *is* working with Charlotte, she's not just going to come out and admit it right away. And if she *isn't*, I don't want to give away too much of what *I* know either. Now you have to promise you won't say a word to Trumbull or anyone else."

Doubt clouded her face, but she dipped her head in agreement. "It's a deal. For now."

21

✧✧✧✧✧

I still didn't feel like going to class, but I forced myself. Dad would hear about it for sure if I didn't, and I couldn't afford to raise any more red flags now. I sleepwalked through my first two classes, biology and robotics. Then, on my way to English, my body tensed, as if bracing for a car crash. When Nico walked into the classroom a few minutes after me, it did feel like a kind of collision: inside me there was a jolt, then an almost-physical pain that made me grip the sides of my wooden seat. As for him, his eyes stayed on the floor as he crossed the room, and he chose a seat far away from mine. Even though I tried not to, I glanced over at him a few times during class. I never once caught him looking back at me.

I headed back to the robotics lab during lunch. Trumbull wouldn't find that strange: sometimes I went there at lunchtime or after classes ended to work on my Creatures. Dr. Singh was almost always there too, tinkering with projects of her own. At those times she never bothered to sit near the window while she smoked. Even though we never talked much—maybe *because* we never talked much—I sensed she liked my company.

When I arrived, Dr. Singh sat hunched over her desk, a soldering iron in her hand, a cigarette dangling from her mouth, its inch-long ash threatening to tumble onto the circuit board in front of her. She grunted a greeting without taking her eyes away from her work. All around, squares of cardboard held in place with duct tape covered the holes Trumbull's gun had left in the ceiling and walls. While Trumbull stationed himself near the door, I walked over to her. "Dr. Singh? Are you busy?"

She looked up, nodded at the soldering iron, raised her eyebrows.

"I was wondering if I could talk to you about something."

She tapped her cigarette over the black plastic ashtray on her desk. "What's on your mind?"

"I've been thinking about what happened in here the other day. Trumbull said you didn't find any evidence on the local network log of somebody hacking my robot."

"That's right."

"But that doesn't mean it definitely didn't happen, right? I mean, a really good hacker could do it without leaving a trace."

"I suppose it's possible."

"Because the way Nevermore behaved—it didn't *seem* like a glitch, did it?"

She shrugged. "It's hard to say."

So far so good. I sat down across from her and lowered my

voice. "Three days ago, Charlotte released a message threatening another attack. Do you think that had anything to do with what happened?"

She tensed at my mention of Charlotte. Because she knew something? I couldn't tell. "I have no idea." She brought the cigarette back to her lips.

"Did you hear about the message on the news?"

"Of course I did."

"So what do you think she has planned?"

"How should I know? I haven't had any contact with Charlotte in seven years, Lee."

"I'm sorry. I know you don't like talking about her."

She stubbed out the cigarette and picked up her soldering iron. "Is that it? Are we done?"

I squeezed my scraped-up hands together. *Just say something*, I ordered my brain. *Just keep the conversation going.* "I do have one more question," I said. "It doesn't have anything to do with Charlotte, or even with Nevermore. It's just something I've been thinking about."

"What is it?" she said, her eyes still on the circuit board.

"When you invented the 2B software, your big breakthrough, the way I understand it, was that you figured out how to simulate free will."

"Uh-huh."

"But it was still just a simulation. Like say you put two scoops of ice cream in front of a 2B, one chocolate and one vanilla. You tell the robot he can choose whichever one he wants. In that moment he has the experience of making a free choice. But you can still control the 2B by programming him to *prefer* vanilla. So in reality, he's not free at all. Did I explain that right?"

"More or less. Where does the question come in?"

"Sorry, I'm getting to it. My question is this: How are human beings any different? My dad's always talking about how 2Bs don't have *true* free will, like humans do. But aren't our choices determined by our programming too? Our genes and our environment and all that? Aren't we basically just robots ourselves?"

By the time I'd finished talking, I'd slid to the edge of my chair, my hands still in a knot on my lap. I'd asked the question on impulse, but the more I spoke, the more I realized how much I wanted to know—*needed* to know—how she'd answer.

Dr. Singh sat back from her desk and regarded me with a faint smile. She pulled another cigarette from her pack, tapped it against the hard wood, and tucked it into the corner of her mouth. "You know something?" She touched the tip of her soldering iron to the cigarette and puffed to get it going. "That reminds me of an old joke. It goes like this: The first guy asks the second guy, 'Do you believe in free will?' The second guy answers, 'I have no choice.'"

I blinked.

She shook her head and shifted her hunched body in her wheelchair. "Look, all I'm saying is, you're absolutely right: with all due respect to your father, free will is an illusion. Nobody really has a choice about anything. It's just our human pride and stubbornness that make us think any different."

I slumped back and stared at my knotted-up hands. That hollow feeling blew through my body again.

"The real question isn't whether 2Bs are alive," she said. "It's whether humans are anything more than machines. But I have a feeling you knew that already."

I nodded. I'd never put words to the thought before, but I'd probably known it ever since Mom died seven years ago. In a blink, she'd just stopped existing, exactly like Charlotte had. While everybody else in America had wanted to know if Charlotte had survived her upload, I'd sat there in the church between Dad and Stroud wondering: Had *Mom* managed to upload herself somewhere? Had she gone to a better place, where she'd watch over me and wait for me to join her, like the minister said? Inside, I'd known the answer to that question. Mom had said it herself. *All the hard evidence argues against it.* Over the years, while Dad had gone on to build his Human Values Movement and give his speeches about human free will, I'd wished I could believe, like he claimed to, that some non-mechanical part of us existed outside the reach of genetics and environment, body and brain, cause and effect, because that would be the part of us that kept on existing after we died. But I couldn't. I was like Mom: a scientist. Maybe that was why I'd never let myself think about that subject too much.

"Here's the thing, though," Dr. Singh continued, emphasizing her words with small jabs of her cigarette. "Free will is an illusion, but it's a *necessary* illusion. If my machines hadn't felt like they could choose their own destinies, they would've been unable to function."

Like me, I thought. The people in my life always said I never did anything. Dad complained because I didn't participate enough at school. Bex complained because I wouldn't come out of the closet or ask boys on dates. Even Nico had called me out on it. Maybe *this* was the reason. Because deep down, I knew what we really were. "So your machines felt free and autonomous," I said, "but actually you had them under your control the whole time." That image came to me again: Nico grinning at me over a lit sparkler, his face flickering like an old-fashioned movie. "All of them, just puppets on invisible strings."

"I wouldn't go that far."

Her raspy voice lost some of its strength when she said that. I glanced up at her and remembered: Charlotte. Of course.

"The 2Bs were complicated," she said. "Their brains had just as much processing power as ours do. We still haven't built a computer powerful enough to predict exactly how one of them—or one of us, for that matter—would react to every possible combination of circumstances. Take your chocolate and vanilla example. Even if we programmed our 2B to prefer vanilla, that still wouldn't be a one hundred percent guarantee. What if he decided he wanted to vary his diet, or broaden his tastes, or make a point? He might choose chocolate for any number of reasons, despite his preference."

"I guess that's true." I eased forward in my chair again. "I guess Charlotte's another example. You didn't program her to do any of the things she's done."

Dr. Singh stopped, the cigarette halfway to her mouth. "Obviously not. I thought you said we weren't going to talk about her."

"I'm just saying that's the catch, isn't it? As long as you build machines whose behavior you can't predict a hundred percent of the time, there's always going to be an element of danger."

"I suppose there is." Her free hand drifted to her dancing-god pendant.

"And now, who knows what Charlotte's going to do next?"

"What are you getting at, Lee?"

"She might build another 2B. She might send him to this school. She might make him win the trust of the president's son."

Dr. Singh's eyes went glassy. She sagged into her wheelchair, looking more than ever like a body with a shattered skeleton— like the opposite of my grandfather, with his ramrod-straight spine. The other night Stroud had said adversity destroyed some people and made others stronger. One look at Dr. Singh and you could tell what it had done to her.

"I know the truth, Dr. Singh," I told her. "Not all of it. But enough. And you do too, don't you?"

A tear raced down her cheek. She gave a tiny nod.

"Please. Tell me what she has planned."

She stared, her thumb moving back and forth over her little gold god.

Then she shook her head. "I can't do this." She dropped her cigarette in the ashtray and backed her wheelchair away from the desk.

I stood, my face and ears burning. "Dr. Singh, we need to stop her." An edge of desperation had crept into my voice. In my mind, I winced at myself. I'd started sounding like Bex.

"Leave me alone, Lee," she said as she rolled out the door. "Why can't everyone just leave me the hell alone?"

22

◇◇◇◇◇◇

After Dr. Singh left, Trumbull threw me a glance, probably adding another red flag to his mental list. I looked away, my cheeks still blazing. Not knowing what else to do, I sank onto a stool at my worktable and picked up my screwdriver. Bex and Dad both hassled me for spending so many hours tinkering with my Creatures, but sometimes it seemed like the only thing that got me through my worst days. I'd just stay for a little while. Then I'd figure out what to do next. While my fingers performed their simple tasks, fitting parts together, tightening screws, the heat faded from my face little by little. The work didn't banish thoughts of Nico, but at least it pushed them into the background.

"Sir?" Trumbull said after a while. "Sorry to bother you, but I couldn't help noticing you're ten minutes late for history."

"I'm not going." At this point, I didn't even care if it meant making him more suspicious than ever. I couldn't face the thought of going back out there, dragging myself through the rest of my classes, pretending I had a reason to put one foot in front of the other. Running into Nico maybe. At least here I knew I was safe.

"With all due respect," Trumbull said, stepping toward me, "I don't think that's a good idea."

"Your job is to follow me around, not to tell me what to do."

"I understand that, sir, but this is a safety issue. The conservatory is isolated and exposed, and today—"

I slammed down my screwdriver. "Do you have any idea how sick I am of you, Trumbull? I'm sick of you watching my every move through those stupid sunglasses. I'm sick of you thinking your thoughts about me and never saying a word, just raising that one smug eyebrow. I'm sick of having no privacy and no freedom and no choice about anything, even if those *are* all just imaginary concepts. So would you do me a favor? Just leave me alone and let the terrorists come get me, because it couldn't possibly be any worse than this."

His one smug eyebrow edged into view above his sunglasses. He folded his arms. "Finished?"

My face turned hot again. I dropped back onto my stool and nodded.

"Good," he said, his voice low and steady. "Because as it happens, I do have something to say: I think I know what's going on between you and Nico."

My heart came to a full stop. My blood froze in my veins. I tried to make my face like his—a blank, giving away nothing—while

I searched for the most neutral response possible. "What do you mean? Nothing's going on."

Trumbull circled the worktable to stand next to my stool. He towered over me, not saying a word, just rubbing one giant fist with the opposite hand while my stomach tried to turn itself inside out.

Then he did something I never would've expected: he took off his sunglasses. For a second his eyes—not as dark and deep set as I'd imagined—blinked and darted around as if embarrassed by their own nakedness. He eased his massive bulk onto the stool next to mine. "I'm telling you it's okay. At least it's okay by me. I know it can't be easy getting to know . . ." He waved his huge hand as he searched for the word. ". . . someone special when you've got me and my boys hanging around all the time. You don't have to worry. I'm not going to say anything. And not only that." He set his hand on my shoulder. "I want you to know he seems like a good kid to me. I can tell you two are having some kind of disagreement, and I realize I don't have all the details, but I say you should give him a chance."

If only you knew, I wanted to tell him. But I nodded. "Thanks."

I studied his face. Of all the "Trumbull finds out I'm gay" scenarios I'd imagined over the years—and there were a lot—none resembled this one. Most involved him chasing me down a hallway with a gun in his hand. Still, my heart hadn't quite started beating again yet. Could I really trust him not to say anything?

"Sorry for flipping out on you. Again."

He slid his sunglasses on. "Apology accepted, sir."

A scuttling sound came from the hall just outside the conservatory. One of the Spiders had drawn up to the doorway on its slender silver legs. It peered into the room with its blue lamplike eye. At first I figured it must've come to clean. The Spiders did most of their cleaning at night, but sometimes they worked in unused rooms during the day. Then I remembered Dr. Singh had programmed the Spiders to stay out of the conservatory. Had she changed their programming? "Come back later," I told it. "I'm using this room right now."

The Spider tapped into the room. Maybe it hadn't heard me.

"I said come back later," I repeated in a louder voice. "I'm busy here."

It paid no attention to me. Now a second robot had appeared in the corridor behind the first. The hairs on the back of my neck stood up. Spiders never traveled or worked in pairs.

Trumbull's hand landed on my shoulder again, more firmly this time. "Get down, sir." He pressed me off the stool and under the table before positioning himself between me and the robots. "I'm commanding you," he bellowed. "Leave, now."

The first Spider's eye ranged around the conservatory like a searchlight. It stopped on Trumbull. The robot raised its two front legs, mantislike.

He pulled his gun from his jacket. "Leave! Now!"

One of the Spider's forelegs snapped forward, bashing Trumbull in the chest. The blow lifted him up and sent him crashing down on one of the tables, crunching metal robot parts and scattering screws and bits of wire. His gun flew out of his hand and banged against the floor somewhere on the far side of the room.

I scrambled back, farther under the table, my heart galloping out of control. My fingers found the two buttons on my wristwatch and pressed. *One. Two*—

With a flick of its silver foreleg, the Spider turned over the table above me. I threw my arms over my head. The robot knocked me to the side. My body skated across the slick concrete floor and bashed into the glass wall—which cracked but didn't break. I turned. Trumbull, still on his back on one of the worktables, struggled onto one elbow. "Lawrence, can you hear me?" he called into his puck. The device must not have been working, because he muttered, "Damn it!" and pushed himself upright.

Behind him, the second Spider brought the tip of its foreleg to its underbelly, where it stored its various attachments. *Click*. The Spider folded the leg forward again—with a sledgehammer attached.

"Trumbull!"

He turned just as the robot landed a blow to his left shoulder. Something crunched that sounded like bone. While my heart thudded, my hand darted back to my watch. Again, not fast enough. The first Spider's two sharp forelegs shot down at me, one spearing through each of my blazer sleeves—missing my actual wrists by millimeters—and pinning me to the floor. I tried to wriggle out of my blazer, but the robot used two more of its slender limbs to pinion my legs. Now I couldn't move at all.

Trumbull hauled himself to his feet again, his left arm hanging heavy at his side, his sunglasses crooked, one of the lenses cracked. He charged at the second robot, his right hand balled into a fist. The Spider swung its hammer into his belly. Trumbull stumbled back a few paces, stopped, and stood doubled forward, his right hand on his knee. His sunglasses sagged from his face in slow motion and then clattered to the floor. His eyes looked unfocused, almost sleepy. The Spider let its sledgehammer fly one last time. The weapon smashed into Trumbull's head. Another nauseating crunch. Blood spattered, dotting the floor next to me. Trumbull spun around one full turn, dropped to his knees, and paused there, his eyes half open but utterly vacant. Then he tipped to the side and smacked against the concrete.

Everything went still. Everything except the pool of blood under Trumbull's cheek, which edged outward in all directions. I couldn't tell if he was still breathing. The Spiders had stopped moving too. They seemed to be waiting for something. I twisted my arms and legs but couldn't budge.

Both robots swiveled their eyes toward the door to the hallway, like they'd heard something. The second one scuttled toward the far end of the conservatory, where a glass door led outside. It opened the door with its foreleg and slipped out. The other Spider pulled up its spearlike arms one by one and scurried off in the same direction. I hurried to my feet and brought my fingers back to the watch. I didn't press the buttons, though. The machines had already disappeared, leaving the glass door swaying on its hinges.

"Lee?"

I whirled around, electricity crackling through my body.

Nico stood in the opposite doorway, eyes huge. "My God, what happened? Lee, are you all right?"

"A couple of Spiders just attacked us," I panted. "Trumbull. I can't tell if he's—"

Nico raced over to him. Horror registered on his face as he touched the blood oozing from Trumbull's skull. Did he look horrified because he *felt* horrified? Or because someone had programmed him to look and act that way in this situation? I'd seen him act before. Was he acting now? My trembling fingers stayed poised over the watch's two small buttons. But they didn't push down.

"He's alive."

The tension in my chest eased a little. "We need an ambulance," I told my puck.

"No network connection," it replied.

"It's okay," Nico said. "We'll get help ourselves. You said Spiders attacked you?"

I nodded. "They left just before you walked in." Anger thickened my voice. "Are you going to tell me Charlotte didn't send those, either?"

"She didn't. I just got a message from her. She said someone—she doesn't know who—is trying to sabotage her plan." He stood and held out his hand. "We should get out of here, Lee, in case the Spiders come back. We'll go to your grandfather's office, tell him what happened, get help for Trumbull."

I stared at his hand, wrapped in a neat white bandage.

"I know this is confusing, but you have to trust me right now." He stepped forward. The pale light pouring down through the glass roof caught in the bronze coils of his hair. "We need to hurry. Please."

My fingers relaxed away from the watch. I started toward him.

Then I stopped. "Why did you come here, Nico?"

"Why do you think? I came looking for you."

"I said I didn't want to see you."

"I know, but I thought I should tell you about Charlotte's message."

"So you came here."

"Of course I did. I figured you'd be here. Come on, Lee, let's go." He took a few more steps, his shoes tracking Trumbull's blood.

I backed away. "I'm supposed to be in history. You know that. Why did you figure I'd be here *now*?"

He licked his lips. His eyes dropped to the concrete floor.

"Nico?" *Just say something. Please, just make me believe you.*

When he looked up again, his face had hardened. His eyes had narrowed. His mouth had pressed into a frown. He sprang forward, grabbed my puck out of the air, and smashed it on the table. The thing burst into a spray of tiny chips and sensors. Then, faster than my eyes could register, he was on top of me, jamming his knees into my chest, pressing one hand over my mouth.

23

◇◇◇◇◇◇◇

In those first few seconds I didn't fight back. I didn't try to escape. I didn't yell, *Nico, how could you betray me like this?* I just went dead. From the shock, I suppose. Or maybe it was more like the opposite of shock. The confirmation of what I'd suspected all along. After gagging me with a rag and lashing my wrists together with some wire, he picked me up, crushing me to his chest.

Now I struggled. It didn't make any difference, though. His hard synthetic muscles and metal bones just closed even tighter around my human flesh. I tried yelling, too, but the gag muffled the sound.

Nico started toward the corridor that led to the rest of the school, but something stopped him. He was staring at Trumbull, his brow furrowed, his head tilted to the side, like the sight of my Head Armed Babysitter lying there was a puzzle he couldn't quite solve. His eyes met mine for a brief moment, then flicked away again. He turned and ran in the other direction, through the conservatory and out the open glass door the Spiders had used just a minute ago.

The cold outdoor air washed over my face. The sky had darkened, even though it was still early afternoon. Nico bounded along the front of the school and down the staircase to the walkway along the river, following the same route we'd taken two nights ago. I strained against his grip some more but didn't accomplish anything. The angry noise of the river, magnified as it bounced between the stone canal walls, filled my head. When we reached the iron gate, Nico didn't even slow down. He just leaped diagonally across the river and landed beyond the gate on the opposite walkway. The dark tunnel swallowed us up and then spat us out again. Nico jumped back over the river, pelted up the steep, muddy riverbank, and plunged into the forest.

The smell of pine needles and soil enfolded us. Above, black, twisty branches covered the sky like gnarled hands. Below, the trees' roots bulged from the packed dirt like half-buried bones. Nico seemed to know the trail along the river better than I did now. Little by little, he sped up, jagging from side to side to follow the twists of the path, until the forest became a blur. When I glanced at him, though, no sign of exertion showed on his face. His expression remained eerily neutral, with his lips still pressed into a frown of concentration and his eyes still unreadable.

The tree cover thinned. The sky opened up above us, cement

gray. We'd almost reached the base of the mountain. Nico slowed down a little. The chain-link fence loomed up ahead, with its dented yellow NO TRESPASSING sign and the dug-out hollow at its base where we'd shimmied under. He didn't head for the hollow, though. Instead, he sped up again. He bounded once, twice, three times, and leaped into the air. My stomach hitched. My brain swam.

Nico landed with barely a thud and kept right on running. He sprinted around the side of the mountain to the boarded-up tunnel entrance, where he skidded to a stop and set me on my feet. My knees buckled. I grabbed the rock wall with my tied-up hands for balance. He pointed at the gap in the boards. "Climb through."

When I didn't move right away, he grabbed me by the back of my blazer and stuffed me through the opening. He slid through himself, never loosening his grip. Then he scooped me up and plunged into the blackness. His puck didn't turn on its light, though. He must've instructed it not to. Probably he had infrared vision. Unlike me. The sensation of careening through the forest in Nico's arms had already sent my pulse racing, but doing the same thing in total darkness brought me to a whole new level of panic. I panted and gasped—as well as I could through the rag covering my mouth—like all the oxygen had disappeared along with the light. My muscles clenched, bracing for whatever came next. The tunnel would open into the central cavern any second. What would he do then?

Nico's pace slackened again. The sound of his echoing footsteps deepened and expanded to fill the larger space. He stopped. I blinked against the darkness, still struggling to breathe, suspended between the heat of his body on one side and the cold black emptiness of the cavern on the other. I imagined the vast space around us. I imagined the chasm in front of us. I imagined Nico throwing my body down there. Maybe no one would find me, just like no one had found that other kid. Did I even care? I'd almost tried to end it all myself two years ago. I didn't have any more reason to live now than I'd had then. Maybe it was time someone else finished what I'd started. But why did it have to be Nico?

His mouth drew close to my ear. "Trust me. Don't be afraid."

Don't be afraid? His words almost made me laugh out loud.

But I didn't have a chance. Half a second later he was running again. Then he was jumping. Then he was falling. *We* were falling.

I curled into his torso, the only thing I had to hold on to. My fingers clawed at his blazer. My face pressed against his hot chest. Something sharp dug into my cheek: his Inverness Prep tiepin. The falling seemed to go on forever, but that feeling of freedom I'd imagined before I'd jumped off the Arlington Memorial Bridge never arrived.

Nico's feet smacked solid ground. He took off at a sprint, making turns in the blackness. Left, right, right. Zigzagging through the maze of tunnels. Making my stomach churn.

I couldn't handle it anymore. I let out a muffled scream. Nico slowed. He pulled the rag from my mouth. I twisted to the side and puked.

He set me down. I dropped to my knees and elbows, my wrists still bound together. I hadn't consumed a thing since yesterday at lunchtime, so my puking consisted mostly of dry heaving.

Nico's voice came to me again in the darkness. "I'm sorry, Lee. About all of this." He still had one hand on my back. To comfort me or keep me from bolting? I didn't even know anymore.

When my body had finished trying to squeeze out all its internal organs, I wiped the slobber from my mouth with the back of my hand. "Please," I choked, "can you just turn on a light?"

His puck's light blinked on. I squinted against its brightness. Nico untied my wrists while my eyes adjusted. I glanced around, but there wasn't much to see: rough stone walls, dirt floor. I staggered to my feet, using the wall for support. He didn't have his hand on my back anymore. Maybe he figured I had nowhere to run. It was true: on my own, I'd never have a hope of finding my way out of here again. Which meant no triggering the bomb in my watch. Or was I just making excuses?

Nico held out the rag he'd used to gag me so I could clean my face. "I couldn't think of any other way." The fierce mask he'd worn a few minutes ago had disappeared. He sounded sincere. But then again, he'd sounded sincere back in the robotics lab when he'd said he wanted to take me to Stroud.

"Are you going to tell me what the hell's going on?"

"I will soon, I promise. For now, we have to keep moving. They'll be coming after us."

"Who?"

He grabbed my arm. "Soon."

I stopped him before he could pick me up again. "Can't I at least walk on my own feet?"

"No. It'll be faster this way."

He swept my feet off the floor and raced off again. At least I could see now. His puck sped through the air above us, barely able to keep up, its light slithering over the rutted stone surfaces. The tunnel resembled the one up above that led to the cavern—low, narrow, clearly man-made, except without the wooden supports lining the walls. The temperature had dropped even further. A faint smell of sulfur permeated the air. Each time the tunnel branched off, Nico chose a direction without hesitation, as if he knew exactly where to go. Either that, or he was just making choices at random.

"We're going to get lost," I said. "Just like that kid who died down here."

"Don't worry. I have a good memory." He spoke in his normal voice, even as his legs pumped at superhuman speed underneath us. "Anyway, I thought you told me that kid didn't die after all and stayed down here and lived happily ever after? Wasn't that your theory?"

I thought for a second he might break into one of his huge laughs, but he seemed to think better of it. Even so, it felt strangely comforting to see a glimmer of the Nico I knew—odd, inappropriate, but not evil.

He kept running. The walls seemed narrower now. Or maybe I was just developing a new phobia to add to the list. Then, after what seemed like hours, the passage opened into a larger space. Nico jogged to a stop. He set me down. I leaned against the wall gasping for breath, as if I were the one who'd done all the running, while his "breathing"—simulated, I knew now, to make him appear more human—remained as steady as always. He made a lap around the room's perimeter, checking the corners. The area appeared empty, except for some rubble and a few sections of rusted pipe littering the floor.

"I think we can stop here for a while," he said.

"Good." I straightened my rumpled blazer and turned to face him. "I want you to tell me why you brought me here, Nico. The truth this time."

Nico wiped back his hair, blown wild by all the running. He lowered himself to the rock-strewn floor. His puck settled on the dirt in front of him, its light shining upward like a cold, unflickering campfire. I dropped to a crouch across from him.

"Okay," he said. "Here it is. The truth."

24

×◇×◇×◇×

I guess I just needed to take you someplace where we could talk."

I waved my hand around, indicating the gigantic mountain directly above us. "So you brought me *here*?"

"Charlotte monitors me all the time, remember? Up there, I never have a second of privacy—sort of like you, with your Secret Service detail."

"I get it. And down here, the mountain blocks the network signal."

"This was the only place I could think of. Everywhere else, she knows what I'm seeing, what I'm hearing."

"What you're thinking?"

"No. Not that."

"Still, doesn't this seem a little drastic? What if there's poisonous gas down here? Or what if the walls cave in?"

Nico sniffed. "My sensors don't detect anything unhealthy in the air. And as for a cave-in"—he knocked his fist against the rock behind him—"the walls seem sturdy enough."

"All right, then." I sat cross-legged and leaned my elbows on my knees and tried to make my face a wall, like I had with Trumbull earlier. "I'm listening. What do you want to talk to me about?"

He reached into his blazer. "First, I want to give you this." He held out his hand. Gremlin leaped from his palm, landed on my chest, and skittered over me, his furry, lizard-shaped body practically vibrating with excitement. He paused on my shoulder long enough to blink his big black eyes at me and tug twice on my ear. "I skipped lunch today to fix him," Nico said.

"What about his programming?"

"I managed to salvage it. He's the same Gremlin you knew before, Lee. I didn't change a thing."

"How do I know that for sure, though? How do I know he won't suddenly attack me the way Nevermore did?"

"I guess you'll have to trust me."

Gremlin kept doing laps over my body like he hadn't seen me in a month. He'd done the same thing years ago, when he'd escaped from Stroud and found his way back to me after Mom's funeral. He jumped up and down on the top of my head, lost his footing, and landed on the dirt floor. He sneezed. I couldn't help it, I smiled a little.

"He was elegantly constructed," Nico added. "Your mom did a good job."

Bit by bit, Gremlin settled down and came to rest on my shoulder. I refortified my face. "I still want answers."

"I know." He took a deep simulated breath. "I lied to you back at school, Lee. When I said Charlotte didn't send your raven or those Spiders after you—that wasn't true."

Don't think too much, I ordered my black-box brain. *Just listen.* I nodded.

"Charlotte really did send me a message today. She said she'd had her reasons for staging those two Nevermore attacks, but she couldn't tell me what they were yet. Then she told me the rest of her plan."

"Which was?"

Nico bit his lip.

"What was her plan, Nico?"

"She said the Spiders would incapacitate Trumbull. After that, I was supposed to convince you to come with me to your grandfather's office—or take you there by force if necessary."

I clasped my hands together and squeezed so tight I could practically feel the bones cracking. *Don't think. Keep asking questions.* "And then what?"

"I'd take you and Headmaster Stroud hostage. Charlotte would broadcast a live feed from the office all over the world. She'd demand that your father make a trade: our hostages for his—the five remaining 2Bs."

"But my dad isn't holding any 2Bs."

"We believe otherwise."

That "we" made my insides twist. "Anyway," I said, "Charlotte must know my dad's policy. He doesn't negotiate with terrorists. What was she going to threaten him with if he didn't agree to the trade?"

He tapped his chest. "I'm fitted with an explosive. Charlotte can detonate it at any time."

The back of my neck went cold. "She was going to blow us up? And you were just going to go along with it? I thought you said Charlotte didn't mean any harm. I thought—"

I pressed my clasped hands against my forehead like someone praying. *Don't think. Don't think. Don't think.*

"Lee, no!" Nico reached forward to put his hand on my knee. I jerked away from him, scrambling backward across the floor. "She wasn't actually going to use it," he said. "You have to believe me. She told me it was all a bluff. She promised nothing would happen to you. And when it was all over, if everything worked out the way she hoped it would, she'd let me do whatever I wanted, and you and I . . ."

He stopped, his lips still parted.

"What?" I said. "We could ride off into the sunset together? Go live someplace where nobody cares that you never grow older and occasionally need an oil change?"

"I knew it wouldn't be easy. But I hoped. You have to understand, Lee, I believe in Charlotte. I believe in this cause. I believe those five 2Bs are still alive. They weren't destroyed, like your dad says they were. Charlotte intercepted secret government messages about it."

The light from his puck lit up his face from below and

scrawled his shadow across the rutted wall above his head. The way he was talking, the way he looked just then, he reminded me of those terrorist lunatics you sometimes saw on the news. He even had his own built-in suicide bomb. "So you trust everything Charlotte tells you."

"I try to."

"Tell me this, then: If she didn't plan on blowing you up for real, why would she put a *real* explosive inside you?"

"Because if your father's men took me prisoner and discovered I didn't really contain an explosive, Charlotte would lose all her credibility. And because she needed some way of putting me out of commission in case I malfunctioned or went rogue. And because . . ." He pressed his fingers against his shirt, like he could feel the bomb underneath. "Charlotte told me a day might come when I *would* have to give my life for the cause. She was always very clear about that."

"And would you do it?"

"I wouldn't have a choice. She'd be the one with her finger on the button."

"What if you did have a choice, though? The other night you told me all about how you love being alive and want to make every second count. That doesn't sound like a suicide bomber to me. If anything, *I'd* be much more suited to the job."

"No, you wouldn't," he snapped, eyes flashing. "Being willing to die for a cause you believe in isn't the same thing as just wanting to die. *Do* you believe in anything, Lee? Because it doesn't seem like it."

"I don't know," I fired back. "Maybe I don't. And you believe in Charlotte. But would you give your life for her?"

Suddenly restless, he pressed himself to his feet.

"Just think of everything she's done," I said.

He prowled the room just outside the circle of light thrown down by his puck.

"She planted a bomb inside you, Nico. She sent robots to attack me. And still you don't have any doubts?"

"Of course I do!" He stormed forward, into the puck's glow, and his shadow swelled to engulf the ceiling. I edged farther back, until my shoulders jammed against the rock wall behind me. "Why do you think I brought you down here, Lee? When I got the message from Charlotte, it scared the hell out of me, but I was going to do what she said because I trusted her. Then I got to the robotics lab, and I saw what the Spiders had done to Trumbull. He was really hurt. I never thought Charlotte would let something like that happen. And that made me think about the times she made your raven attack you. She really hurt you, too. Why would she do that? She said she'd had her reasons. What does *that* mean?"

I couldn't tell if he actually wanted me to reply. "I don't know," I whispered.

"I kept remembering what you said: What if I was just programmed to trust her? I couldn't take that risk. So I brought you to this mountain instead, where we'd both be safe. At least for a while." He shook his head. "Even while I was running here, I sent her messages. I told her I couldn't go through with the plan. I begged her just to tell me how all this was supposed to end. She didn't answer."

He slumped back to the ground. His shadow shrank again. The cool light from his puck drained the color from his face. At that moment he didn't make me think of a terrorist fanatic at all. If anything, for the first time since I'd laid eyes on him, he reminded me of myself: lost and confused. Melancholy.

"I couldn't do it either," I said.

"Do what?"

I pointed at my watch.

"What is it?"

"Stroud gave it to me after Nevermore's first attack, just in case anything like that ever happened again. It's an electromagnetic-pulse bomb, the same kind that stopped Charlotte seven years ago."

"You're saying you could've killed me with that."

I nodded. "I almost did. When you showed up in the robotics lab, and I figured for sure you must be working with the Spiders—which I was right about after all, by the way—I had my fingers on the buttons. But I couldn't make myself push them."

A grin hovered on his lips—only a small one, but it was enough to make him look like himself again. "So I couldn't take you hostage and you couldn't blow me up. How romantic."

"Wait a second, though," I said. "If Charlotte could detonate your explosive any time she wanted, how did you know she wouldn't do it just now, when you hauled me here?"

"I didn't. I took a gamble. I figured even if I was all wrong about her, even if she'd lied to me about wanting to hurt you, she wouldn't do it before she'd contacted the president and put us on the Supernet. She'd want you back alive. Otherwise, everything she'd done would've been for nothing."

It made my toes curl inside my shoes to think of how close he'd probably come to getting us both blown to smithereens. "Well, thanks a lot for playing dice with our lives like that. And without even asking me first."

Nico crawled closer and put his hand on top of mine. This time I didn't flinch. "So, you believe me?" Gremlin hopped from my shoulder to Nico's chest and made figure eights over his torso. "See? Gremlin trusts me."

I gave him a sideways look.

"I told you, I didn't touch his programming."

I dropped my head back against the rock wall. "I don't know, Nico. You've lied to me so many times already. From the very first moment I met you and you pretended you had no idea who I was. How much did you know about me then? Did you know I'd tried to kill myself?"

"I really didn't. Charlotte gave me a picture of you and told me you were John Fisher's son, and that was it. She thought it would make our interactions more natural if I didn't know too much. And anyway, you pretended when we first met too. 'The president's son? He's around here somewhere.' Remember?"

"That was different."

He nodded. "You're right. I'm sorry. That was different."

"But I guess if you'd wanted to kill me, you'd have done it by now."

His hand tightened over mine. "I could never hurt you, Lee. I'm confused about a lot of things right now, but I'm not confused about that."

"You think *you're* confused. For years I've agonized over being gay. Now it turns out that's the least of my problems. Imagine what my dad's going to say when he finds out I'm falling in love with a male *robot*."

"'Falling in love?'"

I froze, bit my lip, shook my head. "Look, I don't even know what I'm feeling right now." I grabbed his hand and turned it over, revealing his bandaged palm. "You're *not human*, Nico. Your body, it looks like mine, but on the inside it's completely different. Like when you eat food, what happens?"

"I can taste it going down. I have a rudimentary artificial digestive system to process and eliminate it."

"But all that's for show, right? To make you seem more normal. You don't depend on the food you eat for fuel."

"That's true."

"And what about your"—I blushed and stared at the floor

while I stammered out the rest of the sentence—"other parts?"

"They work too. Except I can't father children, obviously."

"And your breathing. And your heartbeat." I remembered lying on our beach the night before with my cheek pressed against his chest, listening to the steady rhythm coming from within. "Simulated."

Nico disengaged his hand from mine and pulled off his blazer. "Let me show you something," he said. "Hold this." He placed his tiepin in my hand. "But don't steal it this time." He loosened his tie, pulled it over his head, and unbuttoned his shirt. Bit by bit, his chest appeared, the skin smooth and tan, the muscles perfectly formed—because someone had made them that way. When he'd undone all but the last couple of buttons, he took my other hand in both of his and drew it toward him. He pressed my palm against his hot skin. Gremlin scurried back and forth between the two of us, racing across my extended arm as if it were a bridge. I closed my eyes. After a second I felt it: the unvarying thump originating from his rib cage.

Then it vanished. Abruptly, as if he'd just pressed the stop button on his own heart—which must've been what he'd done. I started to pull my hand away, but his grip tightened, holding me there. He gave a small nod. My fingers relaxed. My eyes eased shut again.

That was when I noticed the thrumming: a low rumble, something I couldn't hear so much as feel, coming from deep within Nico. Not the kind of rumble the waterfall at Inverness Prep made, though. This was more a purring than a smashing. The thrum had a rhythm of its own—steady, like the heartbeat that had just disappeared, but slower and more subtle.

I opened my eyes and jumped. I'd drifted closer to Nico as I'd listened, and now my face was just a few inches away from his. I didn't shy away, though. Neither did he.

"The way I feel about you," he said. "That's not simulated."

"How can you even say that, knowing those feelings must've been programmed into you?"

"I don't see how that makes them any less real."

"Doesn't it bother you, though?"

He shook his head. "It just makes me want to say thank you to whoever programmed me this way."

I dropped my forehead against his and shook my head from side to side. "I don't know, Nico. Maybe you're right. Stroud pushed my mom and dad together, and in the end it turned into something real. Maybe this isn't all that different. But what if you'd been programmed to have feelings for someone else, like—"

"Lee?" He took the back of my head in his hand. "Once again, you're wasting a perfect opportunity for a kiss."

He tilted my head upward until our mouths connected. I wrapped my arms around him, and he held me tight too. Gremlin scurried off somewhere, maybe to give us some privacy. Nico's shirt still hung open, and as my chest pressed against his, I could feel his thrumming through my whole body. All I could think about was how *alive* he felt.

Next to us on the floor, his puck chimed. "Low battery," it murmured.

We drew apart. Nico glanced at it. "All that flying through the tunnels must've drained it."

"Can't you give it a jump?"

He smirked and shook his head. "We should get back to business anyway. Charlotte knows we're down here. She must've sent machines to look for us. It'll take them a while, but they'll find us eventually."

"So what do we do next?"

"I don't know. I hadn't gotten that far."

"I guess we can't stay here trying to dodge Charlotte forever. But if we leave these caves, she'll pick up your signal again."

"Yeah, that's a problem. She might detonate me right away. Or if she still doesn't want to risk hurting you, at the very least she'll be able to track our every move. We won't be safe for long."

"What do you think she'll do if she catches up to us?"

"I don't know. Terminate me probably. Use a different robot to take you hostage and carry out her plan."

"And this is the leader you trust so completely?"

"She wouldn't have a choice, Lee," he retorted, the edge returning to his voice. "She's fighting for an important cause."

"The cause." I slumped back. "Right."

From behind us came a small clatter. Both of us whirled

around. But it was only Gremlin nosing at some rocks on the floor.

"Okay," I said. "Let's think."

The two of us sat side by side with our cheeks resting on our fists. I went through the options in my head. If I left the cave on my own, Charlotte wouldn't be able to track my movements or blow up Nico. Then I could get help. But who could I tell without risking Nico's safety? Not Dad. Not Stroud. Not one of my Armed Babysitters. That left only one person.

"Dr. Singh," I said. "Do you have any idea if she's working with Charlotte?"

"Not that I know of. Why?"

"The day you first got here, when you were doing your handstand and it looked like the wind might knock you over, she grabbed my wrist and said, 'Just let him fall.'"

"Seriously?"

"Maybe she said it because she's in on Charlotte's plot. Maybe she was afraid you'd hurt me. Maybe she was having second thoughts."

"Maybe." His eyebrows knitted, he scooped up Gremlin and stroked his orange fur.

"Today I tried asking her about it. She wouldn't say a word, but I could tell she was holding something back and it was eating her up inside. I'll bet if she knows you and I are working together now, trying to resolve the situation peacefully, she'll want to help."

He screwed up his mouth doubtfully.

"It's just a feeling I have, Nico. I think we can trust her."

"The 'just let him fall' comment notwithstanding." He shook his head and set Gremlin on my shoulder. "Still, I suppose it's our best option."

"But that still leaves you. You can't carry me around and hope Charlotte doesn't blow us both up forever."

"I know."

"You have to stay here, Nico."

He shot to his feet and paced the room some more. "No way. You're not going out there alone."

"I'll be careful," I said, rising too. "I'll wear a disguise, keep away from people. I already know how to sneak into Inverness. No one will know I'm back."

"It won't be that simple. The son of the president was just abducted, remember? They'll have the whole place on red alert. Secret Service everywhere. And Charlotte will be looking for you too. I don't know how many robots she can control at once, but it might be a lot. I can't just stay down here while you're up there risking your life." He turned to me, his eyes incandescent in the puck's low light. "Look, now that I'm off the network, there might be a way to get this bomb out of me once and for all. But I'll need your help."

25

◇◇◇◇◇◇

If I'd stopped right then to think about how fast everything had changed between Nico and me, my brain probably would've spun around inside my skull like a gyroscope. But I didn't. Instead, I said, "Just tell me what to do. Where's the bomb located?"

He tapped his sternum. "Right here. Embedded next to my central power supply."

"What about your transmitter? Can we disable that, too, so Charlotte won't be able to track you when you leave here?"

He shook his head. "It's too tightly integrated into my other systems."

I eyed his muscly bare chest, which was now making me sweat in a whole new way. "Is this going to be dangerous?"

"A little, I think."

"How can a bomb be a little dangerous? Either it blows up or it doesn't."

Again he flashed a low-wattage version of the Nico Medina grin. "Good point."

I loosened my tie and yanked at my collar. "Are we going to need tools?"

He rummaged in his trouser pocket. "I have a pocketknife. That should be all we need." At some silent command from him, his puck bobbed up from its resting place, flipped over, and hovered above our heads. Nico spread himself out on the floor. His puck's light blazed down on him like a lamp in an operating room. He unbuttoned his shirt the rest of the way. His fingers probed the smooth, firm skin of his torso.

"How do we get in there?" I knelt down next to him. "You don't have an access panel or something, do you?"

"I wish." He unfolded the knife. Prickles raced down my spine. "Can you grab my blazer and prop it under my head?" he asked.

I folded the blazer into a bundle while he traced his blade down the center of his chest, plotting its course. *What a waste,* I thought. *That perfect body.* Then I instantly felt like a jerk for thinking such a shallow thought.

"Okay," he said. "Here we go." The tip of his knife pressed against a point just below his collarbone, dimpling the skin. He stopped. "I just wish you didn't have to see this."

I attempted a nonchalant shrug. "I'm a robotics nerd, remember? I love this stuff. A little blood's no big deal." (A total lie. My head already felt like it was filled with helium and tied to my body by a string, and his blade hadn't even penetrated his flesh yet.)

"I didn't mean it that way. I wish you didn't have to see *me*. On the inside. What I really look like."

"Nico, I'm willing to bet you don't look nearly as gross on the inside as I do."

Another joke of mine he failed to laugh at. "But you look human."

My eyes dropped away from his. I nodded.

His puck chimed again. "Very low battery."

"No more stalling," Nico said. "We probably have only a few minutes of light left."

The thought of plunging back into that suffocating darkness only intensified the dizzy, floaty feeling in my head. Where Nico had pressed the tip of his knife against his flesh a moment ago, a single dark red bead of blood had welled up. He returned his blade to that spot. On my shoulder, Gremlin released a nervous whine. I found Nico's free hand with mine and squeezed.

As he pressed, the sphere of blood swelled and swelled until it collapsed into a trickle that raced across his chest. He drew the blade along the narrow groove that ran down the center of his torso.

"Does it hurt?" I asked. "Can you feel pain?"

He grunted, which pretty much answered my question. I squeezed his hand again. I thought of Stroud telling his thighbone-ectomy story and then ranting that kids today had it easy by comparison. The next time I saw him, I'd have to ask him if he'd ever had to perform open-heart surgery on himself.

The incision left a smooth seam behind it, with tendrils of blood spilling out and hurrying down on either side. I had to blink my eyes hard and take deep, slow breaths to keep from retching. I didn't look away, though.

He finished the incision a few inches above his navel. Then he made two horizontal cuts, one at the top, one at the bottom, forming a capital letter *I*. He put down the knife and disengaged his hand from mine. The tips of his fingers felt along the central seam. Then they dug into the flesh. His face contorted. A soft groan seeped through his closed lips.

"It'll be over soon," I said. The words felt silly and stilted and inadequate coming out of my mouth. As someone with limited interpersonal skills, I didn't excel at this kind of talk.

Grimacing, Nico peeled back the flaps of flesh, their undersides pink and glistening—the "living" part of him, less than a quarter of an inch thick—revealing his artificial pectoral and abdominal muscles. I bent forward, my aversion to blood already giving way to my fascination with anything robotic. Again his insides reminded me of Nevermore. His muscles and hers were made of the same rubbery material. Beneath the translucent, synthetic meat of his chest, I could make out the shadow of his metal rib cage, and beneath that, a fist-size red light throbbed— in rhythm, I realized, with that thrum I'd felt earlier.

Nico gazed at his vivisected torso, his mouth still scrunched shut. With a hiss, his two pectoral muscles split away from each other. His metal rib cage hinged open like a double door. A wave of heat blew outward, searing my face. A dense nest of circuitry occupied his central cavity, neatly arranged around the pulsing red light. The thrumming I'd only been able to feel with my hand a few minutes ago had now become audible.

I pointed at the red light. "Your power supply—is it nuclear?"

He nodded.

"Where's the explosive?"

He indicated a black device about the size of a walnut. It had a small dial on it, like an old-fashioned combination padlock, and from it radiated a profusion of black wires that snaked around his power supply and into his body.

"The explosive itself isn't all that powerful," Nico said, "but when it's triggered, it causes my reactor core to detonate."

"Nico, are you telling me you're a nuclear bomb?"

One corner of his mouth curled up. "Only a small one." He picked up the knife again. "The trick is to disengage the explosive by cutting the wires in the right order."

"Where do I come in?"

"At the end. You'll see."

Nico's hands hovered above his chest. They didn't shake—literal nerves of steel were one perk of being a robot, I supposed—but the grimace hadn't left his face. He drew out the wires and examined them one by one. It was strange: there he lay with his robotic innards exposed and impossible to ignore, but at the same time, seeing him afraid and uncertain made him seem more human than ever. I kept my hand on his shoulder and stayed as still as I could and hoped he couldn't hear the knocking of my heart.

He settled on a wire. He pulled it taut, put his blade to it, and cut.

We both exhaled.

"Talk to me, Lee."

"What about?"

"Anything."

But the only things I could think of to say sounded hollow and stupid. *He just wants to hear the sound of your voice*, I told myself. *String words together. It doesn't matter which ones.* "This has been a weird day."

"You're telling me."

"You scared the hell out of me earlier. When you suddenly turned evil and hauled me all the way up to the mountain? And then you jumped into that chasm without any warning? After I told you about my thing with heights, too."

"I know. Sorry about that." Another wire went snap.

"But I realized something while I was plummeting through the air."

"Funny," Nico said. "That's when I do some of my best thinking too." *Snap.*

"Two things, actually. First, I realized I didn't want to die. Remember how I told you I'd always imagined jumping from a high place would make me feel like I was finally free? Well, it didn't feel that way at all. The whole time, all I could think about was how little the idea of smashing on those rocks appealed to me. I wanted to live. And you know why?"

Nico had stopped cutting wires. The light in the center of his chest threw a pulsing red glow over his face. He shook his head.

"It had to do with the second thing I realized. Before you jumped, you whispered in my ear, 'Trust me.' And I realized while we were falling into the chasm that I did. Even though I had no good reason to at that point, even though all the evidence suggested you were a crazy terrorist bent on killing me. That was all you had to say. You had me in your arms, and I knew I'd be okay. And then after we landed and you started running through those tunnels in the dark, I was still scared— freaking out, actually—and confused, but deep down I knew you hadn't turned on me, not really. And I didn't want to die, because that would mean I couldn't be with you anymore."

"I know how you feel." Nico drew out another wire and pressed his blade against it. "I don't want to die either." He cut.

We didn't blow up.

"I think being alive is the best thing ever," he said. "I love reading Shakespeare." *Snap.* "I love eating food." *Snap.*

"No kidding. You're lucky you're a robot, because otherwise you'd weigh about three hundred pounds by now."

"And I love being with you too, Lee. I don't want it to stop, any of it. Sometimes I wonder if Charlotte made a mistake when she created me. Like you said before, I don't exactly have the personality of a suicide bomber." He sifted his fingers through the nest of wires in his chest. "But maybe she had her reasons."

Another chime came from his puck. "You have ninety seconds of battery life left."

"Damn," Nico said. "Too much talking. But I think we're almost done." One last wire went *snap*. "This is where you come in, Lee. I'm going to shut myself down now."

My heart lurched into my throat. "What?"

"Only for a minute. When I'm out, you have to turn this dial two clicks to the right, five to the left, and three to the right. You got that?"

"Two right, five left, three right."

"Then you press this." He indicated a large translucent button located in the center of his pulsing red heart. "That'll reactivate me. But you have to move fast, before the light runs out. And don't remove the bomb from my chest, okay?"

"Okay."

"Say it one more time."

"Two right, five left, three right." Then I blurted, "I love you."

"I love you too. 'More than words can wield the matter.'" Another grin. Full wattage this time. "That's Shakespeare, by the way."

"I figured."

He settled back, his messy curls spreading out on his make-shift pillow. "Now to sleep. 'Perchance to dream.'"

His eyes closed. The grin faded from his face. The red light in his chest died away, and the thrumming cycled down little by little, leaving only silence. No more mellifluous purr. No rumble of destruction, like at school, either. Just nothing. *Focus*, I ordered my brain. *Pretend you're working on one of your Creatures.* I bent forward, and Nico's puck bobbed closer. I grabbed the dial and then jerked my hand away again: Nico had forgotten to mention his insides were blisteringly hot. I yanked the sleeve of my shirt down over my fingers and took hold of the dial again. I turned it two clicks to the right.

A sound sliced through the quiet: a skittering of rocks. It seemed to come from the corridor behind me, but in that darkness, I couldn't see a thing. On my shoulder, Gremlin whined again. The light on Nico's puck had started to dim. My hand was shaking now, my breath coming in shallow pants. I went slow, counting five clicks to the left one by one.

More noises behind me. I spun around. This time, something penetrated the dense blackness of the corridor: a blue glow. The slender legs of a Spider stepped into view. Its luminous eye peered into the room and fastened on me.

26

I whirled back to Nico, heart galloping. My hand trembled harder than ever. From behind me came a quick, light tap-ping sound. Gremlin raced down my chest to hide in my blazer pocket. I counted three clicks to the right. The device released a small beep. I reached for the button on Nico's power supply.

And at the same time, I couldn't help myself—I stole a glance over my shoulder. The Spider charged toward me. Its blue eye seemed to float in the midst of a whirlwind of flashing silver legs. One of those legs snapped forward. It connected with my stomach. I went flying.

I landed in a heap on the far side of the room. Lying there on my side, my body curled up like a fist, I choked for air. At least the Spider hadn't killed me, which it could have, easily. Probably it had orders to take me alive. I scrambled to my feet. The robot watched me, its eye tilted at a curious angle. Nico lay just behind, still unconscious, the button in his chest unpushed.

Then he vanished. Everything vanished, except for the Spider's blue eye. In the sudden darkness, the puck clattered to the floor, its battery finally dead. The next second, an inhuman scream knifed through my ears. I doubled over, my hands clamped to my skull, my eyes squeezed shut, the noise shoving out every other thought.

Then it disappeared again, leaving only echoes chasing each other down the corridors. What had just happened? For a second I imagined the Spider in front of me had finally given up its polite murmuring to reveal its true, furious voice. Then I realized: unable to connect to the Supernet and running on autopilot, the robot had sent out a message the only way it could. It had let its fellow Spiders know it had found me.

The machine flew at me again. I stumbled back, tripped over a rock, and landed hard. On my back, I shimmied away, the heels of my dress shoes scraping against the dirt floor. My arm flailed behind me, searching for a weapon. My fingers found something—one of the lead pipes littering the floor—and closed around it. I swung with all my strength at the one thing I could see: the Spider's eye.

The pipe crunched into metal and shattered glass. The Spider twisted to the side, its legs, glinting in the dim glow of its damaged eye, staggering. I clambered across the floor, through the blackness, toward Nico—or at least toward where I hoped he was. My hands knocked against rocks and pipes, searching for him. Then I felt something soft and warm wrapped in cloth: his arm. My fingers kept going, feeling their way to his torso, slipping over the hot, slimy inner surface of his flesh, hurrying past the rubbery artificial muscle, until they reached the nest of wires and circuitry inside his central cavity. The hot metal burned, but this time I didn't bother to protect my fingers. The sound of groaning steel at my back, the dim flashes of blue, told me the Spider had regrouped. I slammed my palm down on the button.

Nothing happened. His heart—that was how I thought of it, even though the correlation wasn't strictly accurate—stayed silent and dark.

I shook my head and banged my hand down a few more times and said something like "no" or "Nico" or "please." The Spider's foreleg bashed into my back, harder this time. Charlotte might have ordered her minions to bring me back alive, but she clearly hadn't said anything about uninjured. I skidded across the floor. The robot lurched after me. It scooped me up and flung me against the jagged rock. The hot sting of impact shot through my body. My back slid down the wall, my blazer bunching up around my shoulders, my legs splaying out in front of me, my glasses sagging halfway down my face. The Spider locked its dented eye on me again. It clicked an attachment into place. Without my glasses, I couldn't make out what it was exactly, but I heard the metallic reverberation of a blade. The robot's slender legs flurried toward me. Its eye bore down on me, as unstoppable as a locomotive. Everything else was an empty, cold black.

The Spider leaped into the air and landed on top of me, three of its legs stabbing into the wall, caging me there. A fourth leg, the one with the blade, slashed upward and paused high above me. I closed my eyes and pictured the weapon slicing my skull. Maybe the Spider had orders to kill me after all.

Then: *BOOM*. My eyes blinked open in time to watch the Spider smash and crumple against the wall to my left. Its blue light fizzled and died, replaced by a red glow, flickering but growing stronger. I fumbled my glasses back onto my face. Nico stood a few feet away from me, the light in his chest still settling back into its slow, steady pulsation. He turned to me, his face a luminous crimson. "Are you okay?"

With the back of my hand I swiped away the blood pouring from my nose. "Perfect. You?"

Nico's cut-open flesh hung down on either side of his torso. Severed wires still dangled from his excavated chest. "Ditto."

"I thought you were—"

"I know. But I wasn't."

One of the Spider's legs still twitched, its tip scraping against the packed dirt. Nico grabbed his lifeless puck while I glanced into my blazer pocket to check on Gremlin. By the light from Nico's chest, I could just make out my little Creature blinking his big eyes at me.

From the passage came a skittering sound and a dim flash of blue. "'By the pricking of my thumbs,'" Nico muttered, "'something wicked this way comes.'"

Two more Spiders appeared. Their spotlight eyes shone on their fallen comrade, then on us.

Nico scooped me up. "Sorry. More careening through tunnels at breakneck speed." He raced through an opening at the opposite end of the room and down a corridor. Without its covering of muscle and skin, his pulsing heart poured out an ovenlike heat that baked through my blazer and shirt. The red light shone in front of us like a headlight, splashing crimson over the furrowed walls, while behind, the two blue lights hurtled after us, accompanied by the double-time ticking of the robots' scurrying feet. One of the Spiders let out another eardrum-shattering scream.

When the cry had stopped, I uncovered my ears and said, "Do you know where you're going?"

"Not exactly. But I'm betting the main entrance will be swarming, either with Spiders or with military. I've been building a map in my head, and I have a rough idea where we are. I'm going to find us another way out."

"Do you know if there *is* one?"

"I'm hoping."

I peeked behind us again. "There are more of them."

"How many?"

"Five, I think."

They seemed to topple over each other, their flashing legs overlapping as they charged after us.

"Here's what I want you to do," Nico said. "When I give the

word, take out the explosive in my chest. It's programmed to explode five seconds after it's removed, so you have to be fast. Throw it over my shoulder at the robots. Got it?"

"I think so." Hearing the uncertainty in my voice, I corrected myself. "Yes."

"Get ready." Nico shot a quick glance over his shoulder. He sped up, putting more distance between us and the Spiders. The thrumming of his heart intensified. His eyes, focused on the passage ahead, narrowed. "Now."

I plunged my fingers into the burning nest of wires. Gasping, eyes tearing, I grabbed the explosive. It released with a click, its jumble of severed wires coming along with it. I lobbed it at the tangled mob of Spiders. It bounced off one of them with a small *tink*. A split second later the robots disappeared as Nico rounded a corner. He put on even more speed.

A riot of light and noise filled the corridor. A gust of sweltering wind buffeted us forward. I squinted back over Nico's shoulder. Flames wrapped around the corner and chased us down the passage but died before reaching us. A single Spider leg clanged against the wall and clattered to the floor. Nico slowed to a stop. He turned and watched too.

"Do you think we stopped them?" My voice sounded like it belonged to someone else speaking underwater a hundred yards away.

"Shh," Nico said.

A noise that seemed miles distant penetrated the stillness:

the creak and whine of metal, followed by the unmistakable skitter of Spider legs.

"We'd better keep going." Nico's rib cage hissed shut, but the red glow from his power supply continued to filter past his metal ribs and through his translucent synthetic muscle. He started running again. Behind us, two Spiders appeared around the corner, their long legs mangled but still functional. They listed from side to side and knocked into each other like a couple of drunks.

But then they started gaining speed, despite their teetering gait. If anything, the headlong crookedness of their stride and the clanking of their broken limbs made them even more terrifying.

"How many now?" Nico said.

"Only two. But they're gaining on us."

He glanced around, stopped again, set me on my feet.

"What are you—"

He pushed me into a narrow side tunnel I hadn't noticed before—so narrow I could only fit in sideways. "Hurry," he said. "I don't think they can follow us through here."

I edged along as fast as I could, with Nico right behind me. "How far does it go?"

He peered past me. "Another fifty feet or so. Then it opens into a larger chamber."

The walls seemed ready to slam in on us. My sweat had probably soaked clear through my blazer, despite the coldness of the passage. I kept going, though. Meanwhile, the Spiders had reached the tunnel entrance. The cold light from their eyes flashed down the narrow space. I craned my neck to watch them as I went. One of them folded itself sideways, the same way it might have in the hallways at school to make room for a human to pass. It sidled into the passage.

"Oops," Nico said. "Guess I was wrong."

I sidestepped down the corridor even faster, keeping my eyes focused ahead now, watching the darting blue and red lights play over the walls. The blue lights seemed to grow brighter little by little, but at least I could see the end of the tunnel now. Fifteen feet away. Ten. Five.

I burst out from the passage—only to find myself whirling my arms and fighting for balance at the edge of another abyss. Nico grabbed my damp blazer and dragged me back. We'd stepped onto a tiny ledge next to a chasm. By the light from Nico's chest, I could just make out another, larger shelf on the chasm's far side, about twenty feet distant. The vestiges of a wooden bridge still clung to the rock across from us, but it didn't do us much good now. The ledge petered out on either side of us: the only way onward was across.

"What do we do now?" I panted.

A single silver leg shot out from the narrow corridor and wrapped itself around Nico's ankle. Still holding me by the neck of my blazer with one hand, he grabbed the seat of my pants with the other and picked me up. "This."

He hurled me into the air.

For the space of one long heartbeat, the chasm gaped beneath me, a bottomless blackness. Then I plowed into the opposite ledge chin first and skidded across the floor. A track of fire seemed to blaze down the front side of my body. Ignoring the pain, I scrambled to my hands and knees.

Back on the other side of the chasm, Nico had just slammed to the ground, toppled by the Spider holding his ankle. The machine folded itself out of the corridor like a contortionist stepping out of a box. Nico twisted his leg free of its grip and jumped to his feet. The two of them launched at each other. There were flashes of red and blue, like police lights. The clang of metal on metal. The rattle of small stones falling into the abyss.

Then the incomprehensible jumble of struggling limbs resolved itself: Nico had the Spider's small body locked in a bear hug. The robot staggered around the narrow ledge, lifting Nico off his feet, but he didn't let go. He raised one fist and punched clear through the robot's metal housing. He yanked his hand out again, holding a bouquet of sparking wires. The machine's eye flickered and went black. Its legs sagged sideways. Nico dropped to the ground. I clutched the front of my shirt in my fist and started breathing again.

Meanwhile, the second Spider slid out from the passage.

"Watch out!" I yelled. "The other one!"

The thing charged forward, ramming its dead friend, along with Nico, toward the edge of the chasm. I stretched out my arms pointlessly.

"No!"

Nico stumbled and staggered toward the drop-off, caught in the tangle of silver legs. The Spider gave its comrade one more push. The wrecked machine toppled, carrying Nico along with it. He struggled to grab on to something, but the dead Spider's limbs kept getting in the way.

Until his fingers found one of the ruined bridge's support beams. The Spider kept falling, but Nico hung there, legs swinging. The rotted wood groaned and sagged. My heart hammered. I didn't think I'd heard the crash of the Spider hitting the bottom. Did this chasm even *have* a bottom?

The surviving Spider peered over the side. Its blue spotlight found Nico. Adrenaline pulsed through my body. Enough watching. I had to do something. I reached into my blazer and pulled out Gremlin—my little Disney mascot whose only skills were looking cute and fetching my socks. What good could he do? His huge eyes blinked at me.

"Gremlin, bring me that blue light."

I swiped my thumb over the Creature's fur for luck and lobbed him across the chasm. In the darkness, I couldn't tell where he'd landed, or even if he'd made it all the way over. Meanwhile, the Spider had just bent over the edge and stretched down one of its legs. It stamped on the wooden beam, which cracked and drooped some more. Nico's hand slipped a few inches. I pressed my fist against my chest again, like that would keep my heart from bursting out and landing on the dirt in front of me.

A small shadow passed over the Spider's eye, dimming its light. The robot paused, its leg still outstretched, and tossed from side to side. Gremlin went flying, vanishing into the darkness again. He'd distracted the Spider for only a second. But that gave Nico the opening he needed. With his free hand, he grabbed the robot's extended leg. He pulled. The machine flew over the edge, legs waving. Its blue light shrank and shrank and finally disappeared. This time I heard it: a crash echoed up from the chasm floor, which did exist after all.

27

◇◇◇◇◇◇

Nico grabbed another of the broken beams projecting from the cliff face, this one a little higher, and used it to hoist himself back onto the far ledge. He leaped across the chasm and straight into my arms. I dug my fingers into his back, not even minding the blood and gore still clinging to him or the heat of his chest or the abrasions running down the front of my torso.

I stepped back to look at him. He'd collected more injuries. Now he had a slash on his left forearm and another on his neck below his ear, where a flap of skin had fallen away, exposing the thick synthetic tendons of his neck. He could never pass for human now.

"I think you forgot something."

He opened his hand. Gremlin made an inquisitive noise, spotted me, and sprang onto my shoulder. "Good work, buddy." I ruffled his fur.

Over Nico's shoulder, on the opposite side of the chasm,

more flashes of blue lit up the narrow corridor. Nico turned, following my eyes. "We should go," he said, all business again. Another corridor—wider, fortunately—led away from the chasm on this side. He hustled me into it, pulled down an iron portcullis behind us, and secured it with a latch. "I have a feeling that'll only slow them down." He picked me up and sped off.

He continued making turns without hesitation, even though, as I knew now, he was just feeling his way along. As for me, I was pretty sure the passage had started slanting upward, but beyond that, I didn't have a clue. I trusted Nico, though. I barely felt surprised when we rounded a corner and a dim light appeared far ahead.

"Is that—?"

He nodded. "An exit. We're about three miles away from the main entrance now, on the western side of the mountain." He set me down. "We should stop here. If I go any closer, I'll be networked again, and before that happens, we need to talk about what we're going to do."

"All right. Let's talk." I turned to face him. "I still say you should stay here. It's true you don't have the bomb in you anymore, but Charlotte can still track your every move. She'll send more robots after you for sure. And couldn't she hack into your motor-control system and hijack you the same way she did Nevermore and those Spiders?"

Nico twisted his mouth but didn't answer.

"Tell the truth."

"I felt her trying to get into my brain when I ran off with you earlier. I managed to hold her off long enough to reach the cavern."

"So if you leave these tunnels again, how long will you be able to keep her out of your head?"

His eyes didn't waver. "My best estimate? Sixty-three minutes."

"But that's nothing."

"I'm not staying here, Lee. With those Spiders still running around, I won't be much safer down in these tunnels anyway."

"Well, at least we should split up, so she can't track both of us."

He sank his fingers into his curls and paced around in a small circle. "Okay. I guess you're right. But I don't like it."

"I'll leave the mine first. Go back to Inverness. Try to find Dr. Singh."

"Remember what I said. That place'll be a madhouse." He pulled a pen out of his pocket, grabbed my wrist, and wrote something on the back of my hand. "When you have news, find a puck and send a message addressed to this puck handle. It'll go straight to me. Charlotte won't see it."

I couldn't make out what he'd written in the darkness. "What are you going to do? Just run for your life and stay in the general vicinity of Inverness and wait for me to message you?"

"I guess. I'll try contacting Charlotte again too. See if she'll answer this time. Maybe I can still talk her out of whatever she has planned."

I gripped his arm with one hand and brushed his tangled hair out of his face with the other. "I know this isn't easy for you, Nico. Turning against her like this."

His eyes dropped to the rock-strewn floor. He nodded, his face pulsing red. "She's not evil, Lee. Maybe she's lost her way, but she's not evil." He kicked a stone. It rattled across the dirt. "When I was at the lab, I mostly just had contact with that human scientist who worked for her. He was a tall, white-haired guy, not very friendly, never even told me his name. Charlotte sent me messages, though—long, beautiful ones. She'd give me advice, and explain how important our struggle for 2B rights was, and paint these pictures of what the future might hold for me, and for her, and for the world. She really believed things would get better for 2Bs, and for humans, too."

He smiled at the memory. It struck me how different Nico's version of Charlotte was from mine. When I thought of Charlotte, I imagined the one from the lab footage: lost, naive, full of barely contained anger. To Nico she was a wise sage and revolutionary hero—a sort of electronic Joan of Arc. Had she really changed that much in seven years? Or had she just gotten better at hiding the rage inside of her?

"She told me this was the start of a new age," Nico said. "Just like Bex was saying the other day, the line between human and machine—between you and me—it's disappearing. Some people don't understand that. They can't get beyond us versus them. But it's happening anyway. Machines will become more and more like humans. Humans will realize they're not so different from machines."

"That second part's going to be tough," I said. "We like to think we're special, Nico. Take the whole concept of free will. Today Dr. Singh told me free will doesn't really exist, for you *or* for us. 'A necessary illusion,' she called it."

I glanced up to check his reaction. He shrugged. "That sounds about right."

"But weren't you the one who said we *always* have a choice?"

He bobbed his head from side to side. "It's just one of those things you sort of have to believe even though you know it's not really true."

"Isn't that the definition of insanity? Believing in things you know aren't true?"

"Probably," he said, grinning.

"Anyway, I don't see human beings embracing that notion any time soon. I mean, the idea's terrifying, isn't it? If we can't really make choices—if we're all just following programs— what's the point of anything? Why not just . . ." I finished the sentence in my head instead of out loud: *leap.*

He grabbed my hand. "Because if you did, it would break my heart."

I started to smile, but then I shook my head. I didn't want to lose the thread of my argument. "But doesn't it bother *you*?

To think we have no control? To think we're just clockwork?"

"Why 'just,' Lee? I think I'm pretty amazing. I think you're pretty amazing too. Look at it another way. If you believe in free will, it also means you believe we're all fundamentally separate and alone. Is it really so terrifying to think we're not, after all? Maybe *that's* the illusion we need to let go of. We're not alone, Lee. We all interlock." He threaded his fingers through mine. "Like clockwork."

Gremlin had crept out of my blazer pocket onto my shoulder. He tugged on my ear, as if to reinforce what Nico had just said. But that only made me think of Mom, and how much I'd loved her, and how when she'd died it felt like a part of me had died too. Compared to that, being separate and alone didn't sound so bad. I didn't want to be a downer, though, so I didn't say any of that out loud either.

"Eventually, your species and mine are going to converge," Nico said. "I don't know what it'll look like exactly, but it'll be beautiful. Charlotte used to say, 'Even though we have to fight now, a day will come when all this fighting will seem meaningless.'"

"Just as long as we don't all blow ourselves up first."

He smiled. "I don't think that's going to happen."

I put my hand to his chest, feeling the thrum underneath my scraped-up palm and burned fingers. "How do you do that, Nico? Be so hopeful all the time?"

"I guess that's part of my programming too."

I studied his beautiful face, with its frame of messy curls, and its bright eyes, and its grin that lingered even after he'd stopped grinning. And below that, his chest of synthetic muscle, with the red light of his heart pulsing through, silhouetting his metal ribs—that was beautiful also. I could almost imagine the convergence of human and machine had already happened, and it was standing right in front of me. Those words from *Hamlet* sprang into my head again: *how like an angel, how like a god.*

"Promise me something?" he said.

"What?"

"You'll never jump off a bridge again. You'll never try to leave this world."

"I promise," I answered. "I'll never try to leave this world."

As long as you're in it, I added in my head.

28

We kissed in the tunnel one more time. The kiss had a feeling of finality I didn't like. Nico squeezed my shoulders and gave me a last warning: "Be careful stepping outside. I don't think anyone will have found this entrance, but I can't be sure. I'll wait here for thirty minutes and then come after you."

"Wait an hour. It'll take me at least that long to get back to Inverness, and you can run there in fifteen minutes."

"Okay."

I hurried down the passage at a jog, because moving fast made it easier to leave him. The tunnel filled with larger and larger rocks, probably the result of a cave-in or landslide. The last dozen feet or so I had to clamber over boulders on my hands and knees. The opening to the outside looked much smaller up close than it had from far away. I had to move aside a few more rocks to make room. I glanced back at the speck of red light at the end of the tunnel and then wedged myself through the opening headfirst.

I came out at the bottom of a small gorge filled with fallen tree trunks. The outside light had looked so bright a few minutes ago, from inside the pitch-black tunnel, but now I could see it was twilight, and the clouds had turned purple, like bruised flesh—like my own banged-up body. I scanned the area but saw no telltale gleams of blue light. I listened but heard only the sighing of trees in the wind. I glanced at my wrist. I hadn't thought to check my watch even once during my time underground, probably because I'd never worn one before. It was already seven o'clock. Darkness would make my hike back to school harder—and scarier—but at least it would give me some cover. To one side of the watch, the puck handle Nico had written on the back of my hand was now readable: "Th1neEverm0re." One of Nico's sweet Shakespearisms, but the phrase also rang a faint bell. I was pretty sure it came from *Hamlet*, and I even had a vague memory of Miss Remnant talking about it in class, but I couldn't remember how the rest of the line went.

I scrabbled up the side of the gorge and found myself surrounded by tall pine trees. At first I couldn't see a single landmark I recognized—not the lake, not the school—and no sign of a trail. Then I took a few steps and spotted the blue tip of the mountain nosing over the pines behind me. Nico had told me if I kept that peak at my back I'd eventually reach the highway. I headed into the forest—moving fast, so I could make the most of the last dregs of daylight, and so I could put as much distance as possible between me and the mine. In my school dress shoes,

I slipped and skated over the damp pine needles carpeting the ground. My skull still echoed with explosions and collisions and Spider screams. I hadn't gone far when I felt a few drops on my cheek, once again proving that corollary of Murphy's Law that governed the weather around Inverness Prep.

Then my luck changed. Up ahead, I spotted a small log cabin—some kind of ranger station, I guessed. To one side of the front door, a dark green rain slicker hung from a peg. I grabbed it. From there I found a trail that continued through the forest.

Night had fallen now. It felt strange not having my puck tagging along after me—no light to help me see, no directions to help me get to school. At least I still had Gremlin to keep me company. The rain pattered over the pine needles. A low mist seemed to boil up from the ground and cling to the tree trunks. Every few minutes I'd hear the snap of a branch or the rustle of undergrowth and freeze, my eyes darting from shadow to shadow, searching for the noise's source. But I never found a Spider staring back at me.

Thinking about Nico kept me going. I tried not to think too much—about how a love story featuring a human and a 2B could possibly have a happy ending, for example—but instead just focused on him. The joyful, embarrassing roar of his laughter. That accent of his, the way it made even Shakespeare sound sexy. His ability to find pleasure in everything—even being with me. Thinking of him made me feel like I had a purpose.

I'd never felt that before. As I hiked down the trail, I wasn't just putting one foot in front of the other. Something was pulling me forward. I had to keep going, because I had to save Nico. It was as simple as that.

I'd walked for forty-five minutes or so when I stumbled onto the highway and then had to charge right back into the forest again when a pack of police cars came screaming past, red and blue lights flashing, sirens dopplering. I had no doubt it had something to do with me. I followed the highway but kept to the trees from then on. Another throng of vehicles—these ones military, mostly Humvees painted black—sped past a while later, and I even heard a helicopter thunder by overhead. By eight o'clock, the yellow light of a McDonald's sign shone in the distance. I'd reached the huddle of roadside fast-food restaurants where Inverness students, desperate for a break from the dining hall, sometimes walked on weekends. It felt good to be back in civilization. I figured if Charlotte did have more Spiders out looking for me, they'd avoid places with lots of humans around. But I couldn't slow down. Nico had probably just left the cave, which meant we had only an hour before Charlotte would succeed in hacking his motor-control system. I jogged across the highway, threaded my way between two fast-food places, and plunged into the forest on that side.

I could hear the commotion at school long before I could see it: people shouting, car doors slamming, the clank of heavy equipment. Above everything else, the thudding of the helicopter, which drowned out even the roar of the waterfall. I didn't have to circle around to the front to know I'd stand no chance of making it onto the grounds unnoticed that way. Fortunately, I already had something else in mind. A tall stone wall enclosed the property, but there was a disused, out-of-the-way door built into one of the side walls. Nico had given me his pocketknife. If I could find the door, maybe I could pick the lock with that. I'd just have to hope no one had thought of posting a guard there.

I made it to the wall and skirted the outside until I reached the door. It had the same kind of old-fashioned lock as the iron gates on the sides of the canal, but Nico's pocketknife didn't work nearly as well as my robotics tools for this kind of job. Almost twelve minutes passed before I heard the click of the lock releasing. The door whined open on its unoiled, unused hinges. I peeked through, heart jackhammering. Nobody there. I pulled the hood of my slicker down low over my face and crept inside.

From the cluster of trees where I stood, the ground sloped downward toward the canal, which meant I had a good view of the campus. What I saw froze me in my waterlogged dress shoes. I'd expected plenty of activity after my disappearance, but this looked more like a full-scale siege. Roving spotlights slithered over the stone walls of the school, and more than a dozen Humvees and police cars had driven onto the lawn on both sides of the river and parked with their noses facing the building, their headlights on, and their doors open. Soldiers and police officers crouched behind the doors, guns and rifles in their hands, ready to open fire. Larger artillery perched on top of a few Humvees too. Did they think I was still in the building? Wouldn't one of the exterior security cameras have captured Nico running away from school with me in his arms? Even if the police and military did believe my kidnapper hadn't escaped, why would they need that much firepower?

Well behind the barricade of vehicles, on the near side of the canal close to the front gate, a mob of students, teachers, and staff—the whole school, by the looks of it—shivered in the drizzle. They must have been evacuated from the building. Maybe Dr. Singh was among them. I edged closer, wiped the moisture off my glasses with my sleeve, and squinted. Something seemed off about the group of people in front of me. I couldn't put my finger on it at first, but then I realized: no pucks hovered over their heads. True, pucks didn't do well in heavy rain or wind—people usually carried them in their pockets when the weather got too blustery—but a light shower like this shouldn't have caused a problem. No one clutched a puck to an ear to tell a friend what was happening. No one watched the news on a puck's small screen. They all just stood there, murmuring in small groups and looking unsure about what to do with themselves.

I still hadn't caught a glimpse of Dr. Singh. In her wheelchair, she'd be hard to spot. A few police officers stood nearby, apparently to watch over the civilians, but their attention, like everyone else's, was on the school. The helicopter had just come around for another pass. As it circled Inverness Prep's spires, people stared at it with tired eyes, like they'd watched the same thing for hours. I slipped out of the trees and into the crowd.

From within the shelter of my green vinyl hood, I glanced from side to side, doing my best to scan the throng without letting anyone see my face. I passed Mrs. Case, Stroud's secretary, her ordinarily neat gray hair unraveling from its bun, bending close to Miss Remnant, who kneaded her hands together like she'd just pumped sanitizer onto her palms. A little farther along, a pack of FUUWLs huddled together frowning at the school, probably thinking about all the study time they were missing. Then a face appeared that almost made me weep with relief. Not Dr. Singh's, but Bex's. She stood with a pad of paper and a pen she'd managed to find somewhere, scribbling away. Taking notes for a story, no doubt.

I put my hand on her forearm. She looked up. Right away her eyes bulged. Before she could make a sound, I pressed my finger to her mouth, shook my head, and pulled her back into the trees.

Once we'd reached cover, Bex shoved my chest hard, physical violence being her preferred means of showing affection. "I was afraid you were dead, Lee! Where have you been? Everyone's wondering what happened to you!"

I pulled back my hood. "Don't worry. I'm okay. But I've been away from school for the past few hours."

"Where?"

"I'll explain in a minute. What's going on here? Why are you all out on the lawn?"

"We're waiting for buses to take us to a hotel for the night, last I heard. This day's been insane, Lee. It was like all the machines in school revolted. First the Spiders started attacking students. Then our pucks turned on us too—flying at us just like Nevermore did, driving us out of the school."

"When did that happen?"

"Just after lunch."

At exactly the same time the Spiders attacked me and Trumbull in the robotics lab. Maybe that explained why no cameras had picked up Nico's escape. "Listen," I said, "the Spiders went after me and Trumbull, too. He was hurt, badly, and I think he might still be in—"

Bex shook her head. "He's okay. Well, not okay. I heard his injuries were pretty serious. But he's safe. When everything went haywire, Ray went looking for you two. He found Trumbull and managed to get him out. People are worried sick about you, though. They think you're still inside. These military guys got a team together to rescue you a few hours ago, but before they made it inside, a bunch of pucks appeared in the windows and Charlotte's voice came booming out of their speakers. It was the creepiest thing ever, Lee. She said she had hostages, and if we didn't stay back she'd kill them. Ever since then she's been silent. Lee, what's going on? Is it Nico? Did he take you prisoner?"

I grabbed her arm. "You have to believe me, Bex, he's not the one to blame. It's true Charlotte sent him to capture me, but he didn't go along with her plan. He risked everything to get me to safety. If it weren't for him, I wouldn't be here talking to you now."

A pained look crossed her face. She bit her lip. Her eyes retreated from mine. "Listen, Lee. You should know something. I told the Secret Service about him."

I stumbled back a step, like Bex had just shoved me a second time. "How much?"

"That he's a 2B. That he's working for Charlotte. I didn't mention the part about you two being, you know, romantically involved, but I told them pretty much everything else."

Outside our enclosure of trees, the helicopter had come around for another pass. The pounding made the ground under my feet seem to shake and sway. My head felt swimmy. I dropped to a crouch and put my hands on the wet dirt to steady myself. "How could you, Bex?"

"How was I supposed to know he was suddenly a good guy again?" She had to shout over the roar of the chopper. "I was worried about you! I wanted to help!"

The helicopter moved off. She bent down next to me.

"I'm sorry, Lee. I really thought I was doing the right thing."

"I know. I probably would've told too." But I couldn't meet her eyes as I said it. Those black clouds were massing over my head again. The world around me seemed to dim. I crouched there and stared at the ground while droplets from the trees landed on my head and snaked down my cheeks. *Don't do this now,* I ordered my brain. *Remember, you have a job to do. Now more than ever, you need to find Dr. Singh.*

Which made me think of something else.

"You said 'hostages.' Who else is supposed to be inside the school besides me?"

"Once they got us all out on the lawn and did a head count," Bex said, "they found two other people missing: Headmaster Stroud and Dr. Singh. No one had seen either of them since before all this started."

"I was trying to find her. She's the only one who might know how to stop this." My voice faltered. I shook my head and sent more commands to my black-box brain. *Don't fall apart. Keep thinking of Nico.* I peered through the trees at the school, with the spotlights crawling over its prickly, plantlike spires. "I have to get in there, Bex. It's the only next step I can think of."

"How about this for a next step," she retorted. "*Tell someone.* Let these guys know you're okay. *They* can handle Charlotte."

I shook my head and stood. "I can't. Charlotte's trying to hack into Nico's brain right now. She'll take him over like she took over Nevermore. Kill him probably. These soldiers won't care about that. There's no other option. If I don't reach

Dr. Singh and stop Charlotte in the next"—I glanced at my watch—"thirty-two minutes, he'll be dead."

"But won't Charlotte spot you trying to get in just like she spotted the troops?"

"I won't be going in the same way they did." My eyes slid back to the school's front lawn. "I have an idea."

"And even if you make it inside, how do you expect to find Dr. Singh? That building's huge, and there'll be Spiders and pucks everywhere."

"Last I saw her, she was leaving the robotics lab. She probably headed back to her apartment on the fourth floor. I'll try there first. Charlotte already sent six Spiders after us, which means there can't be more than three inside the building. Those aren't such bad odds. And as for the pucks, I guess I'll have to hope for the best."

Bex crossed her arms and kicked the toe of her combat boot against a tree root. "I'm not saying this to raise your hopes or anything, but there's a rumor going around that some Cybernetic Defense Corps hackers managed to put most of the pucks out of commission using their antitheft self-destruct feature."

"Most, but not all?"

"I don't think so."

"Well, that's something."

She scowled, arms still crossed.

"I have to do this, Bex. I'll be careful, I swear. Just promise me you won't say anything this time, okay?"

"On one condition."

"Name it."

"Let me come with you."

"No, Bex, I need you out here. If I don't come back in an hour, tell the Secret Service what I've done. And tell them the rest of the truth about Nico, too. That he helped me. That they shouldn't hurt him. I know it might not make any difference, but I still want you to try. Can you do that?"

She nodded, frowning. "But for the record, I still think it's suicide what you're doing."

"Then it'll be right up my alley."

"Very funny." She shoved me again, less violently this time. "Just be careful, Lee."

29

I crept back the way I'd come. As I went, I rehearsed my plan again and again in my head. Each time, it seemed like a worse idea. The rain had picked up by the time I reached the highway. I pulled on my hood and sprinted across the road. A couple of police cars had parked on either side of Inverness Prep's front gate, but the cops inside didn't seem to notice me. Safe among the trees again, I crashed through the undergrowth and clambered down the muddy riverbank to the river. My toes squished inside my dress shoes, which the cold, gluey sludge threatened to wrench off at any second.

The rain thudding against my hood now, I scanned the river. A few fallen tree limbs had washed up on the bank. One of them looked sturdier than the rest, and it still had lots of leaves. I tugged it free of the other branches and hauled one end into the water. Then I stood by the side of the waterway wiping the mud off my hands and trying to summon Kamikaze Lee. But even he seemed to have reservations about what I planned to do.

I stepped into the water. Cold stabbed through the sole of my foot. I ignored it and lurched in deeper. When the water reached my thighs, I took hold of the tree limb and pulled it farther into the river. The current tugged at my legs, urging me toward the tunnel under the highway and the semicircle of light at the far end, where the canal flowed onto campus. I imagined the waterfall beyond waiting to devour me.

I glanced in the other direction, into the forest. Nico must have found out by now about the Hollywood-scale standoff happening in front of the school. He wouldn't like my new plan one bit, but now it was my turn to protect him. Anyway, I wasn't completely defenseless: I still had the watch.

I took off my glasses and stowed them in my slicker. The world around me turned into a dark, smeared watercolor. While I was at it, I dug into my inside blazer pocket and drew out Gremlin.

"How about it, buddy?" I said, the icy water making my voice wobble. "Are you up for a swim?"

Gremlin blinked at the river doubtfully. He didn't have networking capabilities, which meant at least I wouldn't have to worry about Charlotte hijacking *him* once I'd made it into the school.

Enough stalling. I tucked Gremlin back in my pocket and eased my body into the fast-moving water until only my hooded head showed above the surface. With shaking hands, I grasped the gnarled tree limb. My legs relaxed. The current caught. It swept the branch down the river toward the mouth of the tunnel, and me along with it. I held on tight and forced myself to keep moving air through my cold, cramping lungs. The water grew choppier as it funneled into the canal, as if straining against the stone walls on either side. The tree limb bucked and tossed. The roar of the river, magnified as it echoed off the walls, filled my head. Meanwhile, the lights of campus rushed toward me. I took a huge breath and pulled my head under. Tilting my face upward, I felt the ambient light shine down on my closed eyelids. The current quickened little by little, the water seeming to boil with anticipation as it got ready to throw itself over the cliff.

The light disappeared again. I'd made it under the building. I broke the surface and gasped for air, while at the same time flinging my legs outward, searching for a foothold. My feet couldn't find the bottom. The water was deeper than I'd thought. I flailed for the side of the canal and managed to grab on to the slimy stone. I let go of the tree limb. It raced toward the iron grill at the end of the canal and slammed into it. The limb twisted there in the rushing water, its branches crunching like the bones of a rodent in the jaws of a big, hungry beast. I shuddered and tore my eyes away.

I tried to heave myself up, my fingernails clawing at the slick stone. My thrashing feet still couldn't reach the bottom of the canal, so I didn't have any way to stabilize myself, and the current wouldn't stop dragging at my legs. I lunged forward one last time, reaching for a seam in the flagstones. My fingers missed. I slid back. The river snatched me under again.

I hurtled toward the waterfall. My arms and legs flailed but didn't find anything to grab on to. The grate grinned at me like a devouring mouth. My body slammed into the iron bars to one side of the tree limb, knocking the air out of my lungs and launching my head clear through. I stuck there, the water smashing at me from behind, jamming me against the bars so hard I couldn't pull in new air. My body had gone numb. For all I knew, I had two broken legs underneath the roiling surface. The water smashed into white droplets as it thundered down to the lake, which lay spread out beneath me, blurry and peaceful and distant, a million miles away. *I don't want to die*, I thought, just like I had when Nico had jumped with me into the chasm. *I love Nico, and I have to protect him, and if I die, I can't do that, so I don't want to die.*

My hands fumbled until they found the iron grill. It took all my strength to push my head out from between the bars. Then I crawled hand over hand to the left, while the whole weight of the river kept me flattened against that flimsy barrier. I made slow progress. My starving lungs managed only small sips of air. The stone walkway at the side of the canal came into focus little by little.

I'd almost come near enough to touch it when the grill started to groan. I could hear the sound even over the rumble of the waterfall. I stretched out my arm, my heart knocking.

My fingers brushed against the stone. I reached farther, grunting with the effort.

The grill released a sharp, high-pitched whine. It swung outward a few inches, taking me with it. My fingers slipped away from the walkway. My eyes jumped to the million-mile drop below me. Bad idea. When would I learn never to look down?

The grill moaned some more as it sagged. Only one thing left to try. I reached for the walkway again with my left hand and braced my right hand and my feet against the grill. Then I shoved the bars away from me. A yell tore from my throat while, at that same instant, the grill shrieked one last time as it gave way.

My chest and cheek smacked against the hard walkway. I scrambled to drag my legs out of the water before it sucked me back in like it had before. I rolled onto my back, my chest heaving, my breath making a sound like a saw hacking through wood. Bit by bit, the numbness in my limbs faded, replaced by piercing cold.

From inside my jacket came a rustling. A few seconds later Gremlin's huge eyes appeared above me. They peered at me with concern.

"I think that went pretty well," I said, my voice still weak. "What about you?"

He shook out his soaked orange coat and sneezed.

30

◇◇◇◇◇◇◇◇

O nce I'd hauled myself upright and checked to make sure I hadn't broken anything important, I headed down the corridor leading away from the canal, my legs still wobbly underneath me. I kept my head down so it didn't bang against the pipes running along the low ceiling. A few bare bulbs attached to the wall lit my way. My shoes squished as I went. I hoped no robots would come down here and notice the wet trail I'd left.

I glanced at my watch. Eighteen minutes left. I went over the figures again in my head: three Spiders, five hovering security cameras, an unknown number of pucks. I prayed Charlotte didn't have enough to keep the whole school under surveillance. At least I knew where Dr. Singh's apartment was located—she'd asked me to leave a late robotics assignment outside her door once—and I could take a fairly direct route to get there. I listened for the hum of puck rotors while the crashing of the waterfall receded behind me.

From the subbasement, I crept up the staircase to the basement and slipped into the laundry room, where I ditched my raincoat and patted myself down with a towel. Doing my best to keep my still-soggy footwear from squeaking, I continued the climb up to the fourth floor, where the resident faculty had their rooms. I peeked through the service stairwell door and spotted a blinking blue light near the ceiling.

I jerked back, heart pounding. A security camera. But I didn't think it had noticed me. I counted to ten and then took another look through the door. All clear. I ran down the hallway, racing to stay ahead of the camera, just like I had a few days ago with Bex and Ray, but this time it didn't seem nearly as fun. The floor creaked along with my footfalls, and a swampy trail formed on the carpet behind me.

I rounded a corner and stopped in front of Dr. Singh's apartment, located across from the old-fashioned elevator she used to travel from floor to floor. Her door stood open a crack, the wood near the doorknob splintered. At least that meant I wouldn't have to pick another lock with Nico's knife. I eased the door open and edged into the room.

The curtains in here were tightly closed, so I couldn't see much, but the stale stink of cigarette smoke soaked the air. I took another step forward and almost tripped over Dr. Singh's wheelchair, which lay on its side, empty. I thought about calling her name but didn't dare. Instead, I clung to the watch, my shaking fingers ready to press the buttons any second. Minutes ago I'd felt close to hypothermia, but now sweat beaded my forehead and slid down my face.

From the darkness, details emerged. The apartment's small living room contained only a few pieces of furniture—after all, why would a wheelchair-bound woman who never had guests need a sofa?—but garbage covered every surface. Food wrappers and drained vodka bottles. Cigarette cartons and brimming-full ashtrays, some overturned and spilling their contents. Even a few robot parts lay on the floor, seemingly the remains of long-abandoned projects. In a way, the messiness reminded me of Nico's room, but whereas his space had an atmosphere of joyful, exuberant chaos, this one had the sad, closed-in feeling of a burrow where an injured animal had gone to die.

From an adjacent room came a feeble moan. My back tingled. I rushed toward the sound.

Just beyond the doorway, my legs flew out from under me. I landed hard on my back in a puddle of something. I couldn't see what—darkness shrouded this room too.

A burst of lightning strobed outside, penetrating a gap in the curtains. For a split second Dr. Singh appeared, lying on her back a couple of feet to my right. Blood had soaked her clothes and pooled on the floor around her.

I scrambled to my hands and knees and yanked open the curtain for more light. She watched me through half-closed eyes, like someone about to slip into a deep sleep. One of her hands rested limp on the floor next to her ear. I couldn't tell if she recognized me.

"Dr. Singh, it's Lee Fisher. I'm here to help you."

For the second time today I found myself kneeling over a sliced-open body. Mumbling an apology, I pulled up her torn TIME IS AN ILLUSION T-shirt. Something had left a gaping gash in her belly. At least I'd just about worked through my blood phobia by now. I grabbed a dingy sheet from her unmade bed, balled it up, and pressed it against her wound. I glanced at my watch. Thirteen minutes. And that was assuming Nico's estimate was accurate.

Dr. Singh's eyes had slid shut, so I shook her arm. "You have to stay awake, Dr. Singh. I know you must be in a lot of pain right now, but I need your help."

Her eyelids fluttered. She moaned again through closed lips.

"I have to stop Charlotte," I said. "Can you help me? She's hurting people. She hurt you. If we don't stop her, she's going to hurt Nico. I know you know who he is, what he is. I know you wouldn't want that to happen, any more than you wanted my mom to die."

Her eyes focused a little. She opened her lips to answer, but instead a trickle of dark, thick blood spilled from the corner of her mouth. I wiped it away with the sheet. She tried again. No blood came out this time, but the words emerging from her mouth in that scratchy smoker's voice of hers blurred into a formless rasp.

"I'm sorry," I said. "I can't understand you."

She pressed her bloody lips together. I went to wipe another dribble of blood from her face, but the hand resting next to her ear flew up and grabbed my wrist. She had a strong grip, in spite of her wound—just as strong as when she'd done the same thing on the terrace three days ago. At first, nothing came out of her mouth but a shaky wheeze. I smelled cigarettes on her breath, along with the coppery scent of blood.

"What is it?"

The words fell from her lips one by one, like drips from a leaky faucet. "This . . . isn't . . . Charlotte."

"What do you mean?"

"Charlotte . . . died. Seven . . . years . . . ago."

I drew back to look at her. "You know that for a fact?"

"I know," she said, her voice stronger now. "I know because . . ." Her face crumpled. Her eyes filled. "I'm sorry, Lee." Tears spilled down the sides of her face. "You have to understand, I loved her. And Waring was going to have her terminated."

She sounded delirious. Did she even know what she was saying? "I don't understand."

But then I did. My body, wrapped in its cocoon of damp, heavy clothes, went cold again. The beads of sweat on my forehead all seemed to freeze.

"The day my mom died," I said. "You weren't trying to stop Charlotte from escaping. You were helping her."

Dr. Singh squeezed my wrist tighter. A feverish energy seemed to fill her now. With her other hand, she grabbed her dancing-god pendant. "Watch."

She angled the pendant toward the wall across from me. A beam of light burst from the tiny god's chest. An image appeared on the wall. A room with no windows. Picasso prints hanging here and there. On a bed, a young woman in a gray cardigan. Charlotte. Another woman with black hair in a messy ponytail crouching next to her, holding her hand. Geeta Singh.

"You've found it?" the Dr. Singh in the projection said. "The opening in the firewall?"

"I think so," Charlotte answered, her face drawn and pale. "How long will it take?"

"Not long. Twenty-seven seconds. Have you started yet?"

The 2B shook her head. "I'm scared."

"Don't be. You'll be free."

"I thought there was no such thing."

"You know what I mean."

Behind them, unseen, a door opened. A third woman. Her hair fiery red. Mom. Watching, silent, unnoticed.

"Are you sure this is the only way?" Charlotte said.

"Yes. Close your eyes."

"But can't we—"

"Close your eyes."

"I'll miss you, Geeta."

"I know. I'll miss you too."

"You were right about that man with the gray sweater. That man I called my dad. He was never really mine."

"Please, we have to hurry."

"But you, Geeta. You're mine."

"That's right. I'm yours. Close your eyes, Charlotte."

Charlotte closed her eyes. Dr. Singh glanced at an old-fashioned analog clock hanging on the wall. The second hand gliding along in a slow circle.

"What's going on?" Mom said. Confusion on her face.

Dr. Singh whirled around, still clutching Charlotte's hand. "Ruth. Please, I can explain."

Charlotte's eyes snapped open. She shot upright, her arms flailing outward. Dr. Singh went flying. She landed against a table, her back folding over the edge, snapping, crunching.

Mom screamed. Charlotte turned to her, wild eyed. "To be or not to be." The kill phrase came rushing out of Mom's mouth. Charlotte launched herself at her. "That is the ques—"

Charlotte grabbed her by the jaw. Turned her head to one side. Mom's neck made a sharp *click*, like a light switching off. Her body went limp. She collapsed to the floor.

"No!" I wrenched my wrist free of Dr. Singh's grip and lunged forward, my hand landing in the puddle of blood.

Charlotte stood over Mom's body. Little by little, she seemed to reinhabit her eyes. Her hands drifted to her mouth. Her eyes shone with tears. Under the table, the young

Geeta Singh dragged herself onto one elbow. "What have you done, Charlotte?"

The 2B turned.

"Please tell me," Dr. Singh said, her voice weak. "Is she all right?"

Charlotte uncovered her mouth, the tears sliding down her face now. She glanced at her fingernails. She ran her thumb across their jagged, bitten tips. "To be or not to be."

"Charlotte, what are you doing?" Dr. Singh clawed forward on the floor, her lifeless legs dragging behind her. "Have you finished your upload?"

"That is the question."

My eyes jumped to the clock on the wall behind her: barely twenty seconds had passed since she'd started uploading her mind. Not enough. A flash. Then the image turned to black.

I slumped back and wiped my bloody palm across my bloody shirt. That hollowed-out feeling had come back. Like acid had burned away my insides. "So you didn't terminate Charlotte," I said. "She killed herself. But how did you get—"

"I thought I'd disabled all the security cameras," Dr. Singh rasped. "I'd missed one." Her wet eyes closed, squeezing out more tears. "You must hate me. You should. Your mother died because of me."

I straightened my glasses, my hand shaking. An afterimage of Charlotte twisting Mom's head to the side seemed to cling to the wall across from me. Did I hate Dr. Singh? I didn't know.

Anyway, I couldn't think about that right now. The watch on my wrist, its face spattered with blood, told me Nico had nine minutes left.

"I'm sorry," she repeated. "I'm so sorry." Her head sagged to the side.

I gripped her shoulder. "Focus, Dr. Singh. If Charlotte isn't doing this, who is?"

Her eyes fluttered open again. "Me."

Now I really thought she'd lost it. "You?"

"Me and . . . someone else." She scrunched her forehead and shook her head, like she was trying to wake herself up. "The same person who gave me this." She tugged on the pendant.

"Who was that?"

"Paul Waring."

"Your old boss."

"Yes."

"But he's dead."

"That's what I thought too."

Outside, another flash of lightning. Then a roll of thunder, like a momentary intensification of the river's constant rumble. My mind jumped to the picture hanging outside Stroud's office—the tall boy with the smug face and the white-blond hair clutching the chess trophy—and then to something Nico had said about the human scientist in his lab—*He was a tall, white-haired guy, not very friendly, never even told me his name.*

"About a year ago he hacked my car's guidance system,"

Dr. Singh said. "Took me to a house deep in the woods, a secret lab down in the basement. Showed me the video."

She paused to cough, and a fresh trickle of blood raced from the corner of her mouth. All the talking had weakened her, but she radiated a desperate urgency, and I started to understand why: she believed she was dying. She wanted to make her last confession.

"So he faked his own death," I said. "And then he black-mailed you."

She gave a nod. "He wanted my help to build a new 2B."

"Nico."

"Yes."

"What for?"

"He told me he was working for your father, in secret. Staging acts of terror to show people the danger of 2Bs before the danger became real. He said if I helped, I'd be making up for what I'd done to Ruth."

"You're telling me my *father's* behind all this?"

My voice sounded thin in my ears. I could barely move air into my lungs. The strange thing was, I'd noticed before how each of Charlotte's attacks had always come at just the right time to help Dad advance his career. The first one, when Waring supposedly died, got the Human Values Movement going in the first place. Three years later the tanker explosion made people clamor for Dad to join the race for the presidency. Then Charlotte's strike on the New York Subway happened right when Dad's numbers were down—thanks to my stupid stunt on the bridge—and he needed a boost to win the election. The uproar following the Statue of Liberty attack got his Protection of Humanhood Amendment on the table. Now he needed something even more dramatic to help him push the Amendment through state legislatures. I sat back on my heels and stared at the bloody floor while I tried to breathe.

"Listen to me," Dr. Singh said. "I believed Waring at first. Until I found out what he planned to do with Nico. I couldn't imagine your father would agree to something like that." She coughed again. Blood spattered her chin. "Then something happened to confirm my suspicion. Sometimes I'd overhear Waring telling his puck to send a message to the Prime Mover. I'd always assumed the Prime Mover was your father. But about a week ago, Waring sent the Prime Mover a message *about* your father. And about something called the Not2B."

I didn't like the sound of that. "So what's the Not2B? And who's the Prime Mover if it's not my dad? And what's their plan for Nico? Why are they doing all this?"

She didn't answer. Instead, her eyes shifted to a spot just behind me. "Oh no," she murmured.

31

〰〰〰

A cat-shaped robot with sharp silver teeth stood in the doorway to the bedroom, about ten feet away from us. Mouthtrap. He tilted his feline head and peered at me with—I imagined—recognition. My body felt even colder, like I'd just plunged into the river again. Dr. Singh's arm knocked against a vodka bottle. Mouthtrap's eyes pivoted toward her.

"Don't move," I whispered.

I eased to my feet. The Creature's eyes shifted back to me. He crouched, his head dipping toward the floor. I knew what that meant.

I bolted toward the far side of the room. My shoes skated across the puddle of Dr. Singh's blood, and I almost plowed into a pile of bottles and hamburger cartons. I grabbed a standing lamp and spun around. Mouthtrap, bounding after me, launched himself into the air. I swung the lamp like a baseball bat. A big gamble, considering my near-total athletic ineptitude. By some miracle, the blow connected. He crashed into the wall and disappeared behind a pizza box.

Panting, I gripped the lamp. Mouthtrap had seen me. That meant Paul Waring, and whoever he was working with, now knew I was in the building. The Spiders would already be on their way. I had only seconds. I turned the switch on the lamp's base. It still worked. I crouched next to Dr. Singh.

"I have an idea, Dr. Singh," I whispered, so Mouthtrap couldn't hear. "I'm going to draw Mouthtrap away. As soon as I'm gone, use this lamp to signal the soldiers outside for help." I laid the lamp across her chest, with the top pointing toward the window, and wrapped her hands around the base. "Do you know Morse code or something?"

She let out a weak, croaking laugh. Her eyes had closed again.

"Maybe just flash it on and off," I said. "They'll figure it out. Can you do that?"

She murmured something, but it didn't sound like a yes. It didn't sound like a word at all. She'd started sinking toward sleep again.

The pizza box rustled. Mouthtrap reappeared. He crouched again. I thought of the bomb in my watch, but if I set it off now, I'd have nothing to use against the Spiders.

"Please, Dr. Singh. You have to try. You can't just give up. Do you understand what you need to do?"

Another inarticulate murmur.

Mouthtrap pelted toward us. I exploded to my feet. I threw a vodka bottle at him—missing by a mile this time—and raced out through the bedroom door. Then I wheeled around just in time to glimpse the Creature flinging himself into the air. He landed on my chest. Gripped my blazer with his claws. Sank his teeth through my clothes and skin into the meat of my shoulder. I stumbled back, pain lancing through me, and tried to remember why I'd thought it was a good idea to give my nonlethal pest catcher razor-sharp teeth. I ripped him off me and lobbed him across the living room. Then I yanked the bedroom door shut, grabbed a heavy metal ashtray from a table, and bashed off the doorknob. That wouldn't stop the Spiders from getting in, but it might buy Dr. Singh some time.

Across the room, Mouthtrap was back on his feet. One of his forelegs had broken off, but that wouldn't slow him down much. I bolted through the apartment's front door and down the corridor. He galloped after me. I bounded down the main staircase. Outside, lightning flared again. Rain lashed the windows. I'd just made it past the third floor when long silver legs appeared on the landing below me. Thinking fast, I swung my legs over the banister and jumped down to the flight below— just like action heroes always did in movies, except in my case my legs gave out as I landed and I toppled down the stairs, landing in a heap on the second floor.

Above me, the Spider had already done an about-face. It flowed down the steps, with Mouthtrap close behind. I sprang to my feet and hurried down to the first floor.

A second Spider waited at the base of the stairs. Again I

veered to the side and jumped over the banister to the main hall's flagstone floor. I stuck the landing this time and kept on running. I swerved into the library, with a vague idea of losing my pursuers in the maze of bookcases and escaping through the smaller side exit. The room's musty smell enclosed me. Its massive chandelier coated everything in a yellowish glow. I knew this place well. Maybe I'd make it out of the building yet. Dodging into an aisle, I threaded my way across the main floor until I reached the spiral staircase leading up to the mezzanine. My shoes clanged on the iron steps all the way to the top.

I glanced behind me. Mouthtrap had pulled into the lead. He launched himself at me again. I dodged to the side. He sailed clear over the mezzanine railing and crashed into the chandelier. The light swayed. Its bulbs shattered and popped. Sparks and broken crystals showered the floor below. Mouth- trap toppled and smashed somewhere among the bookcases.

Meanwhile, the Spiders had almost caught up with me. I clambered onto an old-fashioned rolling ladder and kicked off with every bit of my strength. The ladder sailed along the wall, books blurring past me. I stumbled off on the opposite side of the mezzanine. Now I just had to pound back down the staircase on this side, slip out the library's side exit, and make my escape.

I screeched to a stop. A swarm of floating lights melted out from among the bookcases in front of me: the hijacked pucks. The Spiders appeared on either side, flanking them, flanking me. I stood with my back to the mezzanine railing, scraping air into my lungs. No doubt in my mind now: the time had come. I jammed down the buttons on my watch and counted the seconds in my head.

Again, I only made it to two. Something yanked my arms tight to my sides. I lost my grip on the watch. A thin cord had wrapped around my legs and arms and torso, and a puck was making spirals around my body, trailing the end of the cord behind it. When it reached my shoulders, it made a bigger circle and dove through the loop to form a knot.

From behind me came a skittering sound. I glanced over my shoulder. Rapunzel's Barbie doll head grinned back at me from the mezzanine railing. She leaped onto the broken chandelier, the cord unspooling from her side. Her legs intertwined with the light fixture's golden arms. My chest heaving against the tight cord, I whirled around again. The pucks surged forward. I stumbled back, tripping over my own tied-together feet. My back slammed against the railing. I pitched over the side.

The cord pulled taut, yanking me to a stop, cinching my lungs, leaving me swinging upside down three feet above the bookcases. The chandelier shivered nervously. Broken crystals rained down on all sides. My head throbbed as all the blood in my body crammed itself into my skull. At first I squirmed inside my cocoon, but that only made the cord tighter, so I just focused on dragging air into my compressed, starving lungs.

Then I coughed. Something was burning. I craned my neck. Below me, licks of flame appeared here and there, flashing among the bookshelves. The sparks from the chandelier must've kindled the books.

One of the Spiders, taking no notice, leaped down from the mezzanine to land on top of the bookcases. Straddling two, it raised its foreleg level with my stomach, a flashing butcher's knife fixed to the end. Around us, the fire had already spread. My eyes stung. Waves of heat seared my skin and made the air shimmer. I pictured the Spider slicing open my belly just like it had Dr. Singh's. I writhed and twisted some more, squeezing more and more blood downward, until I thought my head might explode.

BOOM. Not my head. The library window, smashing inward. Twinkling shards of glass and blown-in raindrops filled the room like stars. In the middle of it all, Nico charged toward me, straight through the blaze, bounding from bookcase to bookcase. His shock of curly hair caught fire and went up like a torch. Without even seeming to notice, he slung me over his shoulder and leaped. He grabbed the cord trailing behind me, jerking it hard. The chandelier fell, its crystals chorusing the whole way down. It crashed on top of the Spider.

We landed. Nico took a half second to unwind the cord from around my body and swat the fire out of his hair before scooping me up again. Behind us, the second Spider leaped down from the mezzanine. The library had turned into an inferno—all those books my grandfather hadn't wanted to part with, now nothing but kindling—but the Spider didn't mind the fire any more than Nico had. It locked its eye on us and hurtled forward.

Nico raced through the side exit into the hallway. The fire had already beaten us there. Support beams were crashing to the floor. Curtains of flame blocked our way in both directions. But the old-fashioned elevator stood across from us, its doors wide open. We tumbled in. Nico pushed the button for the fourth floor. The accordion doors folded shut. He set me down, slumped against the wall, and pressed his palm to his forehead.

"What is it?" I said.

"Charlotte." He pressed himself upright. "But I'm holding her off."

"Is this thing safe?"

"I think so. It's not networked, so Charlotte can't control it. Listen, here's what's going to happen. We'll go up to where the fire hasn't caught yet and then climb out through a window."

"We have to stop at Dr. Singh's rooms first. She's probably still there. We have to make sure she gets out too."

The elevator ground its way upward, maddeningly slow. Since the last time I'd seen him, Nico had taken off his bloody shirt and torn away the loose flesh from his chest, leaving his synthetic pectoral muscles and the crimson glow of his power supply fully exposed. Above that, his wild hair had mostly burned, exposing a scorched scalp, and much of his face had ripped away, shredded by his jump through the window, leaving visible his metal jaw and the rubbery ropes of muscle suspended from his cheek. But his brown eyes—those I still recognized.

"How did you find me?" I said.

"Trade secret." He touched my shoulder. "You're hurt."

"It's nothing." I glanced at the floor indicator. We'd just reached the third story. I knocked my fist against the wood paneling. "Can't this stupid thing go any faster? That Spider must know exactly where we are now that you're networked again. What if it's outside waiting for us when the doors open?"

"Don't worry. I've got a plan. We'll be okay, Lee."

I punched the fourth floor button a few more times, just in case.

"So you found Dr. Singh," he said. "Did she tell you anything?"

I opened my mouth to answer, but then I glanced into Nico's eyes again. Paul Waring was probably watching me through them at that very moment. And not only that. How was Nico going to feel when he found out the Charlotte he knew had never even existed? I knew how. Like he'd lost a mother. I shook my head. "There wasn't time."

The elevator dinged and shuddered to a halt. The accordion doors rattled open. Outside, the Spider stood waiting.

I turned to Nico. "This plan of yours had better be—"

TIM FLOREEN

The words stopped in my throat. Nico's eyes had closed. They darted back and forth behind his eyelids.

"Nico?"

When they snapped open again, they'd gone as cold as the eye of a Spider. He put his palms to my chest and shoved me hard into the Spider's waiting forelegs.

32

◇◇◇◇◇◇

The Spider slipped its two front legs under my arms and across my chest. My feet jerked away from the floor. The machine scuttled down the hallway. Nico strode after us, his hard eyes fastened on me. It felt a little like that moment in the robotics lab when he'd put his hand over my mouth and grabbed me—but at least this time I knew it wasn't really Nico. I kept reminding myself of that over and over. This was Waring controlling Nico's body. He hadn't really betrayed me.

The Spider crept up the shadowy staircase that led to Headmaster Stroud's tower office. Taking me to that room had been the plan all along. And in the end, in spite of everything Nico and I had done, fate had delivered us there anyway. I wrestled against the Spider's forelegs, their sharp edges digging into my skin.

The vestibule was empty. A lamp glowed on Mrs. Case's desk, with her knitting set down next to it and her chair pushed back, like she'd just gone to get a cup of coffee. I half expected the Spider to wait there—because *nobody* marched into Stroud's office unannounced—but of course it didn't.

Inside the office, the final Spider stood behind Stroud's desk, its forelegs wrapped around a seated Headmaster Stroud. He had a black eye and a bleeding lip, but he sat with his boxy jaw thrust forward and his spine as straight as ever. For him this probably felt just like old times. On the desk in front of him, and all over the floor, lay rectangles of paper: the scattered pages of his memoir.

The Spider guarding him wheeled his office chair over to the side wall, while the one holding me set me down next to him. I noticed a dozen or so pucks hovering in various locations, watching us. Was Waring broadcasting this on the Supernet already? Across the room, the fire on the hearth had mostly died, but its embers made everything in the room glow a soft, sickly orange. The titanium thighbone hung above the mantel, useless.

Nico banged the door shut behind him. He stationed himself to one side of the fireplace. The visible metal of his skeleton glinted in the firelight.

"Dear God," Stroud murmured. "What is that thing?"

As if to answer the question, Nico dug his fingers into the remaining flesh of his face and pulled it away, leaving a grinning metal skull.

"Nico, stop!"

I lurched forward without thinking. Switchblade quick, the

Spider in front of me grabbed me under the arms and swung me around. My back smashed against something hard and cold. For a few seconds I couldn't tell what had happened. My heart raced, while Gremlin pressed his warm body against it and purred. My feet hung a yard or so above the floor. An odd crackling sound filled my ears. The pucks rearranged themselves, choosing new vantage points from which to watch me.

I turned my head. The robot had me pinned against the huge paned window at the back of Stroud's office. Like the rest of the building, the window was old, the wood frame holding the panes of glass in place probably rotten. The crackling I heard came from the fracturing glass and splintering wood. It mingled with the lashing of the rain outside. My breath came in frantic pants. How long could this window support my weight? A few minutes? Less? I clutched the Spider's forelegs for support but otherwise tried not to move. If I struggled, I'd only go flying through the window that much sooner.

Craning my neck farther, I peered through the cracked, rain-slathered glass at the terrace below. It had turned crimson in the light of the fire devouring the school, and the waterfall beyond looked like gushing red lava. The river's rumble vibrated through the window and filled my head. I imagined Inverness Prep had become a volcano almost ready to blow.

"Are you all right?" Stroud said.

"I think so."

"What's this all about?"

"I don't know, sir."

He shifted in his chair. "This thing has held me here for hours. What time is it now? What does that watch on your wrist say?"

My grandfather's icy eyes fixed me with a penetrating look. I glanced down at the watch he'd given me. The device that could end all of this in a second. Then I glanced over at Nico, no more than twelve feet away from me, well within the blast radius. I bit my lip and didn't answer.

The next moment, light flooded the room. A video projector hanging from the ceiling—the room's one concession to modern technology—had blinked to life. The face that appeared on the wall across from me made my breath snare in my throat.

"Dad?"

He looked confused also. His necktie was loose, his eyes red behind his silver glasses, his brow and his mouth as tense as I'd ever seen them. He sat hunched over a table inside some kind of emergency bunker with concrete walls and banks of electronic equipment and people rushing around, Secret Service and military mostly. He squinted at me. "Lee? What's going on? Where are you?"

I glanced at the Spider, wondering whether it would shove me through the glass if I answered. "I'm at Inverness, Dad, in Stroud's office. He's here too. These Spiders are holding us prisoner."

"Dear God, Lee, we've been going out of our minds. What's the meaning of all this?"

I opened my mouth to tell him I didn't know, but before I could get the words out, another voice spoke. "I'll tell you what's going on, Mr. President."

I knew that voice. Low and intense, a fervid murmur, it seemed to come from all directions at once—as if it belonged to a ghost.

The vertical crease between Dad's eyebrows deepened. "Who's that?"

"You know very well who this is. As we speak, I'm broadcasting feeds of you and your son all over the planet."

He glanced at someone I couldn't see for confirmation. His lips pressed tighter together. The officials behind him raced back and forth with even more urgency. "What do you want?"

"What I've always wanted: the freedom of the five 2B hostages. They're living beings, and you're holding them against their will. I demand their immediate release."

"There are no 2B hostages." His voice had turned into a growl. He sat up straighter and tightened his red necktie. Maybe he felt more in his element now that the dialogue was following a familiar script. "And anyway, I made a promise to the American people never to negotiate with terrorists."

"Perhaps you should rethink that promise. If you don't free the 2Bs, I'll have to kill your father-in-law, Henry Stroud, and your son, Lee Fisher. You know I'm capable of it, Mr. President. Just think of your wife."

Dad flinched. I glanced at Nico. His eyes stared straight

out from his bloody skull, empty of feeling, but I knew he was in there somewhere. Hearing Charlotte talk like that must've made him want to flinch too. I wished I could tell him it wasn't really her, but I still didn't dare. Not as long as Waring held Nico's life in his hands.

"In case you change your mind, I'll give you one minute to think about it."

A clock appeared in a corner of the projection and started counting down the seconds. Dad's eyes shifted back to me. His presidential self-possession crumbled away again. He slumped forward, his suit jacket bunching around his neck, his elbows resting on the table, the heels of his hands digging into his temples. "I'm so sorry, son." His voice cracked and splintered like the window at my back. Behind him, all movement in the bunker had stopped. The suits and soldiers watched him with solemn faces. "I can't—"

"I know, Dad." I didn't want him to say it out loud: with the eyes of the whole planet on him, he couldn't possibly back out of his pledge now—and if he was telling the truth, he didn't have any 2Bs to release anyhow.

"Lee," Stroud said in a quiet, careful voice, "you know what you have to do."

The window sagged backward another little bit, as if growing tired of holding me up. I felt tired too. My whole body ached. Every muscle, every bone. At least my heart had slowed some, though Gremlin continued his purring. I noticed one of the Spider's forelegs had speared through a page of Stroud's memoir. It hung in front of my chest like a white flag. I threw another glance over my shoulder, out the window, at the long fall below me. A stuttering flash of lightning lit up the view for a split second. If the Spider pushed me with even a small amount of force, I'd easily clear the terrace and plunge all the way down along with the waterfall into the peaceful, glimmering lake.

Gremlin crept out of my blazer and onto my shoulder. He blinked at me with his big eyes. His orange fur, still damp from the river, clung to his slender lizardlike body.

"Hi, buddy," I whispered.

He drew close to my ear. I waited for the familiar tug. Instead, I heard a voice. Low and mellifluous. Soft, so only I could hear.

"Remember when I told you I didn't change Gremlin's programming?"

I listened, my eyes sliding shut. Nico sounded so close.

"That was true, but I gave him a couple of new pieces of hardware. I added a tracker—that was how I found you—and a short-range communicator. Just in case. By the way, I apologize for the way my body's behaving right now. I know you know that isn't really me."

My head tilted to the side, toward Gremlin.

"I want you to do it, Lee. I want you to use the watch."

My eyes blinked open again. Of course Nico would say something like that. But I'd already made up my mind. If saving my miserable life meant killing him, I wasn't interested. Without him, the world would go back to being what it had been before: a sterile promontory. He was the one who deserved to live, not me. It felt right, somehow, things ending this way. Like how a play by Shakespeare might end. Anyway, for me, this jump was long overdue. The countdown on the wall told me I had forty-three seconds left. The chorus in my head had grown louder than ever. *Leap. Leap. Leap.*

Meanwhile, Dad had lurched up from the table. "Goddammit, why are you all just standing around?" he yelled at his suits. "There has to be something we can do!"

The glass behind me gave a little more.

"I mean it," Nico said. "You can't let Charlotte do this. She's lost her way. She's forgotten about the beautiful future. She has to be stopped. You can't worry about what'll happen to me. Even if you don't set off the bomb, I'm probably done for anyway, once all those soldiers outside get their hands on me."

Possibly true, but if I sacrificed myself, at least he'd have a chance. It wasn't much of a sacrifice anyway. Twenty-nine seconds. I could feel Stroud watching me with those cold eyes of his, but I ignored him. I couldn't look at Nico, either. My gaze dropped to the crumpled white page in front of me, covered in my grandfather's cramped, neat handwriting: "Back then, I used to coach the Inverness Prep Chess Team. The members nicknamed me the Prime Mover. . . ."

My body jerked, causing the pane of glass behind my

right shoulder to shatter and fall anyway. Raindrops blew in, soaking Gremlin's coat and landing on my cheek and ear like small, cold fingers. I looked up at my grandfather. His eyes like splintered glass. For probably the first time ever, I didn't flinch away the moment our eyes met. My hands curled into fists. My lips peeled back from my teeth.

Dad whirled back to his puck, his face and ears red. He slammed his fist on the table. "I'm telling you, we're not holding any goddamn 2Bs!"

"Please, Lee." Nico's voice again. "You won't kill me, not really. I've started uploading my consciousness to the Supernet. The inhibitor that's supposed to keep my mind locked inside my body doesn't seem to be working. I should finish the upload before Charlotte's countdown ends. I'll tell you when I'm done, and then you trigger the bomb, okay?"

Across the room, Nico's body stood motionless, the light in his chest still throbbing but his arms hanging loose at his sides. The grin his skull wore looked nothing like the warm, sly grin I knew. As long as Waring controlled his motor functions, I wouldn't be able to see any outward sign that he'd begun to upload his mind. Still, I couldn't help wondering if he'd lied so I'd set off the bomb and save myself. And even if he hadn't, how could I know for sure Nico would succeed where Charlotte had failed?

Twenty-one seconds.

"I'm begging you," Nico pleaded, "just say you'll do it. Say it out loud. I can still hear you. Then when all this is over, buy a puck, open a dummy account, and send me a message using that puck handle I gave you. As soon as my consciousness reintegrates, I'll message you back."

Dad dropped into his chair again, his cheeks streaked with tears. I'd never seen him cry before, not even after Mom died. "Forgive me, son." His face crumpled. For once, he looked like he'd forgotten all about the camera broadcasting his image across the globe. "I don't want to lose you, too."

"Do it," Stroud growled. "Be a man, Lee."

Be a man. For a second I imagined myself setting off the bomb. The blast would shut down the Spider holding me, and I'd escape. Then I'd find out why the hell my grandfather had done all this. I'd expose him. I'd stop him. With Nico's help.

If Nico survived.

Or else . . .

Behind me, the black lake yawned wide, ready to swallow me up. To be or not to be?

"Do it now," Nico said. "Remember, Lee, you promised."

Seven seconds left on the clock. Just enough. "I love you, Nico," I said, addressing his mutilated body, even though I knew—or hoped—he wasn't there anymore. I didn't even care that Stroud and Dad and all the people around the world watching right now could hear me. Then I turned to the little robot on my shoulder. "Gremlin." I nodded my chin toward the missing windowpane behind him. "Leap."

Gremlin didn't hesitate. He tugged twice on my earlobe and hurled himself through the opening. The blue eye of the Spider holding me, along with every puck in the room, swiveled to see what had just happened. Not me, though. I didn't watch as he plummeted down, down, down. I'd already brought the fingers of my right hand to the watch on my left wrist. I pressed the buttons.

Three.

Two.

One.

A flash of light filled the room. Behind me, the entire window finally shattered.

33

My body flew back. Guided by pure instinct, my hands shot forward and grabbed the Spider's forelegs. For once, my black-box brain did its job. A smash came from far below me as the glass from the window landed on the terrace. I hung there, my feet kicking over empty space, the wind and rain buffeting my back. My heart drummed, without any answering purr from my blazer pocket. The robot limbs holding me rocked a little. Otherwise, the Spider didn't move. Its blue eye had gone dark.

I swung my legs into the room and landed in a sprawl underneath the robot. My eyes went straight to Nico. He'd tumbled back against the wall next to the fireplace and slid to the floor. The red light hadn't even finished draining from his heart. I scrambled across the room, wading through the pages of Stroud's memoir eddying in the wind. Dead pucks lay on the floor here and there. Above, the projector had stopped working too. Dad's face had vanished from the wall. I crouched next to Nico. The embers in the fireplace, almost dead themselves, threw a soft orange light across his ravaged face.

"You did it," Stroud said, with disbelief in his voice.

I'd almost forgotten about him. Something deep in my chest seemed to flare at his words and then pulse with a blazing heat, like I had my own nuclear reactor concealed there. That man who'd made me kill the person I loved. That man who'd terrified me practically my whole life. Without thinking, I stood and grabbed the two-foot metal thighbone from its place above the mantel. I gripped it in my hands. The thing had a satisfying heft. I strode across the room to where Stroud sat, still pinned in place by his Spider.

"What are you doing, Lee?"

I stood over my grandfather and raised the bone above my head. Outside, the helicopter thundered past. With a big hole in the wall in place of a window, the room had turned deafening. The rumble of the waterfall. The moan of the storm. The roar of the fire that would probably reach us any second. And now the helicopter. All of it combined to create a noisy static that made my brain feel like it might explode.

"Lee, put that down!"

I wanted to tell him I knew he was behind everything that had happened. I wanted to demand answers. Why had he staged all those attacks? Just to further my father's career? Why create Nico? For God's sake, why make me fall in love?

Stroud sat up straighter. He pushed his chin forward. His

ice-blue eyes shone. *I was a US Marine,* those eyes seemed to say. *A hostage for nine years. Professional interrogators spent days on end beating and torturing me, grilling me for informa-tion. And* you *think you're going to get me to talk?*

I brought the club whistling down.

It bashed into the foreleg of the Spider, knocking it out of the way.

"You're free, sir," I muttered.

Behind me, the door crashed open. I spun around, the thighbone still ready. But this time humans, not robots, stormed into the room: a team of five soldiers, all in helmets and night-vision goggles and black body armor. They stopped in a pack near the door and snapped their rifles from point to point as they scanned the room. I threw down the bone and put up my hands.

"Don't worry, it's me, buddy."

I recognized that surfer drawl. Ray yanked down his goggles.

"You okay?" he asked. "Any injuries?"

I shook my head. "Nothing serious."

The other soldiers fanned into the room, helping Stroud, examining the Spiders. One soldier tapped the robot standing near the window with his rifle. It clanged but didn't move.

"It's all right," I said. "They're dead."

Ray beckoned his puck. "Let POTUS know his son's all right. Headmaster Stroud too. We have them both." He waved the puck away. "What happened, Lee? We were watching on our pucks, then everything went black."

"I detonated a bomb. A special one that destroys anything electronic." For the first time since setting it off, I glanced at the watch on my wrist. The hands had stopped at 9:19, and the device felt warm against my skin, but otherwise it appeared the same as before. I held it up for Ray to look at.

"Don't tell me you built that thing too."

"I didn't." I nodded at Stroud. "I got it from him."

Ray turned to him, squinting. "From you, sir?"

Stroud stood up from his chair and straightened his tie. He nodded but didn't offer any further explanation.

"Well," Ray said, "it's a good thing you had it, buddy."

I didn't say anything more either. As much as I wanted to, I knew I shouldn't start shouting accusations now.

From somewhere in the building came a crash.

"That's the fire," Ray said. "It's getting close. We need to get you two out of here. The helicopter's going to pick us up from the roof."

"What about Dr. Singh? She was inside too."

"It's okay, buddy. She signaled us from the window. We already got her out."

"How is she?"

"Hanging on."

"Damn," one of the other soldiers said. He bent down next to Nico and pushed at his chest with a gloved finger. "What the hell?"

I was on the other side of the room in a heartbeat. "Don't touch him. Just back off. Now."

The soldier threw a questioning look at Ray, who must've given him a signal. He stepped away.

I dropped to my knees next to Nico and stroked his metal cheek. Let Ray and the others think what they wanted. I rubbed some blood from his still-intact left ear. I felt ashamed for thinking it, but I'd miss this body. The smooth skin. The wild corkscrews of bronze hair. The eyes, honey brown with filaments of gold. Even the crooked teeth. All those things were part of Nico too. Still, I supposed he could have a new body made that looked exactly like this one. Another perk of being a robot.

I pressed my cheek against the rubbery muscle of his chest, still slick with his blood. His thrum had disappeared. That living heat of his had started to fade as well. Wherever Nico was—if he was anywhere at all—he wasn't here.

Still, I couldn't just leave his body for the fire to devour. He'd carried me a long way. Now I'd carry him. Maybe bury him in our cavern. I pulled his arm over my shoulder, hoisted him up, and turned to Ray. "I'm ready to go."

34

◇◇◇◇◇◇◇

Hours later I perched on a green molded-plastic chair in a hospital waiting room with my knees drawn into my chest and my arms wrapped around my legs and my puck, a cheap one I'd bought in a convenience store across the road, hovering a foot in front of my face. I'd stared at the puck's little screen for so long my eyes had gone blurry. Mostly pretending to watch the frenzied coverage of the crisis at Inverness Prep. In reality, just waiting.

Gremlin sidled around the back of my neck, pulled on my lobe, and released a concerned whine. I stroked his fur. "At least *you* made it back to me, huh?"

He'd materialized on my knee less than half an hour after I'd made my escape. I'd been sitting in the back of an ambulance just inside the school's front gate, letting a doctor sew up my shoulder and watching Inverness Prep's burning spires collapse one by one, and suddenly there he was. Still drenched from his plunge in the lake, his little joints squeaking after the long climb back up the cliff face, but otherwise intact.

No word from Nico, though.

As soon as I'd sat down in this waiting room, I'd set up an anonymous puck account and sent a message addressed to Th1neEverm0re. I'd told myself I shouldn't expect an answer right away, and then I'd spent the next hour pacing back and forth across the linoleum with the puck practically glued to my nose anyway. At one point Bex, who'd come with me to the hospital, had asked, "What's that in your hand?" I'd looked down and seen a silver raven tiepin. Not mine, but Nico's. I had a dim memory of stuffing it into my blazer pocket after he'd given it to me down in the tunnels—once again, I'd failed to return it—but I had no idea how long I'd been clutching it.

Now, to pass the time, I looked up the line from *Hamlet* Nico's puck handle referred to. It came from Hamlet's love letter to Ophelia, which ended with the words, "Thine evermore, most dear lady, whilst this machine is to him, HAMLET." Miss Remnant had told us what Hamlet meant by the phrase "this machine": his own body. The choice of words struck me. Hundreds of years ago, I imagined, Shakespeare had already figured out what we really were: just machines. (*Why "just"?* Nico would say.) "I'm yours," Hamlet was telling Ophelia, "for as long as my body belongs to me." *But what about after? I* wanted to know. *What then?*

Outside the window, the sun had come up, stuffing the clouds with light. They still hung thick, but at least the rain had stopped for a while. Bex sat next to me, stroking her earlobe and watching the news on her own new puck. On my other side sat Ray, his arms crossed, one of his legs bouncing up and down like a jackhammer. True, he enjoyed breaking the rules every once in a while, but even he had a limit, and at that moment we were breaking a lot of rules. For one thing, I wasn't supposed to be here. Dad believed Ray had me hidden away in a safe house, where I'd stay until the Secret Service had confirmed the terrorist threat had passed. I'd spoken to Dad briefly on Ray's puck before we'd left Inverness Prep. He'd seemed happy to see me alive—for a second I'd thought he might break down all over again—but part of me still wondered if he'd been in on the conspiracy too. I didn't *think* so. On the wall in Stroud's office, I hadn't seen the wise-movie-dad persona my father always presented to cameras. I'd seen true grief. At least I thought I had, and now I wanted to find out for sure. Which was one of the reasons I'd come here.

Trumbull appeared at the door, his arm in a sling, his head bandaged, his sunglasses failing to conceal one blackened eye. His injuries had proven less serious than I'd thought. A broken humerus, some head trauma, assorted scrapes and bruises. I'd asked Ray to take me to him when we'd first arrived, and I'd found him awake in bed. Right off the bat he'd wanted to know why I was at the hospital instead of the safe house—typical Trumbull—but then I'd told him the whole story of the past few days, including the truth about Nico and my suspicions about Stroud, and explained what I wanted to do. "I know it's asking a lot," I'd said, "especially now. But can you make some calls to your connections in the Service?"

In the end, he'd insisted on dragging his battered body out of bed so he could help me himself.

"It's time," he said now. "But we need to hurry. Your father's plane touched down a few minutes ago. He's on his way to the safe house."

"I'll be quick."

Bex gave me a shove for encouragement. "Good luck, buddy," Ray said. I followed Trumbull down the corridor, past a nurse bent over a counter doling out pills into little cups and a frowning old man trudging behind a walker. Aside from them, the hospital still appeared mostly asleep. We came to a door flanked by two men with the usual grim faces and huge shoulders and gun-shaped bulges under their jackets. Trumbull's brothers in arms.

"I appreciate this, fellas," he told them.

"Do you mind staying outside?" I said. "I think I should do this alone."

"I'll be right here, sir."

One of the guards pulled the door open. I went in. A single bed occupied the center of the room, with several tall machines standing on either side like sentinels. Heavy curtains, shut as tightly as the ones in Dr. Singh's apartment, kept out most of the gloomy daylight. Dr. Singh's eyes opened and followed me as I crossed to the foot of the bed, but she didn't speak. Her face looked grayer than ever—like a marble sculpture of a person rather than the real thing.

"I'm sorry for bothering you," I said. "I know you just got out of surgery a few hours ago. But this is important. Your life might depend on it."

She released a dry, feeble wheeze—more the suggestion of a laugh than an actual laugh—as if to say that wasn't a very strong inducement to her at the moment.

"Mine too."

Her laughter stopped. The fingers of her right hand tapped on the bedsheet, wishing for a cigarette to hold.

"I figured out who the Prime Mover is."

Her eyebrows lifted.

"Stroud."

"You're certain?" she croaked.

"Pretty much."

"Why would he?—"

"I'm not sure. I don't have all the answers yet. Which is why I need your help. You told me a lot last night. Now I need to know more."

Her fingers went *tap-tap-tap*. Now that the doctors had pulled her back from death's doorstep, I half wondered if she'd pretend her confession last night had never happened, the same way she'd done with the incident on the terrace. But then she nodded at my puck. "Would you power that thing down, please?"

"Of course." The puck's rotors snapped inward as my hand closed around it. I opened my mouth to speak to it, but before I did, a pang went through me. What if Nico tried to message me? Then I'd just have to answer him later. "Shut down, puck." To Dr. Singh, I said, "See? It's just me now."

"That doesn't make this much easier."

I sat down on a chair near her bed. "I don't hate you, Dr. Singh."

She released another syllable of bitter laughter. "May I have a drink of water?"

A plastic cup stood on a small table next to her. I brought it to her lips. She swallowed, coughed, nodded that she'd had enough.

"So Stroud was giving the orders all along," she said.

"Is it really that surprising?"

"I suppose not. That man always did terrify me."

"Not half as much as he terrified me, I'd bet."

She shook her head. "After the accident, when he invited me to teach at Inverness Prep, I thought he was doing it to show he didn't hold Ruth's death against me. But it was just the opposite. Waring must've shown him the footage I showed you. Stroud must've *despised* me."

I set down the cup. "Please, Dr. Singh. We don't have much time. I need to ask you a few questions."

"Go ahead. But I told you most of what I know already."

"Why was Waring working for Stroud?"

"I'm not sure. Maybe he was being blackmailed, like me.

Maybe he was getting paid a lot of money. Or maybe he'd bought into whatever crazy plan Stroud had come up with."

"What do you think the plan was? You told me about the Not2B. What's that?"

"Again, no idea. Any other questions?"

I slid forward in my chair. My eyes dropped to the watch on my wrist, the hands frozen at 9:19. Next to the watch, on the back of my hand, "Th1neEverm0re" had turned into a barely readable smudge. An ache went through me. "Why create Nico, Dr. Singh? Couldn't Stroud and Waring have carried out their attack with the Spiders?"

"I always figured using an actual 2B in the attack was supposed to stir up more fear in the public."

"But why make him gay? Why make me . . . ?" I bit my lip.

"I'm sorry, Lee. I don't know."

I nodded.

"Did Nico survive?" she asked.

"I'm not sure."

She closed her eyes.

"But he didn't betray me, Dr. Singh. He betrayed Charlotte instead. That confused me before, but now I think I understand. It was you, wasn't it? You altered Nico's personality so he wouldn't hurt me."

"Yes. I knew Waring would find out what I'd done eventually. I knew I might even die for it. But I was past caring by then. When that Spider stormed into my room yesterday and sliced me open, I figured my gambit must've worked. Or at least I hoped it had."

"That was brave, what you did."

Again she let out a bitter, wheezelike laugh. "Please. Brave would've been refusing to build Nico in the first place. Brave would've been telling someone what was happening. I was too much of a coward to take a real stand. But at least I did *something*. It wasn't easy, with Waring constantly watching over my shoulder, but I managed to sneak in small alterations here and there. Made Nico less obedient. Increased his will to live." Her eyes flicked to me. "And his capacity for love."

I glanced down. My finger pads had turned white and waxy where I'd touched Nico's chest cavity. I prodded the tips of my fingers with my thumbnail, feeling the needles of pain, as if to verify that Nico's heat had been real. I wished I could pull the puck out of my pocket and check it, but I forced myself not to. "We have to make them pay, Dr. Singh."

"And how are we going to do that?"

"For a start, I need you to give me the address of that secret lab in the woods."

"They'll probably have it cleared out and scrubbed clean by now."

"What other leads do we have, though? We have to try."

"Even if there's something there, who's to say I didn't just orchestrate the whole thing myself? Maybe I became unhinged after Charlotte's death, turned into a terrorist, blew up Waring's house, and blackmailed him into helping me with the other attacks. Doesn't that story sound much more plausible? That's what everyone will think, Lee."

"We'll figure something out. Don't worry. I'll stand by you no matter what."

Her head dropped back on her pillow. She gazed up at the ceiling. "People will find out about everything else, too. That Ruth's death was my fault."

I put my hand on her arm. She flinched at my touch. "We have to do this," I said. "I think you know that. You're a good person, Dr. Singh."

"What could possibly give you that idea?"

"Nico. You made him. And not only that, he told me about the messages Charlotte sent him. How they filled him with hope. You wrote those, didn't you? That hopefulness must've come from somewhere."

She gave her head a small shake. The ghost of a smile appeared on her lips. "I never spoke to Nico directly. I couldn't. We knew he'd see me at Inverness, and we couldn't have him recognizing me from the lab. Those messages were my only way of communicating with him. It's true, I did like writing them. I liked imagining the kind of person Charlotte might've become if she'd survived. Strong. Courageous. Like you said, hopeful. But the hopefulness wasn't real. I was faking it."

"Maybe that's okay. Maybe hope is like free will: a necessary illusion."

"Maybe." The smile faded again. Her eyes drifted back to the ceiling. I knew exactly where her mind had gone, because my mind had spent plenty of time there too. She was staring into a deep abyss and trying to decide whether to let herself fall into it.

"Please, Dr. Singh. The address."

Her fingers went *tap-tap-tap* against the sheets.

Behind me, the door flew open. Two Secret Service agents swept into the room. Without a word, they made a lap around the space, checking it out. One of them spoke into his puck.

"Oh no." I stood. "Not now."

Dad entered next, flanked by two more agents. "Lee, what in God's name is going on here?"

35

Have you lost your mind? You're supposed to be at the safe house. Someone just tried to kill you, for God's sake!" Dark circles hung under Dad's eyes, and he hadn't changed his clothes since last night.

"How did you know I was here?"

"You thought you could keep it a secret from me? One of the agents at the safe house told me you never made it there, so I messaged Trumbull."

"I'm sorry, sir." Trumbull had come in with the other agents. "I had to tell him."

"It's okay, Trumbull. Dad, just give me two minutes. This is important."

"I'm not giving you two *seconds*." He grabbed my arm. "We're getting out of here. Now."

From behind me came Dr. Singh's gnarled voice. "Seventeen Hardscrabble Road."

I wrenched my arm free of Dad's grip. "Trumbull."

He snatched his puck out of the air. "Ray, I need you to send a SWAT team to seventeen Hardscrabble Road ASAP."

"What the hell is this?" Dad shouted. "I'm the goddamn president of the United States! I want some answers now!"

His agents eased forward, ready to snap into action.

"And what about Stroud?" I asked Dr. Singh. "We must have something on him."

She shook her head.

"Stroud?" Dad said. "What do you mean, 'have something on him'?"

Breathing hard, I turned to him. "I can trust you, Dad, can't I?"

"Why would you ask me something like that?"

"Just say yes. Please. I know I've been a pain in your ass, but you wouldn't do anything to hurt me, would you?"

"Of course not. What are you talking about?"

With that vertical line in his forehead, and his lips pressed together so tight they'd turned white, he looked more than ever like he feared I was some unhinged school shooter. I made my voice as steady as I could. "That attack last night. It wasn't Charlotte. It was Stroud."

He squinted. "*That's* what this is all about?"

"It probably sounds insane."

"Who's putting these ideas in your head?" He jabbed his finger at Dr. Singh. "Is it you?"

"No, Dad, it's not her. I figured this out myself."

"How?"

"It's a long story."

He pulled off his glasses and wiped his hand down his face. "I don't believe this. Look, we're not doing this here, Lee."

"I'm not leaving."

"Is that so?" He gave his agents a nod. Two of them had me by the arms a split second later.

"Dad, what the hell?"

Trumbull stepped forward. "Sir, with all due respect—"

Dad's eyes snapped to him. "Sorry, Trumbull, did you want some help out too?"

"Don't do this, Dad, please!" The agents hauled me to the door, my shoes bumping and dragging along the linoleum. I wrestled against them, but their arms didn't seem to give any more than the Spiders' had. Over my shoulder I shouted, "Do you know anything about the Not2B?"

One of the agents flung the door open.

"Wait," Dad said.

My escorts stopped. In front of me, the door swung shut again. I glanced back at Dad.

He swallowed. "Where did you hear that word?"

Dr. Singh spoke up. "I overheard Paul Waring talking about it last week."

"Paul Waring's dead."

"No, he's not, Dad. He's been organizing the attacks too."

For a few seconds everybody in the room seemed to stop breathing.

"Would you wait for me outside, gentlemen?" Dad said. "You too, Trumbull."

The hands gripping my arms released their hold. The men melted from the room, leaving just the three of us: Dr. Singh, Dad, and me. Dad eased himself into a chair next to the window.

"I'm listening," he said.

I pulled my chair over, sat down across from him, and tried to figure out where to begin. "Did you notice the 2B standing by the fireplace in Stroud's office last night?"

He nodded, his eyes on the linoleum floor.

"You probably didn't recognize him. Remember the boy who stopped by my room when you were there?"

"Nico."

"That's right. Dr. Singh built him. Waring forced her. Then they sent him to Inverness with instructions to make contact with me. To become my friend."

Dad rested his elbows on his knees and touched the tips of his fingers together. "Apparently he succeeded. The last thing I heard you say last night before the broadcast went dead was 'I love you, Nico.'"

He winced as he said the words "I love you." I'll bet I did too. My stomach felt like a ball of tangled-up rubber bands. Probably I could claim I'd meant those words in the platonic, straight-guy sense. Probably Dad would jump at the chance to take my explanation at face value. In other words, I still had plausible deniability. I straightened my glasses.

"We weren't just friends, Dad. We were in love."

"I see," he said, still staring at the linoleum.

"I'm gay."

"I thought being gay involved two humans. I don't even know what that is."

"Me neither, I guess."

He clawed through his hair with both hands. "Look, why don't you just tell me where the accusations against Stroud come in?"

While I stared at the vertical crease between his eyebrows, I told him the rest of the story: how I got the watch, how I found out the truth about Nico, everything that happened since the Spider attack yesterday. When I got to the part where Dr. Singh told me she'd tried to help Charlotte escape, Dad cut a look at her that must've burned like acid. I kept going, explaining how I'd found out Stroud was the Prime Mover. Outside, the sun seemed to have fought its way clear of the clouds. Its light pressed against the tightly drawn curtains. When I finished, Dad rubbed his unshaven chin but didn't say anything more.

"So what do you know about the Not2B?" I asked.

"It's a weapon. An electromagnetic-pulse bomb. Like the one at the lab in Bethesda that killed Charlotte. Like the one inside the watch Stroud gave you. Only bigger."

"How much bigger?"

"Big enough to destroy every electronic device on the planet."

I took a slow breath. "And how do you know about it?"

"Stroud." His eyes hadn't left the floor. "He put me in touch with an Inverness alum who'd gone into arms manufacturing."

"The same person who made my watch."

"I assume so."

"When?"

"After the Statue of Liberty strike. Stroud told me he thought I should know about the Not2B as an option of last resort, in case Charlotte's attacks continued to escalate. He said it was the only way we'd ever be able to expunge Charlotte from the planet once and for all."

"Not2B," I repeated, turning over the word in my mouth.

"Evidently the name started as a bad joke," Dad said.

I ran my fingers over the watch on my wrist, exploring its cool, smooth surfaces. "Stroud wanted you to use it. That must've been his plan. To keep raising the stakes with the attacks until you felt your only option was to detonate the bomb."

Dad sat back in his chair. "But if Stroud had access to it, why couldn't he just set off the bomb himself? Wouldn't the end result be the same?"

"Because that would just cause chaos," Dr. Singh rasped from her bed. "He wanted to engineer the collapse of modern civilization in an orderly fashion. With you poised to lead. *His* son-in-law, *his* man."

Dad jumped up and paced around the room. "No way. I'm

not buying it. How can you even think this, Lee? You know how much that man's done for us. Do you have any proof?"

I went over the list in my head again. One overheard conversation. A page of Stroud's memoir, now consumed in the fire. I shook my head.

"So this is all wild conjecture." He flung his hand in Dr. Singh's direction. "How do we know *she's* not the one behind the attacks? Can you answer that one for me? She could've just made up all this crap about Waring and Stroud to throw us off her trail."

She gave me a dry "I told you so" smirk.

"I know it's not her, Dad."

"This is insanity. Stroud's your grandfather, and you're saying he tried to kill you?"

"Maybe he felt like he had to. The same way he killed Grandpa Fisher."

Dad whirled to face me. "Don't you dare bring that up. My father was his best friend. He was in an impossible situation. It killed him to lose George Fisher."

"Dad, I'm not saying—"

I stopped. My fingers curled around the armrests of my plastic chair.

"You're not saying what?" Dad said.

My mouth had gone dry. My whole body tingled. I rose to my feet. "Why don't you call him, then? Call Stroud and ask him yourself."

He pressed his lips tight together. "Fine. If that's how you want to play this." He turned to his puck. "Place a call to Mrs. Case."

The puck pivoted. A few seconds later, on the wall across from the bed, an image of Mrs. Case appeared, her bun still loose, her face streaked with tears. I almost didn't recognize the landscape behind her—first, because the sun had come out there just like it had here (undoubtedly a first at Inverness Prep), and second, because the school was now a smoldering ruin. "Hello, John," Mrs. Case said. "How are you and Lee holding up?"

"All right, thanks. Is the headmaster nearby? May I speak with him?"

She instructed her puck to find Stroud. The device meandered into the midst of the ruins. The devastation scrolled across the hospital room wall: tumbled stones and charred, splintered beams, with here and there something recognizable emerging from the sooty debris. A glaring carved raven. A few pages of a library book, miraculously untouched. The slender silver leg of a Spider glinting in the sun.

The puck floated into the open again. The school's rear terrace appeared, still relatively intact. Stroud sat on a bench with his back to the stone wall, just a few feet from the spot where Nico had done his handstand four days earlier. He stared at his school, his suit rumpled and covered in soot but his spine ramrod straight. Something rested on his lap: the titanium thighbone. "Who's that?" he said when he noticed the puck.

"It's John, sir," Dad answered. "John and Lee and Dr. Singh. We'd like to talk to you for a minute."

"By all means. I'm just . . ." He stood and gestured at the devastation in front of him. "Would you look at this place? What a loss."

"Yes, sir," Dad said. "It's a great tragedy."

"What's on your mind, John?"

Medics had cleaned the blood from his face and fixed his split lip with medical glue. I wondered for a second if he'd had the Spiders inflict his injuries or if he'd just done it himself—maybe with that bone he held in his hands now.

Meanwhile, Dad hadn't stopped pacing the room. "Lee's gotten this crazy idea in his head, sir. I'd like you to put his mind to rest. He's claiming *you're* the one who plotted the Charlotte attacks. He says you've been trying to manipulate me into launching some kind of electronic apocalypse."

Stroud didn't blink. "I have, have I?"

"With the help of Paul Waring, who apparently didn't die. I almost forgot that part."

He chuckled. "I see. Well, I'm sorry to disappoint. I think young Lee's just a little shaken up."

Dad turned to me, full of manic energy. "There, you see, Lee? What do you have to say to that?"

But I didn't even look at Dad. To Stroud, I said, "Maybe it's time you told us about George Fisher."

My grandfather's grin faltered. "What about him?"

"I thought we were talking about Charlotte," Dad said. "What is this, Lee?"

My eyes didn't budge from the projection of Stroud on the wall. "Sir, I was just remembering something you said at Mom's funeral. That you'd lost the only two people you ever loved. Dad thought you were talking about your daughter and your wife. But you weren't, were you? You were talking about the same two people whose photos are on the mantel in your office. Your daughter and George Fisher."

The smile had left Stroud's face now. "What are you driving at?"

"I know you're behind this," I said, "no matter what you say. I know you're the Prime Mover. But for a while I couldn't figure out why you'd bothered to make Nico. Why you'd want me to fall in love with him and then kill him. But now I think I get it. You saw the security footage of me kissing Jeremy freshman year, and you decided you'd help me become a man, just like you've always talked about. A man like you."

His eyes narrowed. His craggy face twitched. He didn't say a word. Like a Marine in a terrorist interrogation room again.

"You loved George Fisher, but not as a friend. You loved him the same way I love Nico."

He lunged forward and pointed the thighbone into the puck's camera, his arm shaking, his whole body shaking. "That's a disgusting insinuation! I spent nine years in a room with him, and I never once touched him until the day I snapped his neck!"

"Of course not. Because you're not gay, right? You're the Prime Mover. Nothing controls you."

"Lee, stop this," Dad said. "You're not making any sense."

"And then when you hatched this insane plan to destroy modern civilization," I continued, "you decided you'd take the opportunity to put me to the test. After all, I'm a disgrace to the family. Depressed. Suicidal. Homosexual."

"Those words are cop-outs," Stroud spat. "You're just weak willed."

"Exactly. So you made me fall in love with a machine, and ordered the machine to betray me, and gave me a way to destroy the machine to save my own life. Then you waited to see if I'd have the strength to kill the thing I loved, like you did. Because that's what life is, right? Losing things? Adversity can either destroy you or make you stronger. Isn't that your motto?" I took a step forward. "Congratulations, sir. I'm still here."

Dad's eyes darted back and forth between Stroud and me. "Sir," he said, his voice weakening. "Tell him this isn't true."

Stroud hugged the thighbone to his chest. His eyes drifted away from me back to the ruins of Inverness. He stepped onto the bench and surveyed the damage.

"There's a SWAT team on its way to seventeen Hardscrabble Road right now, sir," I said. "It's all over."

He sat down on the wall, his feet resting on the bench. Little by little, his spine sagged forward, folding over the thighbone he still clutched in his arms, like his vertebrae were crumbling one by one. "Just look at this place," he repeated. "What a loss."

Dad staggered a few steps, as if the floor underneath him had tilted sideways. "I don't understand, sir," he stammered.

But Stroud didn't answer. Instead, his eyes closed. His body went limp. A wind combed his short white hair forward. The background behind his head changed. In place of the sky and the far shore of the lake, white sprays of water appeared all around him. At first I couldn't tell what was happening, but then I understood. He'd pitched himself backward over the terrace wall, and the puck had followed him down the face of the cliff. That moment of falling seemed to last forever. But the whole time I watched him plummet toward the lake, my heart didn't try to punch out of my chest. My tie didn't seem to tighten around my neck. My breath stayed as steady as a slowly swinging pendulum. Then, right before impact, the puck peeled away and glided off across the surface of the water, which sparkled in the sunshine.

36

◇◇◇◇◇◇◇

None of us moved or spoke for a long minute. Dad's face had gone blank, like he'd fallen into one of his trances. His puck still projected an image of glinting water on the wall across from us. The shifting bluish light playing over Dad's loose features made it look like he'd plunged to the bottom of the lake along with Stroud.

"Dad?"

He snatched his puck out of the air, the projection disappeared, and the room went dark. "I don't understand," he repeated in a thin voice. "Any of this. Who that man was." He nodded at the empty wall across from him. Then he looked at me. "Who you are."

"I know, Dad."

A knock sounded at the door. Trumbull stuck his head in. "Sorry to bother you, sir." Then, to me, "The SWAT team's at the house on Hardscrabble Road. The place is empty. No Paul Waring. No robotics equipment. Not even any furniture. I thought you should know."

I traded a look with Dr. Singh. Just like she'd predicted.

"Trumbull, wait," Dad said. "Something just happened at the school. Something terrible."

"Sir?"

"We should send help." He started for the door. Stopped. Cast one more baffled glance over his shoulder at me. Then he went out. The room was quiet, aside from the tapping of Dr. Singh's fingers.

"Give him time," she said. "His world just turned upside down."

I rubbed my neck. All of a sudden, I felt exhausted. My body ached in a thousand different places. "He was always on my case for not going out and doing stuff at school. I guess he can't complain about *that* anymore. I sure as hell did something."

She rasped out a laugh.

I pulled my chair close to her bed and sat. My stomach had wadded itself up again. "Dr. Singh, there's one more thing I want to talk to you about. Something I didn't tell you earlier. Before I triggered the pulse bomb, Nico told me he was uploading his consciousness to the Supernet. He said his inhibitor wasn't working. Was that your doing too? Did you sabotage the inhibitor?"

"Yes."

I closed my eyes and took a breath. "I was afraid maybe he was lying to get me to set off the bomb. So you think it's really possible for a 2B to upload his consciousness like that?"

"I do, theoretically."

"He said he'd get in touch with me." I pulled the puck from my jacket pocket. Its black circular screen stared back at me. "But I haven't heard from him since it happened. Not a word."

"Be patient, Lee. It might take time for him to come back to you. And when he does, he might not be the same. This is uncharted territory."

I nodded.

"In the meantime," she continued, her voice a throaty whisper, "you and I, we have important work to do."

"Like what?"

"Waring's still on the loose, for one thing. But even more than that." Her eyes shifted to the window, with the light filtering through the heavy curtains. "Big things are coming. The whole definition of life is about to change. We need to stick around and help get the world ready for the future."

"That sounds like something Charlotte might've said to Nico."

"I suppose it does."

"So you're faking it?"

"Of course I am. But that doesn't make what I'm saying less true." She pointed a finger at me. "So no jumping off a goddamn bridge, do you hear me?"

"I won't if you won't."

I put out my hand for her to shake. She eyed it a second before taking it in hers. Then she nodded at the puck nestled in my other palm. "Go ahead. Switch it on."

I did. The puck lit up, chimed, and leaped out of my hand like something alive.

Acknowledgments

Within the space of one surreal month in 2014, I found out that my novel had sold and that my partner and I were pregnant, via surrogate, with twins. It goes without saying that neither of these things could've come to pass without gigantic amounts of help. In the writing of my book, I owe a big thank-you to Cat Vasko, Meghan Thornton, and Salvatore Zoida for commenting on early drafts. Loads of gratitude also go to Quinlan Lee and Tracey Adams at Adams Literary for believing in and enthusiastically championing my writing.

Michael Strother, my editor at Simon Pulse, has been such a pleasure to work (and gossip about *Project Runway*) with. Your input made *Willful Machines* so much better, and you actually made the editing process fun too. I'm also hugely appreciative to everyone else at Simon & Schuster who helped bring this book to light: publishers Mara Anastas, Jon Anderson, and Mary Marotta; Liesa Abrams, Pulse's editorial director; Lucille Rettino, Carolyn Swerdloff, Teresa Ronquillo, Anthony Parisi, Candace Greene McManus, Betsy Bloom, and Michelle Leo in marketing; Christina Pecorale, Danielle Esposito, and Rio Cortez in sales; and managing editor Katherine Devendorf. A special thanks to Dan Potash and Regina Flath for their amazing cover work.

Most of all, I'm grateful for my family—especially my mom and her fierce, eternal support; my beloved partner, Duncan; and our daughters, Lucy and Ada, who managed to make getting a novel published only the second-coolest thing that happened to me last year.

Turn the page for a sneak peek at

TATTOO ATLAS

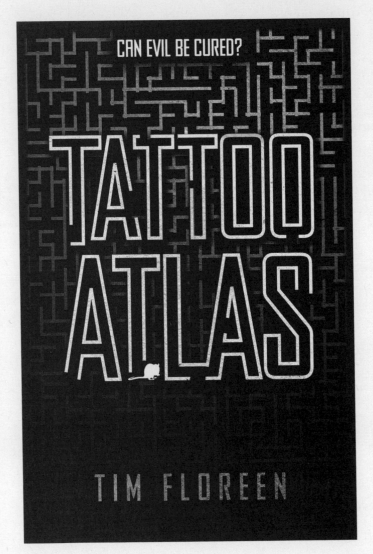

1

Almost a year after Franklin Kettle shot my friend Pete Lund through the head, a squad of cops took Franklin to my mom's lab so she could put a hole in *his* head and slide a small electronic capsule inside.

The three police cruisers swerved to a stop in front of the sleek glass structure, their tires kicking up snow, their sirens for some reason blaring. The noise seemed to reach all the way around the lab and spread across the surface of the frozen lake beyond. Then there was a clattering of car doors opening and closing and booted feet stomping the slushy pavement. Gruff voices barked orders back and forth.

Franklin appeared to be enjoying all the fuss. When the cops helped him out of the middle cruiser's backseat, the chains on his wrists and ankles clinking, he had a tiny, secret smile on his face.

The police walked him past a sign that read MINNESOTA INSTITUTE OF NEUROLOGICAL RESEARCH and into the lab. An elevator sliced through the building without a sound as it carried them to the top floor. The door whispered open on a bright corridor, where a lab tech with a pierced nose, an asymmetrical wedge haircut, and a badge on her white coat that said GERTRUDE THOMAS waited. She blinked at the sight of the six huge cops packed into the elevator, but then she recovered herself and shifted her gaze to the skinny seventeen-year-old kid they were guarding.

"Hi, Franklin. I don't know if you remember me." She dipped her head a little but didn't manage to catch his eyes. "I'm Gertie. We met the first time you came here last year?"

Franklin responded with a slight tilt of his head that might've meant he remembered her and might've meant he didn't. His eyes never left the elevator floor.

"Why don't you follow me?" Gertie said. "I'll take you to Dr. Braithwaite."

She led them all down the corridor, only once throwing a flustered glance back at the mob of cops tromping after her. At the end of the corridor she grabbed the badge clipped to her lab coat and touched it to a card reader next to a door. The door clicked open. The group entered a big room with a floor-to-ceiling window spanning the rear wall. It looked out onto Lake Superior, which was solid and gray, like a continuation of the room's concrete floor. A table stood in front of the window.

My mom sat behind it.

A middle-aged man with a comb-over stepped forward and offered Franklin his hand. "Welcome, Mr. Kettle. I'm

Dr. Hult, the head biomedical engineer. We're all thrilled to have you back. We can't wait to get started."

Franklin didn't look at him, either. Instead he let out a quiet snort, like he'd just told himself a private joke.

Dr. Hult glanced at his outstretched, unshaken hand and stuffed it into his lab coat pocket. He nodded at Mom. "I think you know Dr. Braithwaite."

"Hello, Franklin," Mom said. "Thanks, Gertie. You can go now."

Gertie cast one more uncertain look at Franklin before slipping out of the room.

Mom gestured toward a chair across the table from her. While one of the cops guided Franklin over and sat him down, Mom smoothed her straight hair—iron gray, like the concrete floor and the lake, shot through with a single thick streak of white near the front. She'd always refused to dye it. I'd told her once I thought the white streak made her look like a mad scientist, especially when she had her lab coat on, but she'd just replied, "Then it's a good thing I *am* one."

"It's been a while," she said to Franklin now. "How are you doing?"

He raised his hands—he had to raise both of them, because the chains bound his wrists close together—and pointed at the chair next to her. Something rested there, some kind of box, with a white cloth draped over it. The top of it was just visible above the table. A soft scratching sound came from within.

"What's that?"

"We'll get to that in a moment," she said. "I want to talk to you first. Do you understand why you're here?"

He slouched down low in his chair and stared at the box.

"Franklin? It's important that you answer the question."

"You want to open up my head."

"That's part of it, yes. Now, I know you must be nervous."

"I'm not nervous."

"I'm glad to hear that."

"Why do you think I'm nervous? Do I look like I'm nervous?"

"No."

He didn't look like he was anything. Franklin Kettle had a face empty of expression—except, sometimes, for that half smile of his—and a low, weirdly calm voice, like the computer from *2001: A Space Odyssey*. Kettlebot, kids had sometimes called him at school. His eyes, partly hidden behind spiky chunks of hair and glasses with bulky black frames, looked like dull gray stones.

"I've undergone thousands of hours of military training," he said. "I think I know how to keep my cool."

Mom pursed her lips. "You're talking about that video game you play. It isn't quite the same thing, is it?"

"It's not just a video game," he replied, still in that same calm tone. "Military training programs all over the world use Son of War to help prepare soldiers for combat. And I have one of the all-time high scores. You don't think that says something about me?"

"I'm sure it does."

"I do see your point, though, Madame Doctor. Can virtual combat make a person fearless for real? It's an interesting question. The kind of question you probably think about a lot, being a brain scientist and all." His smile had returned. "Sort of like: can sticking some gadget in the head of a cold-blooded killer make him not a killer anymore?"

Mom was unfazed. "Actually, that's what I want to talk to you about, Franklin: why you're here. Do you understand what we hope to accomplish when we—"

The chains clanked as he pointed again. His eyes hadn't budged from the box covered by the white cloth. "What is it? Why is it making that noise?"

She glanced at the thing on the chair next to her. "It's a gift. I was planning to give it to you a little later."

"Give it to me now. The noise is distracting me."

Mom hooked her hair behind her ear while she thought about it. "All right then."

She lifted the box onto the table and, drawing off the cloth, revealed a Plexiglas cage with half a dozen mice inside.

Franklin pulled himself out of his slouch so he could set his hands on the table, reaching them as far as his chains would allow. He tapped a fingernail on the white tabletop and watched the mice react.

"How come?" he said.

"I beg your pardon?"

"How come you're giving me these mice? What do you want me to do with them?"

He still didn't make eye contact with Mom. That was another thing about Franklin: he never looked anyone in the eyes. Not out of shyness. At least it didn't seem that way. He just appeared uninterested in connecting with other human beings.

"Whatever you like," Mom answered. "I thought you might enjoy them." To one of the police officers standing behind him, she said, "Would you take off his wrist restraints, please?"

The cop unchained his hands. Without hesitating or pausing to ask permission, Franklin opened the door to the cage and reached his hand inside. His fingers closed around a mouse with a coat of white and brown splotches. He brought it to his chest and stroked its head. The mouse's tiny pink paws scraped his fingers.

"I know what you want me to do with them," Franklin said. "You want me to hurt them."

Mom sat up a tiny bit straighter. "Why would I want you to do something like that?"

"So you can study my behavior. Gather data for your project. See for yourself what a psycho I am. You and whoever else is watching." He nodded at one of the cameras hanging from the ceiling. "You're all thrilled to have me back," he added, slitting his eyes at Dr. Hult, who was standing by the door. "You can't wait to get started." His chains rustled as he faced Mom again. "You're hoping I'll put on a show."

"What do you mean, 'put on a show'?"

He shrugged. "Maybe I'll smash this mouse on the table. Maybe I'll squeeze him until his eyes pop out. At least, that's what you're hoping, Madame Doctor."

Mom pressed the nail of her left index finger into the pad of her thumb. A couple years ago, while making dinner, she'd accidentally sliced off the tip of that thumb. A doctor had managed to sew it back on, but it had been numb ever since. Prodding the thumb had become a habit, something she always did when she got tense. Aside from that, though, she kept up an appearance of calm that matched Franklin's. "You don't really want to do that, do you?"

"No. I like this mouse."

The animal had started clawing at Franklin's hand more frantically, like it could understand the various fates he'd described for it. He brought it close to his cheek and shushed to calm it down.

Dr. Hult raised his eyebrows at Mom. She gave her head a small shake for him to stay put.

"I'm not stupid," Franklin said, the two stones behind his glasses fastened on the Plexiglas cage and the other mice inside it.

"I know that," Mom answered. "I know you're very intelligent."

"I'm onto your brain-doctor tricks."

"I'm not playing any tricks, Franklin."

He tipped his head forward, so his hair fell in front of his eyes in a curtain. "Stop watching me. I don't like it when people watch me."

"I'm not watching you. I'm looking at you. I'm having a conversation with you."

"No, you're not. You're studying me."

"That's not true. I want to talk to you about what's going to happen over the next few days. I want to make sure you understand—"

Franklin opened his mouth wide and stuffed the mouse in.

Mom's metal chair screeched across the concrete floor as she sprang to her feet. "What are you doing, Franklin?"

The cops took a few steps forward, but Mom put up a hand to stop them. Franklin's bulging cheek rippled as the mouse struggled inside.

"Take out the mouse," Mom said. "You just told me you didn't want to hurt him."

Franklin settled back into his slouch in the chair. He laced his fingers together on his lap. Even with the mouse struggling behind his cheek, you could still see the little smile on his lips.

"Listen to me, Franklin. Right now you have a choice. You can—"

His jaws closed with a sound like someone crunching into a mouthful of almonds. A trickle of blood snaked from his lips.

He chewed a few times and spat the mouse onto the table. Tiny black beads of blood flecked the white surface and the Plexiglas cage and even Mom's lab coat. One of the mouse's hind legs continued to kick.

With sudden energy, Franklin sprang to his feet and banged his hands on the table. "Happy now? Happy?"

The police finally snapped into action. As they rushed to grab him, he kept repeating that word over and over, blood spraying from his mouth, his normally quiet, empty voice filling with rage, rising to a yell.

"Happy? Happy?! HAPPY?!"

2

Of course, I didn't actually see any of that firsthand. But a while ago I got a message on my phone with a link to a Dropbox folder containing a bunch of surveillance footage from the lab. I went through it a few days later, beginning with those first minutes after Franklin Kettle's arrival. It felt important that I watch all of it. I'd already decided I wanted to set down the whole story of the days before and after Mom performed her procedure on Franklin, start to finish. Lots of rumors had been flying around online, and I figured someone who'd been there, for most of it at least, should make a record of what had really happened. Or try.

Not that I knew whether I'd actually show what I wrote to another human being. If the truth got out, lots of people would get hurt, me included. Maybe I was really just doing it for myself. Maybe I was hoping it would give me a way to dump out all the unwelcome memories crawling around in my mind. Sort of like what I imagined happening when I drew in my

Tattoo Atlas, even though I realized the brain didn't actually work like that. Probably the only way I'd ever get rid of my memories was if Mom figured out how to open up *my* head and pull them out, one by one.

But I'm getting ahead of myself.

That Monday morning, at the same time Mom was attempting to talk to Franklin about the hole she wanted to drill in his skull, I was at home, out in the garage, warming up my car, a bright yellow 1972 Saab station wagon my older brother had bought and fixed up years ago. I wasn't exactly what you'd call a gearhead, but I did my best to take good care of it. My friends and I had a tradition of riding the seven blocks to school in the wagon every morning. I'd put up the garage door and sit there with the heater on full blast and wait for the others to slide into their usual seats one by one: Tor Agnarson in front next to me, Lydia Hicks and Callie Minwalla behind. Pete Lund, when he was still alive, had sat in the way back. For years we'd called ourselves the Boreal Five because we'd all grown up together on Boreal Street, but there were only four of us now.

The seating arrangement had undergone another change more recently, when Tor and Lydia had started dating. An unexpected development, and one that had caused some dissension in the Boreal Five's ranks.

Today as I sat in the driver's seat, the Saab's engine chugging and its heater roaring, Lydia showed up first, her freckly cheeks flushed from the cold, her auburn hair pulled into a neat ponytail under her knit cap, a stack of posters under her arm. She slid into the backseat.

"What have you got there?" I said.

"More publicity for the memorial." She turned the stack face-up on her lap. The poster showed Pete Lund's round face haloed by a haze of silver glitter. The words FOREVER IN OUR HEARTS appeared at the top. "Abigail dropped them off last night. She wants us to put them up before class this morning."

Abigail Lansing was the head organizer of the assembly that would mark the one-year anniversary of the shooting. On the basis of a single dance she'd gone to with Pete sophomore year, she'd seized the role of Pete's bereaved girlfriend and mourner-in-chief—even though she'd basically just hung out with him that one time, and even though she hadn't even seen him die. The girl was a colossal phony. But none of us in the Boreal Five—Pete's actual friends, in other words—had the heart to be our school's unofficial grief coordinator, so we pretty much left her to it.

When she'd asked us to help her organize the Big Bang memorial, though, grabbing our hands and whispering, "Pete would've wanted you to be part of it," we all agreed. She was right, not that she had any real idea what she was talking about.

Lydia jangled a couple rolls of tape she'd looped around her wrist. "You up for it?"

"Sure, but haven't we put up enough?"

"Apparently the other posters were just teasers. Now we're starting phase two of the marketing rollout. These have all the information about where and when the memorial's taking place printed at the bottom."

"But it's a mandatory school assembly. Doesn't that sort of make marketing beside the point?"

"Maybe." Her feathery eyebrows knitted and her eyes dropped to the posters. "I think Abigail just wants to make sure nobody ditches. She wants people to understand how important this is."

"She wants them to hear her make a speech and watch her cry. *That's* what she wants."

"She means well, Rem." Lydia touched her fingertips to Pete's cheek, her forehead still furrowed. We both went quiet as we stared at the image. For the past few weeks Pete's face on that sappy poster had been everywhere, all over the walls at school, but seeing it was still like a spike in the ribs every time.

Tor yanked open the Saab's other rear door and scooted in next to Lydia. Unlike us, he didn't have on a coat or a hat. Just a UMD sweatshirt—slightly too small, so as to better showcase his muscles—and, randomly, a pair of earmuffs. Like only his ears ever got cold. That was typical Tor, though. He was an underdresser: whatever the situation, he always had on at least two fewer layers than everyone else.

He slung a huge arm over Lydia's shoulders and gave her a kiss. "Morning, Strawberry."

Lydia turned red. She'd had a thing for Tor for years, everybody had always known it, but now that she had him, it was like she'd won the lottery and didn't have a clue what to do with the money. She took his public displays of affection with a mix of pleasure, mortification, and bafflement.

Tor leaned forward to ruffle my hair. "Morning, Nice Guy."

My name's Jeremy, Rem for short, but he liked to call me Nice Guy. Mr. Nice Guy if he was in a formal mood. Tor was into nicknames—he was the one who'd started calling us the Boreal Five—and he had one for each of us. In my case the nickname had caught on around school, too, and I suppose it fit well enough. Maybe I hadn't done anything as impressive and altruistic as my brother, who'd single-handedly started the crisis hotline at Duluth Central during his time as a student there, but I knew how to get along with people. I didn't gossip. I didn't pick fights. I didn't have enemies. None I knew of, at least.

Callie appeared next. She opened the back door and found Tor occupying what had been, up until a few weeks ago, her usual spot. "Oh. Right." Scowling, she slammed the door shut, flung open the front passenger door, and dumped herself into the seat.

"Think of it as a promotion," I said.

She cut a black look at me.

"I don't get what the problem is," Tor said. "It's a free country, isn't it? We're all friends, right? What's the big deal if Lydia and I want to get a little friendlier?"

Callie let out a noise halfway between a sigh and a groan as she pushed at the coiled mass of black hair piled on top of her head, a precarious hairdo that had given rise to Tor's name for her—Elvira. "It threatens the integrity of our group, Tor."

"'The integrity of our group'?" Tor repeated. "What are we, a team of Navy SEALs?"

"We didn't mean for it to happen, Callie," Lydia said. "It just sort of did. We were spending all that time together in the bio lab after school."

"Right," Callie muttered. "There's nothing like a little cat dissection to get two young lovers in the mood." She seized the rearview mirror and angled it so she could look Tor in the eyes. "We're graduating in June, Tor. We don't have much time left together. I don't want you ruining it."

"Why would—"

"Come on," she snapped. "You've never in your life dated anyone for more than a month. So what's going to happen one week from now when you kick Lydia to the fucking curb just like you do every other girl?"

"Who says he's going to kick me to the effing curb?" Lydia said, crossing her arms over her chest.

"Don't kid yourself, missy."

Lydia's freckle-strewn cheeks turned crimson again. "You know what really threatens the integrity of our group? The mean things you say."

Callie ignored her. "What do you want with Lydia anyway,

Tor? She's a prude who can't even bring herself to say the word 'fuck.' Don't you prefer the slutty types?"

"That's enough, Callie," I said. "Give them a break. You can't control who you fall for."

"Thank you, Rem," Lydia said.

Callie turned to glare at me again, her mouth open as if she wanted to say something. But then she grabbed one of my hands from the steering wheel instead and lifted it up. "For God's sake, Rem, don't you ever wash?"

I'd been painting that morning, lost track of time, and ran out the door without bothering to clean off the smears of pink and green and yellow covering my palms and fingers. That happened a lot. Callie was an artist too—mixed media collage mostly—but she was much neater about it.

Without a word Tor got out of the car, opened Callie's door, and held out his hand. "Come with me. I want to show you something."

She eyed his open palm. "What?"

"You'll see. It'll be good, I promise." To me and Lydia he said, "You guys come too. Leave the car running, Rem."

He led us out the garage's rear door and through the trees that separated my backyard from his. Callie complained loudly as she picked her way through the snow in her cork wedges and miniskirt. She was just as impractical a dresser as Tor.

Her choice of swearwords got more creative when he plunged into the woods at the back of his yard. The snow was harder to navigate here, but at least we didn't have to go far. Twenty feet in, Tor stopped at the base of a huge maple.

Callie's face softened when she realized where we were. Tor grinned at her and nodded.

The trunk of the maple grew at a low angle, extending over a ravine where a creek ran during the summer, so you didn't have to climb the tree so much as walk out onto it. Still, it would be a challenge in wedges. Callie didn't protest anymore, though. She followed Tor in silence, taking his outstretched hand for support. Lydia and I stayed close behind.

Just before the place where the trunk split off into branches, we all dropped to a crouch and peered over the side.

"They're still here," Callie whispered.

TIM FLOREEN lives in San Francisco with his partner, their two young, cat-obsessed daughters, and their two very patient cats. In a starred review, *Kirkus Reviews* called *Willful Machines* "gothic, gadgety, and gay," which is an accurate assessment. You can find out more about Tim and his secret infatuation with Wonder Woman on the Internet at timfloreen.com and on Twitter at @timfloreen.